BY MARTIN COPELAND

NOVELS

The Boys from Dogtown
Manhunt in France

PHOTOPLAYS

River of Doubt
Right Proud: the Buffalo Soldiers

LA LOVE STORIES

Martin Copeland

RAINBOW BRIDGE

ISBN: 978-1-7341123-1-3
Rainbow Bridge Books

LA LOVE STORIES

CONTENTS

1. A HIT MOVIE, MEANT TO BE

Love can be a hurting thing.

When his wife lay dying, on the last day of life she'd shared with him for 20 full, loving years, Harold Kile made a confession.

He'd been avoiding it ever since the moment in their youth, all those years ago, when he realized he might have a chance to make love to her. In fact, his confession concerned that moment.

Harold had moved to Los Angeles at 22, fresh from a stellar academic career at UT Austin where he'd made a name for himself as an actor in campus productions. Quite a name. He'd starred in comedies and dramas and even handled brilliantly the lead in a southern version of West Side Story which he'd liberally helped adapt with the writer.

Armed with such an outstanding resume, he'd followed the Okie trail and landed at a co-rental in West Hollywood with a member of the Texas Mafia, the network of ex-Lone Star staters that helped each other find work in Hollywood.

With such moral and practical support, word of mouth casting tips and his own confidence in self and his talent, Harold worked his way into the Biz. Baby step by baby step. He'd changed his screen name to Harry, figuring rightly that one has to be Humphrey Bogart to survive an awkward monicker, and as time marched on, her realized he wasn't. He plateaued as a gifted, versatile secondary player. He could do everything well, from villain to goody two shoes, but when he looked into a mirror, as all actors anxiously did, he saw no constellations blinking brightly around his head.

Still, he dreamed like all the other thousands and thousands of aspirants who came every year to LA from around the world and never fell into what he'd read about in one of his UT lit classes— some classic work that bored the hell out of everyone and would never make for a feature—the "Slough of Despond." He made a deliberate and constant effort to meet as many directors and aspiring directors as he could. Directors drove the industry, and if his career were ever going to truly take off, one of them would have to provide the propulsion.

He rented an apartment in Santa Monica near the beach, and through the actor's grapevine he heard about a Sunday volleyball game where Biz folk unwound after a week of most usually, flat-out indifferent rejection. It was cathartic to pound the ball, imagining it to be a producer's hatrack head.

In between games, surf dips to cool off and a lot of jokes and gibes about the Industry, they swapped contacts and anecdotes even while pretending to avoid that very same.

"It's chill out time, Big Guy," said Peter, who'd become Harry's best bud among the group. "Sunday at the beach with Pete. Oh shit, isn't that a French flick?"

Peter was the actual Big Guy, almost 6'4" and one hell of a volleyball frontliner, but he liked to tell Harry, "You're going to be big in this Biz, and that's good because you could use a few inches."

Harold—or Harry as he was now known—wasn't short, except in comparison to Peter, who towered over most people in many ways. He was a writer/director with several TV films on his credits and it was only a matter of time—short time—before he landed his first feature.

He could afford to be generous, and he was, a rarity in LA where despite "wanting your friend to do well" so they could help you do well, if you listened close, you could hear teeth gnashing whenever someone announced he'd got a deal.

Harry never forgot the tale, sworn truth, about when George Lucas screened the very first Star Wars film back in the 1970s—a galaxy far away but still relevant—despite the phony encouragements and "I liked it " and ritual criticisms that weren't, one could smell apocalypse in the room, as if Verdun had come to Gower.

Jealousy will out. For all the carping and humming and hawing, everyone knew that something new had come to town and it would be a hit. Their buddy George was headed toward a different universe, one they would never join unless he invited them. And why would he? Unless for the rest of their lives, if they were able to maintain contact—not a given, and as early as tomorrow cords could be severed—they sucked up to him. The King was alive, long live the King, and as soon as the royal ring slipped on his finger, no lack of lips would queue up to kiss it. Or whatever body part.

Harry had learned the ropes that quickly and hoped he wouldn't hang himself one day.

That was why Peter seemed so different. With him Harry felt at ease and comfortable on a human level. They would usually play on the same team, and Harry became outstanding at setting up Peter for the vicious spikes at which he was even more outstanding. At breaks they sat on the sand relaxing and talking, and during the infrequent times they played against each other, excelled at talking shit to each other.

Peter was also different from most all the others at the game in that he had a wife, and one day he announced with tears in his eyes, a baby daughter.

Harry sometimes brought a girl friend du jour, but they came and went like the Santa Monica sands. He had never been the type, which it seemed grew in LA like mushrooms in a tropical forest, who chose partners either for their looks or how they could advance their careers, and ideally both. He cultivated sincerity in his personal relations, as deep down, he felt he needed a partner who could support him emotionally during the frequent downs of a second-role actor's career.

Every day in LA he heard of another flavor of a past month who'd hit the singles circuit again after a scandal or box office flop had put the kibosh on his prospects, and, ergo, been dumped by his erstwhile lover who could not abide sleeping with failure.

Harry read the LA Times and Hollywood Reporter assiduously, first thing each morning, scanning films and future films for info which meant network power. He even memorized credits, especially after the cocktail party his first days in town when he hadn't recognized a soap star and gotten the coldest shoulder of his young life, as well as sneers and contempt from his date. He became a walking catalogue of contacts—virtually none of whom gave him a call on his cell.

He'd noticed despite his career concentration that the Times rarely discussed a film without mentioning its budget and box office, in lieu of any artistic merit. Million dollar salaries got upfront attention, and the paper carried a continuing feature about the latest fab real estate purchases, none of which concerned an East LA bungalow (though here prices were skyrocketing too). Rather, jillion-dollar homes on Malibu bluffs or gated and guarded in Holmby Hills or the Canyons.

Harry doubted he'd ever be mentioned for his mortgage. Neither did he want to stay permanently in his overpriced one bedroom. He stubbornly kept looking for true love that didn't involve real estate.

He had many stands of varying length, from one night to a year, the longest, which ended when he hit a casting slump. He liked to shed his sandals for hiking boots and go off on weekly treks to the Southwest, different canyons indeed but perfect for shaking off

LA's tinsel. He'd had a couple of hot and heavy affairs during and after these trips, but couldn't manage the long distance involved. As much as he recognized the superficiality of Los Angeles, he still dreamed of making his mark on the Screen.

Not for money or power or glory, though he would welcome all of the above, but for whatever posterity he or the world might have. He wanted to cast himself large in a story that would make people laugh or cry years and years hence, moments captured in time and tale, long after the physical Harry had moved on to whatever six feet of dirt or potted cinders waited.

So he stayed in LA, plugging away at auditions and encounters with the opposite sex—and one or two of the same, as after all, everybody else with the exception of someone like Peter was doing it. The city stank of serial predators "jumping out of bed faster than into it, and hardly giving their oldshoe lover time to dress before spraying the premises with Lysol."

Harsh words, spoken by Harry's friend Stevo, a man who'd been around, though never as much as he claimed, which was everywhere.

He was a wannabe, Type A variety, and made it his business to know the Business without ever having actually worked in it. He was however great company for a single man, as he had a gift for approaching and meeting members of the opposite sex without being threatening. A huge consideration in LA, where phone numbers often directed one to more automated answering systems than PG&E.

Harry liked the lonely heart underneath Stevo's BS. He liked to say about Harry's latest failed relationship, "It wasn't meant to be. If it's meant to be, it will work out."

Thus far nothing in Harry's love life had been meant to be. He countered to Stevo that he didn't believe in fate and believed you made your own destiny. "If that's true," Stevo said, "you'd better beat the hell out of yourself because you ain't delivering."

Stevo felt one had to impress a date, first last and always. Harry thought that only confirmed what he said about creating one's fate. "It's an exhausting way to live, always trying to impress your lover. She should accept you and make your life easier."

"Right. Nail on the head. Your head. Think about it. If it's meant to be, she will."

#

One Sunday afternoon the weekly volleyball game went long. It was early September, often the hottest month in LA's annual sun drench, and after a listless round of games earlier when the heat seemed to turn ball and players into de facto zombies, a slight breeze of marine air began to cool the grateful who had lingered— because they were too baked to budge, or simply waiting in the late summer torpor for just this kind of break in the heat.

Harry had stayed on, first because he had no one to go home to and no place in particular on his agenda, and second Peter had clued him in on a new series project.

"If it goes, you're first in line for a part, Big Guy. And I'm talking regular."

"What's the concept?"

"An aging grandmother who turns into a Hit Woman. But she only offs bad guys. Kind of a vigilante. Think Death Wish with Granny. Every time she blows somebody away, she removes her dentures."

Harry thought it one of the most ridiculous ideas he'd ever heard. Which meant it had a good chance to get made.

"It's got interest out the wazoo. People are lining up. This deal's going to get done. I'm telling you, send out the good vibes, okay? Let them feel the energy. It's real, you know. You make your own destiny."

Harry listened hard, nodding assent like he really believed in the concept, whereas he mainly cared about the promised part, and was on the point of asking Peter which role that might be—

"Hey, my better half. Much better."

Over Peter's shoulder Harry saw a darkhaired woman walking toward them. She walked bathed in the rays of the descending sun, like in a movie where a goddess first appears to man. Harry had to shade his eyes to see her more clearly, and when he did, as she came closer and shaded from the bright band of sunlight, he felt a breathless thrill, almost a physical blow.

She was the most attractive woman to his eyes he had ever seen. Not classically beautiful, but naturally beautiful. Everything about her drove him wild with attraction. He'd never believed in the literary conceit "heart stopping," but she'd almost done that to him.

He'd almost missed that she was carrying her baby. Peter cooed over her and the child while Harry stared. So patent she turned to him full on.

"Hi, I'm Ariane," she said to him, plain and simple, smiling. Her voice had a melody that played on his heartstrings as well.

"Like the rocket," Peter chimed. "Space rocket, for non-scientists like you. Harry can't spike for shit honey but he's a good guy. Watch out for his hands. He's a batch on the make, 24/24."

"He looks like a real gentleman."

"He's never been a real gentleman, real or otherwise. Lucky for him he can act a little bit."

"Nice to meet you," Harry said, almost stuttering the banality.

Peter took the baby and began showing her off to the other players, who crowded around the happy father and his daughter. Harry was left with Ariane, trying to find something to say. She had tied his tongue into knots.

She helped him out. "He's so proud. He's going to spoil her crazy. And I'll probably let him."

"She's beautiful already. Your daughter."

In his mind he meant her. Ariane. He wondered if she felt his attraction.

"Can you believe he wanted to name her Scarlett? There I had to put my foot down. We compromised on Melanie."

Nothing profound, but Harry found her utterly charming, with a quality so rare to find in LA, at least in his experience—she was genuine and genuinely sweet, just a very very nice person. She was also married, and when Peter came over he said, "Before she got pregnant we'd have this game, race each other home. She'd always beat me."

"You? You're a gazelle," he said. "In the speed sense. Gazelles are handsomer."

"There goes your part," Peter jibed back.

Ariane laughed and said to Peter, "That's clever. You should take notes."

"We hire writers for that."

"So nice to meet you, Harry." She held out her hand and they shook. A strange, astounding sensation coursed through his body from his hand, which when he thought about later—and he would replay the moment many many times—he could only describe as a current of physical and sexual electricity. And in a bizarre sense, premonition. He felt they were meant to make love.

"Break a leg," Peter said, "you've got two, you know."

Ariane was wrong, Harry thought as they walked off, Peter can be clever too. But maybe she was just flattering him because she liked him?

He watched them—her—walk back into the sunlight from where she'd come, just a few short minutes ago when she'd changed his life, and it occurred to him like a blow that in a moment she'll disappear, FADE OUT from FRAME like in a film script, and this might be the one and only time he'd see her.

But it wasn't. She came more often to the Sunday volleyball games, never playing—"Hand-eye, I'm such a klutz"—just nurturing the baby and cheering on whoever made a good shot.

Harry tried not to make it obvious that he'd fallen completely, hopelessly and helplessly for her, crazy as that appeared to worldly souls like Stevo, who only got the broad stroke outlines from his friend after several glasses of a strong Italian red. "Tell her," Stevo said. "Let her know. Not that she doesn't know already. Women know these things. Trust your old buddy."

When Harry recounted the moment of when they'd shook hands, Stevo said, "Meant to be. End of story."

"The story hasn't even begun," Harry countered.

"Trust your old buddy. Destiny will find a way."

Harry bought the thickest shades on the market, so no one could spot him staring at her. They did his volleyball game no good, and more than once he just avoided getting smacked in the face by a spike. But when she was there he could care less about winning or losing. And when she wasn't, he cared even less. He lived for Sundays.

Ariane was exceedingly attractive, the kind of looks that appealed to him more than anyone else he'd ever met, but he could no more define the why and wherefore than how he'd felt the electric attraction surging through him that first day when they touched hands.

Whenever his mind cleared somewhat, he saw little hope. Ariane was married, Peter was his friend and even more in LA, a meal ticket.

As smoothly as he could however, Harry did everything to ingratiate himself with Peter. If his series project got a green light, it meant they'd see each other much more often and given odds and numbers, Ariane. Harry said to himself, maybe they're not as happy as they seem—which was very. But he hoped. Hollywood being Hollywood, he dreamed.

Ariane was never less than ebullient, charming and pleasant. He thought she liked talking to him and after each beach afternoon he made a calculation of their together time, what percentage of the day's conversation she'd spent talking to him in lieu of his teammates. He always came out ahead.

Peter, never, but he didn't have to. Race or walk home, he'd go with her and Harry would trudge alone back to his apartment and whatever casual date he'd set up for the evening—if. If not, a burger grilled on his small terrace balcony and a Sunday night film.

The volleyball group played year-round—God bless LA—but when winter came Peter and Ariane suddenly didn't.

As the weeks went by, Harry panicked. When he couldn't bear any more suspense, he called Peter on his cellphone. It took several days before he returned the call, a wait that panicked Harry even more.

He knew well how one could suddenly be dropped from a friend's social circle. Maybe from some offense they hardly realized at the time. Maybe because said friend had made a deal and instantly arrived at a circle richer, more famous, more successful. More. And the sludge had to be wiped from the boots. Goodbye Falstaff, and don't bother to write or call.

Such is LA, Harry thought. A city paved with eggshells.

When Peter finally came on the line he sounded rushed, busy and occupied. Which meant—"We've got a deal. The series. Hey, I've just been swamped. Been meaning to call you. You're still head of the pack when we start casting. Hey, I'm giving a little garden party next Sunday. Kind of the calm before the hurricane. Love to have you come. The producers will be there and all kinds of other assholes. You'll fit right in. Here's my gofer—he'll give you the address. Later, Big Guy."

It occurred to Harry that Peter hadn't doubted for a second that he would accept, or miracle of miracles, have other more important plans.

It was a big bash. Peter and Ariane had gotten lucky—Harry said to himself, they're always lucky—and found a superb home in the Palisades with an ocean view and orange and lemon trees, small fish pond and large enough lawn to accommodate all manner of Hollywood assholes who'd come out en masse.

Ariane had greeted him. "So glad you could come, Harry, it's been too long," and though he was not as sensitive as radar, he thought he saw genuine delight in her eyes. For damn sure it was in his.

Spring had come, and a light Santa Ana, and she wore a light floral dress of impeccable taste revealing her form and sexuality that almost overwhelmed him with excitement. He had to restrain himself from giving her a hug that might last all afternoon.

Instead he fell to the ritual of working the party—what one did in film land, bullshit small talk until vital info about name and career status could be divulged, and consequently cards. He'd worn the shades, and could keep her in his field of vision. Thus happy, absolutely agog at sight of her, he exuded confidence and attracted admirers and potential future colleagues who, like everyone in Town who didn't have a deal in place, sought out someone, anyone who could get them same.

Peter said in passing—he was like a dervish this day, as is the wont of a writer-director with a big project in the hopper—"Ariane organized everything—if it'd been me I'd have had 17 types of chips and dip."

"She has great taste," Harry said, indicating Ariane who'd arranged the extensive and scrumptious hors d'oeuvres that kept on coming.

"Yeah, except she likes you," Peter replied. Then he was off again, leaving Harry to wonder at the remark. And dream.

The party wound down at dusk, the Biz folk having other gigs on their agenda.

Ariane had been a perfect host, speaking to everyone, arranging the food and drink with the caterers, and Harry found barely a moment with her, but as the event waned she came over and said, "Don't leave yet. We've got some questions for you, ok? My big hiker guy."

He thrilled at the "my" and lingered—as if he'd ever had a nanosecond of impatience and desire to leave.

Harry was standing alone with his drink, watching the sun dip down toward sunset. For once in LA, some clouds had gathered and scattered the sunlight, and the rays struck the garden like a strobe at times.

Out of the corner of his eye, he saw Ariane tugging at Peter, who broke off his conversation with a producer type.

They came over to Harry, Peter waving toward a director as he left.

"Had a good time?" Peter asked.

"Fun."

"Some big shots asked me about you. The handsome guy in the shitty Hawaiian shirt. I said you were the Japanese gardener."

"Peter…" Ariane said.

He got down to the point. "Listen, we're going to get away before the shit hits the fan on this series. We've never toured the West, you know, that circle tour you always talk about."

"Right, Zion and Bryce and then the Big One."

"Got to see Monument Valley, John Ford country."

"It's a detour but if you've got the time…"

"We're going to take the time," Ariane said. "Do some hiking."

"No extreme shit," Peter said. He asked about non-extreme hikes. Harry had done some extremes, week-long backpacks, but he knew the easier tourist trails and listed them.

"I'll do up an itinerary and email you."

"You're so sweet," Ariane said, so sweetly he was surprised the following wasn't gibberish.

"When are you leaving?"

"This Tuesday," Peter said. "Two days. Time gets crowded, you know."

"Don't put yourself out, Harry," Ariane said.

"Be glad to do it," Harry said.

"What's to see at the Grand Canyon?" Peter asked. "Just a big hole in the ground, no?"

Ariane rolled her eyes.

"Kind of a romantic trip," Peter said, spotting the roll. "Got to put the romance back."

Despite himself Harry felt his hopes rise a notch. Such was love and war and LA, where friends and partners ogled wives and husbands from sunrise to sunrise. He was different, he thought. He wanted Ariane physically and sexually and emotionally, sincerely, deeply. There in the garden with his friend and her husband he admitted it silently and proudly.

"I wanted to camp," Peter was saying as Harry half-listened, his eyes on her through the filtering shades, "You know, sleeping bags and all that. But she wants to stay in those expensive UNESCO lodges built by the robber barons, where the beds are so big you have to hike toward your honey."

"Where can we hike at the Grand Canyon, Harry?" Ariane asked. "Something scenic but not too strenuous."

Harry thought a moment. "The Rim Trail."

Peter said, "Let me guess. It follows the rim."

"Yeah. It's flat and spectacular. Great photo ops. Watch your step though. It's not a 4-lane highway."

In mid-sentence Harry had a thought for which he was ashamed, and which would haunt him for years and years. Like a flash cut in a movie, an image that came and went in a second, he imagined Peter slipping and falling into the canyon depths. And Harry, himself, sad but content because it left Ariane for himself.

"Hey, you're a champ," Peter said, breaking off the conversation. He'd gotten the info. To Ariane: "Hey, we've got to say goodbye to the Bittermans."

Ariane smiled. "That's better than hello."

He had never heard her say something so biting, albeit utterly true. He knew the Bittermans, though only by reputation as huge Power Players in the Biz.

"Too bad you can't come with us, Harry," Ariane said. "Knowing how you love to hike the canyons."

"Three's a crowd," he heard himself say. He had a vision of himself alone in a motel room watching TV or in the campground among the bears and his fellow citizens while Peter made love to Ariane in the historic lodge with Rim view and bed large enough to accommodate a wagonload of pioneers.

"Not when you're the Number Three," she said. "You're so easy to be with."

As she went off to the Bittermans, Harry chugged his wine, trying to remove the despicable thought he'd had. She wouldn't think him so nice if she knew. She would detest him, and she would be right.

Reality was reality, and Ariane was not available. She had a husband and child and on this trip they would no doubt conceive another and he'd be off in a tent somewhere, real or symbolic. Alone.

Harry left the party while his friends were still making nice with the Bittermans. He waved to Peter who responded in kind. Harry pointed to his watch and mouthed, "Plans." The Bittermans ignored him. Ariane smiled and threw him a kiss.

"Have a great trip," he muttered to himself.

#

A few days later Harry had a pro forma meeting with one of the producers of Peter's TV series.

Pre-production would soon be in full swing, and at the party Peter informed his friend that he'd set up this meeting. He was determined to cast Harry in a continuing role, though the producer hemmed and hawed that nothing was definite yet and all the contracts hadn't been signed etc. It was looking good for a green light though.

Harry mentioned that he had a lot of gigs on his resume, to which the Producer said without enthusiasm, "Great, that's a plus," meaning he hadn't bothered to read the resume and wouldn't be doing so anytime soon in this century. TV was a producer's medium, but if the director wanted him, he had an in and Peter had been true to his word in arranging the meeting. Unlike about 99% of the people in Tinseltown, he kept his promises.

Which made Harry feel even more guilty that he'd welcomed even for an instant the prospect of Peter's death. Because he had. He tried to rationalize. He'd drunk quite a bit during the day, and with the hot sun and stress of networking and the vision of loveliness that was Ariane...

Harry had met some other of the couple's friends at the party, and he was glad to BS with the volleyball crowd who'd come in force. Some of them had known Peter much longer than he. They all exchanged numbers.

But Hollywood being Hollywood, where news often traveled first through the trades, Harry opened the Hollywood Reporter as per diem over his morning coffee and learned that Peter had slipped and fallen to his death on the Grand Canyon Rim trail.

His body had already arrived back in LA, accompanied by his widow.

In a series of frantic phone calls, Harry managed to gather some sparse information. Ariane was under a doctor's care. She'd been hiking with Peter, who'd been snapping photos, and typically of a man who went full bore enthusiasm through life and work and damn the torpedos, he hadn't bothered to notice the loose gravel and sand and how close he was to the rim.

He was gone without a sound, Ariane said to the police, and vanished so quickly it took a moment for her to realize what had happened. She wanted to follow him and almost did, but just managed to restrain herself at thought of their child, innocently waiting back in Los Angeles.

Was it fate that had killed Peter? Harry thought not. His wish had given force to the wind or whatever loose rock and shale had sent Peter to his death, had led him to choose the one spot on the Rim trail that would not hold his weight. Perhaps the wind had begun to rise that moment at the party when Harry described the trail and said to be careful. Speculation grew into fatality, a monstrous accident fomented by a monster.

Because he hadn't changed. His first flashcut thought after the shock of news he was reading in the paper was, "Now she's available."

And the second: "There goes the TV series."

He hated himself. Praire scum, except the prairie would have spit him up in disgust.

#

The funeral was an ultra-private affair strictly limited to close family, and Harry thanked God for that, even though he knew God would need a long long time to pardon him. And her, never.

He sent a condolence card to Ariane and was deeply hurt when she did not reply, though he understood. Even if she didn't suspect his perfidy within, she would forever associate the Rim Trail and Peter's death with him, the so-called friend.

Just as well, he concluded. At first sight of her, even more beautiful and soft and desirable, with depths of soul deepened by tragedy, he would not be able to control himself from taking her in his arms and holding on for life.

And she, seeing the guilt writ large all over his face, screaming "Murderer! Assassin! Traitor."

#

He called his agent and said, don't be choosy. Get me anything and everything, I'll audition till the cows come home and take whatever's offered. No discrimination. I want to bury myself in work. He found himself doing decent projects and utter schlock, risking to confuse producers so much their heads wouldn't be able to wrap around his resume.

The months went by. About a year after Peter's death, at one of the jobs he knew he'd be ashamed of when he looked back, between takes he noticed a voice message. He sourced it and was stunned to hear the sweet, melodious, vulnerable voice of Ariane. Wondering if he'd like to have a drink or coffee. She apologized for not staying in contact for so long. "Recovering, you know."

He would very much like that, he told her when he called back, assuring her over and over that he understood she needed time and he'd respected that. Avoiding saying what he really thought, that she'd been so much braver than he in taking the first step out of grief, and that he was not worthy of her.

But just for that reason, paradoxically, he desired nothing so much as to see her, and where a worthy person would have not done so out of principle, he could not help himself. As always with her.

Coffee shops came few and far between in LA if they weren't named Starbuck's, and Ariane was nothing if not classy.

She chose a bar/restaurant a stone's throw from the beach, but many stone throws from the site of the volleyball game where Harry played only sporadically now.

The days were stretching longer and Harry figured what Ariane confirmed—she wanted to have a late afternoon drink and decide later if and when she and Harry wanted to prolong to dinner time.

"It's been hard," she said. "I feel so fragile."

Harry found her subdued at first, then pleasant and amiable, her fragility to him only putting into high relief her bravery in surviving a wound that would never heal completely. Those were her words, her only reference to the preceding months when she'd tried to "rebound and go on, for the baby's sake."

As if Harry needed any more proofs of her infinite charm, he had only to look around the trendy bar and fail to find anyone who could match her. She had the same hold over him, so much he could well imagine himself melting like the Wicked Witch of the West.

He deserved to, he reflected, for the evils I've done in spirit and maybe reality.

She read him well.

"Don't blame yourself, Harry."

He was stunned. Did she know?

"We loved the Rim trail. The minute we saw it. We'd have taken it even if you'd never existed."

She took a drink and smiled. "But I'm glad you do."

"I can't ever tell you how sorry I am."

"I know you are."

"But I'm…"

He interrupted himself. He meant to say, I'm glad you didn't go over the edge as well. But couldn't. It would have been too awful taste.

"I know you are." Then added after a moment: "I've done enough sorrowing for us both."

They stayed for dinner. For the first time, Harry had her all to himself, and the evening passed in a bright golden light for him, both literally when a brilliant sunset lit up the sidewalk table where they sat, and symbolically. He'd never felt so happy and content to be exactly this place in the world, above all others, because he was with her, even if he had no reason to consider the evening anything more than renewed friendship. Ariane gave nothing away.

With some hesitation, but determined not to let the chance pass with a woman he found irresistible, he relied on an LA trope so common it virtually guaranteed a yes, as it ranked with breathing salt air at the beach—he invited her to a movie, the proverbial highly anticipated sequel to a blockbuster romantic comedy. She accepted instantly and suggested they catch an early screening so she could fix him an alfresco dinner.

"It's warm enough outside and I've found a buyer. We'll kiss the place goodbye."

She'd said matter-of-factly that the house was too big for her and the baby and she wanted to move to Santa Monica.

"A real city," she said, "to make different memories."

He welcomed this with a thrill, as it would bring her closer—at least geographically. and without being said, he knew she wanted to change her life. Maybe, he worried, he was a loose thread from her time with Peter and she was preparing to pack him up for the movers as well. Hence the dinner. A farewell.

He found it stressful, the evening meal in the same splendid back yard where he'd last seen Peter and in one horrendous moment, wished for his death. If karma existed, he would be struck dead and at any moment he expected her to stand and shout "*J'accuse.*"

But she didn't, and they had a pleasant evening under the stars and a cool marine breeze. They walked to the cliff edge to observe the great wide ocean under a full moon.

"Last glass," he said, pouring the champagne he'd brought and grateful she hadn't found it in bad form. "A gift," he said of the Dom Perignon, "been sitting around. I couldn't just drink it myself in front of the Dodgers."

For the first time, they just watched and wondered, with nothing to say. Harry had one thought only in mind—how to embrace her with the intention of never letting go.

When she finished the last of her champagne, she again made it easy for him. She turned and kissed him, not a polite kiss but direct and passionate.

Boxes had already been piled up in the bedrooms, even the baby's, but the beds remained, for the baby and hers in the guest room where she'd been sleeping. They made love there, and Harry was happy not to be in the room where she'd slept with Peter. He felt awkward at first, amazed that a dream came true, but again she made it easier for him, loving with a startling fervor.

When he found enough sense to reflect, he rationalized that she'd been bottling up desire for a year—she'd sworn he was her first date since the accident—but the next time and the time after that, she made love as if it were the last time and each second had to be savored with all the love and feeling she had in body and soul.

They spent one day as perfect as he could ever imagine, at the beach under supernal skies, mood made divine with happiness, an evening of lovemaking that went on and on, in her new Santa Monica apartment that seemed to liberate both of them.

When dawn began to light their room where they hadn't slept a second, she suddenly broke down in tears, shaking and sobbing until he began to worry she'd finally broken under the strain of denial and tragedy, and their idyll would end under the realization it had been a rebound fantasy.

"I love you," she managed to say.

Having said that, she looked away. "They brought him in all bloody and mashed up and broken. So horrible. How could I identify him? They forced me to look and look, but he wasn't a person any more. I will never look at him again. Never never. I won't. Don't let me. Make me happy."

They married soon, in a small private ceremony with no beach crowd present, just family and baby Caroline as bridesmaid.

Harry had some savings and spent a good chunk on a honeymoon in Europe. They loved Venice and Rome and adored the Italian coast south of Naples, less visited by the rich and famous but a perfect getaway for those whose private, personal universe closed in more and more as time went by.

With her love supporting him and the confidence she had in him, Harry went back to work with the strutting assurance that made producers and directors notice and respond.

"You're a grounded guy," a bigwig once told him.

Harry felt grounded but on the other hand, as close to 7th heaven as could be. Sometimes when he woke up before her, he would just stare at her, marveling at her beauty. When they went to industry parties—rarer and rarer as the years went by—he could glance at a packed room of beautiful people, starlets and wannabes from around the globe, and still laser-focus on the one woman in the room who lit all the fires he had in him.

He lost touch with Stevo, still on the make and prowling singles bars, a galaxy that now seemed far, far away.

They bought a house in Santa Monica and consolidated households. Their son John was born, conceived somewhere on the Italian coast, grew up loved and pampered and got along well with Caroline, whom Harry succeeded in raising as his own daughter. She remembered almost nothing of her natural father. The children survived adolescence along with their parents and moved into adulthood as solid hardworking citizens. And fine human beings. Harry attributed it to Ariane having chosen this little island in Santa Monica, far from the craziness of Hollywood.

He got more and more parts, roles in TV series and sometimes a feature. He reconciled himself to being a secondary player, never a star. But once he renounced such foolish ambitions, à la Hollywood, he got a continuing role in a hit series and for five years became a household name. He'd become familiar to audiences over the years, and the role fit him perfectly.

Ariane had no ambitions to become rich or famous and enjoyed their life on a quiet section of town north of Wilshire and south of Montana, with pine trees and a small garden. She learned relaxation therapies, and specialized in individual sessions where her empathy and humanity gave new life physically and psychologically. In a town where insecurity came with every day's breakfast, she thrived and found many celebrities knocking on her door. When she expanded to psychomotor therapy, she thrived even more, to the point where Harry worried for her health. "You're exhausting yourself and you don't need to," Harry said.

"I can help these people,"Ariane smiled. "Pay for my sins, you know."

"You've never sinned in your life," he said, and he meant it. Even their arguments resembled spirited debates.

Harry would sometimes feel so glad to be alive he wondered how he could ever die. "What's the point?" he chuckled.

The past had receded. LA was a great place to bury guilt. Dinner parties and days and days came and went where conversations turned around current movies, gigs and possible gigs, scandals, Malibu fires and mudslides, who was making how much money. One basked in the superficial like the constant sun, and Harry liked it that way.

"Existentialism got stopped at LAX customs," he liked to say, without fully knowing what it meant.

At 45, still so lovely she was often taken for her sister when she went out with her daughter, Ariane learned her growing and sometimes almost unbearable abdominal pains came from ovarian cancer.

It went very fast, so fast nothing worked, no chemo, no surgery.

"I deserve this," she said. "I was too happy."

She went into hospital when the pain became too great and needed painkillers that only wounded the pain. Harry refused to believe she would leave him and spent whole days at the hospital.

On one of those sad, miserable days, he woke up very early, unable to sleep much as usual since she'd fallen ill. He went to the hospital.

When he arrived, the night duty doctor announced she'd had a bad night, gone down fast and he wasn't sure she'd make it through the day. "She's fading into a coma," he said.

Trembling, Harry managed to call the children with the news.

He sat at her bedside, waiting for them to arrive and whatever time would bring.

He took his wife by the hand. Any time he spoke to her, he got no response. She slept a deep profound sleep.

Desperate, Harry had a revelation. He told himself, if my wish could make it happen at the Grand Canyon, maybe if I exorcise my guilt and sin, the gods will take pity and save her. She was wrong. She doesn't deserve this. I do.

"I wanted him to die," Harry blurted out to her. "As soon as I said, take this trail, I saw him falling. And I wanted it. A part of me loved him but a part of me hated him because he had you. I wanted you for myself. I loved you so much. I've always loved you. My wish made it happen. He fell because of me. And I've never had the courage to tell you. Because you'd hate me. And then I couldn't live, seeing the pain in your eyes."

He was sobbing now, staring into the past.

Something told him to turn.

Her eyes were open. Harry looked deep into them.

And as if on a big film screen, he saw the scene: Peter squatting low on the rim, the Canyon below, snapping pictures of the resplendent colors, when a hand came into FRAME, pressed onto his back and pushed him into the void. He fell out of sight without a sound, perhaps silenced by shock and despair.

Ariane struggled to whisper, and he leaned closer so he could just hear, "He didn't fall."

Her eyes closed again. She died before the children arrived, leaving him in the dark.

#

He mourned for a year. Lost and floundering, he sleptwalked through a couple of small roles. Hollywood being a small town, word got out, and despite the sympathy he got for "having a rough time"—much of it was token and expressed in the same breath with "he can't give you 100%." Others could, and offers stopped coming despite Harry's berating of his longtime agent, who responded by acknowledging his grief but subtexting that he needed to get over it.

Harry tried, but besides missing her each and every second of his days and nights, the beauty he could always find on the pillow next to his—he remained stunned and wondering at the thought she might have killed for him.

Had she? Had he misinterpreted her dying words? It seemed incredible but at the time, that moment when she left him, he believed her.

One day, a day he thought he would go mad—he'd avoided shrinks because if he would really and truly get help, he'd have to relate the problem and this being Hollywood, he felt sure the tale would turn up and a treatment and pitch—he sat down at his computer.

The story of their love poured out in 8 hours of nonstop recollections.

When it was done, Harry reread them. He felt if not cleansed, at least exorcised. Of himself and his dear darling and everything that had happened. Once again he saw her walking out of the late afternoon sunlight on the beach and into his life, a vision straight out of the most romantic gauze-doctored film he had ever seen.

Once again the thought crossed his mind, if someone gets a look at this—shrink, gardener, candlestick maker—that's exactly what they'll think too. Film. They'll stampede to every wannabe producer in town.

And that, he could not abide. It was his story. He got in touch with his friend from the Texas mafia with whom he'd worked in college, now writing adaptations of romance novels for TV films.

Together they worked up a script for a feature. Harry's friend suspected he was working from a true life story, but was discreet enough to never pose the question upfront. Harry was paying his fee out of his own pocket with his depleting savings, and a big backend participation if the film got made.

Which it did. Harry couldn't bring himself to play any role, least of all the lead—it would be too much for his fragile emotions—but equally he couldn't entrust the story to anyone else to direct. So he held out, refusing to sell until the producers agreed to give him the shot.

The script attracted a lot of interest, and the budget for this character-oriented film involved few if any special effects—though the death scene at Big Sur would involve some location shooting—and Harry got the gig.

Surprisingly, some big names lined up to play the leads—including the hottest actress in town, the star du jour who nevertheless was perfect for the part and put heart and soul into it.

The film was put into limited release, the distributors rightly figuring that it would have to be handled delicately, given the controversy that might follow.

Harry Kile never could get outside of himself enough to see the story as others might see it. The film for him represented first and last his tribute to Ariane, and his best attempt at catharsis.

Debate raged. Between those who admired what a woman would do for true love, and those who reviled her as a heartless killer. They doubted she could ever be genuine in her love. Many references were made to film noir and the evil vamp quite willing to off her husband to be with her lover. But critics countered that in this film, the character had not even kissed before killing. "No woman would ever do that!" screamed the consensus of doubters and moralists.

All agreed however that the woman's part merited an Oscar nom. Suffering from guilt, hiding it from her husband and children, and when she could not repress it completely and let pass a flashcut into her haunted soul, having to endure her husband's barely controlled anger and jealousy over what he thought was her un-dying love for her first husband.

Whereas she had let it die when he did.

As ever, the controversy drove spectators to the cinema. The film became a massive worldwide hit. Harry Kile was besieged with projects and offers.

He could afford to pick and choose. One film had made him a rich man, and as a major film director now, he no longer had to worry about money or the primal fear of an actor, age.

Speculation had never ceased to identify the film story with his own. Harry said ruefully to his co-writer, "Maybe somebody on the upper steppes of Upper Mongolia thinks it's all fiction, but he's the only one." But he never came forward with an admission. Harry, né Harold, had gotten used to stalling confessions.

And after all, why should he? He'd begun dating again, and LA being what it is, here too he could pick and choose. The Times ran a story on his new home in the Canyons.

Sometimes he would reflect on his life and how much he owed to Ariane, and how fortunate he'd been that she decided to choose him. He could only conclude that she too had been unable and unwilling to resist their attraction.

But like her, he never allowed himself to envision how Peter looked when they brought up his crushed body from the rocky canyon depths.

2. FIRST LOVE. PART 1.

When a New York doctor and LA film director fall in love on a hiking trip they must manage dream and reality across the wide continent that separates them.

Rachel rarely reminisced about her youth. There was too much to occupy her time, from husband and 4 children to a schedule chockfull of work, charitable causes, her medical practice and events like the conference she was flying to attend in Los Angeles.

She was nearing retirement age but determined to keep on working as long as she wanted. She was in excellent health, thanks greatly to her regime of gym and the yearly treks she organized with a group of likeminded New York City friends who loved to escape the Big Apple and spend several days hiking and camping in the wilderness.

She'd brushed up on the conference agenda during the flight, and just as she'd finished reading, the pilot announced that they'd soon be crossing over the Grand Canyon. The crystal clear weather and sharp sunlight this spring day would allow for great viewing of the natural wonder.

Rachel looked out from her window seat but she had another sight she wanted to see, before they arrived at the Grand Canyon, and worried that they'd already passed over it. But no, there it was.

Down below in the welter of gullied brown terrain that she recognized as plateau and canyonland, flattened out from this perspective, but not at all flat as she well knew, she spotted a dark circular disc. It stood out because it was a mountain, Navajo Mountain, and to the north she could see how the land was cut into creases which she knew were deep canyons.

She knew those canyons. She'd been in them once.

#

When Rachel turned 27 on a frigid spring day in New York, she had yet to have a serious love affair. She'd grown up on her parents' farm in Pennsylvania and knew how to milk cows and gather eggs and all kinds of farm chores and though she reveled in the rural life outdoors, it had furnished few men capable of matching her vivacity and brilliance. Her parents had fled Poland to escape the Holocaust and she cared passionately and fervently about her Jewish heritage and could not conceive of ever marrying someone who did not share her faith. Jewish men had not come droving for her favors at the rural farm.

She went to college and excelled academically as always, and promptly moved to New York to finish her studies. She had settled on the medical profession.

As a doctor, she saw herself becoming a holistic practitioner who could combine physiological, traditional medical care with psychological insights rooted in the age-old traditions and values of her religion. They gave her an anchor, and she wanted to give back.

At university she studied hard and usually did not have great amounts of time to meet men. She did take two long backpack holidays to Europe, solo——though she wasn't fearless, few things or men intimidated her. On the contrary, that was the problem—she intimidated them. She managed to lose her virginity in her ancestral homeland of Poland, but it and the whole country she found depressing, still recovering from the effects of the war and Communism, grayness everywhere, and somehow the sexual act with an ardent young Polish student didn't light flames.

Back home in New York where she had settled in blissfully, she dated as frequently as she could tolerate whoever she'd met or been set up with, but still, Mr. Right did not come along, or even close.

She confided to her friend and confidant Karen, "At this point I'd settle for Mr. Maybe."

She realized that she was no great classic beauty, but she was attractive and had a wonderful smile and laugh, so the man who could bring out her innate optimism and joy would be treated to many delightful moments just being around her. But borrowing from another religion, she said ruefully one day to Karen, to whom she could confide a bit more of her "crass worldly concerns," as she called them, than to her very orthodox devout friends Isaac and Sarah, "Mohamed isn't coming to the mountain. Am I that fat or just so hard to climb?"

She meant it half seriously, as she thought she was a bit chubby and hadn't had a chance to work off all her baby fat. "And every other kind of fat."

So she began working out and riding her bicycle everywhere.

Then on her birthday she had a wild hair of an idea. "If Mohamed isn't coming to the mountain, maybe he doesn't like mountains. Maybe he prefers canyons."

She had joined the Sierra Club and done some dayhikes with the local chapter. She sensed a great deal of rapport with the people she met and they brought a satisfying weekend change to her intensive weekly routine of classes and study and lab work.

She'd been throughout Europe but the rest of the USA remained terra incognito; by now an avowed New Yorker, she saw no reason to live anywhere else. One day a girl friend from Pennsylvania had come for a visit and dropped over for coffee. They'd been discussing the City That Never Sleeps and just after Rachel had excused herself for a moment, she came back from the bathroom: "Come here," she said, "got to show you something."

Her friend followed her to the bathroom and Rachel pointed toward the tub. Scuttling around on the porcelain that probably dated back 50 years was "A New York in all its authenticity," Rachel proclaimed. A large, and to most eyes ugly, cockroach.

Her friend had trouble hiding her disgust, but to Rachel, this was the city in all its highs and lows. One lived with Lincoln Center culture just down the street from where she lived and cockroaches from time to time in the bathtub.

The Sierra Club organized weeklong backpacking trips open to members from all over the country, and Rachel saw this as a chance to take a break from everything and for a few days maneuver past a land new to her of scorpions and cactus.

Plus, she had another motive. A couple of months ago she had met a guy named Jim at a party who interested her. He didn't seem the One at first glance and conversation but he was handsome and eligible and she was attracted to him. He lived in Phoenix and had returned home the day after the party, too soon for them to get anything going but enough to tease.

She saw that the Sierra Club was offering a trip to Rainbow Bridge National Monument in Utah, in the heart of canyon country. Two women were leading it, meaning if she found herself surrounded by unsympathetic horny males, she would have a lifeline.

The trip fell between exams, and she calculated she could take a few days afterward to visit Jim in Phoenix. She knew that he'd be expecting more than polite conversation when she arrived and crashed at his apartment with him for three days. But she was ready for adventure.

To Karen she confided: "I'm 27. I've been working and studying non-stop since I was seven. On the farm they called me Miss

Chore. Out there in the Wild West I'm going to tie one on, and I don't mean alcohol."

The Club had a list of essentials and she made sure to pack them, as well as her sleeping bag and just enough clothes in her new backpack to get through seven days on the trail where they might not encounter enough running water to bathe in. She had no problem contemplating this deprivation, which appalled Isaac and Sarah. "Remember, I grew up on a farm."

In her valise she packed the dress clothes she'd wear after the hike, and particularly a white nightgown, tastefully revealing, for the sojourn in Phoenix. She flew in to the city and gave Jim a call from the airport. He said he was expecting her after the backpack trip. She'd have liked to hear a tad more excitement in his voice, but she told herself, she'd work on charging him up next week.

It had been exciting just to fly over Arizona's desert mountains and land in the sprawling city that radiated enough heat even these first days of May to give her an idea of the Armageddon that was the summer here.

Fellow tripsters Frida and Joe Smith picked her up. They were from California, all-American, WASP and seasoned hikers, even though Joe had let his gut pot out considerably. He said to Rachel, "We don't look like hikers but we can pick 'em up and lay 'em down."

Anyway, Frida said, "After the first day it doesn't look so strenuous." Rachel realized she hadn't even thought much about whether she'd be able to shoulder a heavy pack and march over rugged rocky canyon terrain. She'd just counted on the excitement, her customary energy and adrenaline to see her through.

As they left the megalopolis Phoenix was becoming and headed north on the freeway, she felt a few tremors, no panic but a healthy fear she hoped would help lead her down a canyon trail. While she waited for the rush, she talked up the storm she was quite capable of doing when the occasion demanded, drawing out Frida and Joe about their daily lives.

Nothing she heard gave her any desire to take up their mellow Southern Cal lifestyle, but they added to her range of life experience and they were very nice and generous, insisting on buying her lunch when they reached the northern town of Kayenta.

Rachel admired the green high national forest country they traversed after climbing out of the Phoenix valley megalopolis. It seemed deep, dark and endless. When they reached Flagstaff, snowflakes coated the city. "Never been here once when it wasn't snowing, and I've been here for a few," Joe said.

Soon after the town of Cameron they turned and headed east, and now Rachel was stunned by the vast scrubland emptiness under a hot cloudless sky that stretched for miles and miles wherever she looked in all directions. Occasionally she glimpsed a smallish rounded dome hut far in the distance, which Joe said was a Navajo hogan.

"On the res now," he said. It was the loneliest landscape she had ever seen, and to an adopted New Yorker who loved the proximity of people and community, it was an almost visceral shock. "It's the culture," Frida added sympathetically. "The Navajo like space and distance between their dwellings."

"Culture? It's more like their religion. Nature and all. Sure easy to get lonely out here," Joe added.

Rachel thought, in that way it's not so different from New York. She rarely permitted herself to get lonely, but she knew that deep down she was and wondered if living in a hogan was so very much a change from a single young woman in a single apartment on the West Side.

After what seemed hours but was probably no more than one— after a time the landscape became interchangeable in Rachel's eyes —Joe announced, "Look careful now."

"For what?" Rachel asked.

"Where we're going. See that dome?" Rachel looked left and just could make out an oval shape on the northern horizon.

"Navajo Mountain. Rainbow Bridge lies in a canyon on one of its flanks."

"Sacred mountain," Frida added, and Rachel liked the idea of sacredness even though she doubted she could ever feel what the Navajo felt. Theirs she knew was an earth-centered religion, if it could even be called religion by her own definition of the word. To her understanding, she confided to Joe and Frida, it was more about respect for Mother Earth. No gods but nature, in all its wonder.

"That's poetry," Frida said. "Never thought of it that way."

"Where we're going, Rainbow Bridge, that's sacred too for them," Joe added.

"Yeah, like some big energy vortex," Frida added.

Rachel was just impish enough to imagine a vortex whisking Frida away into the sky like Dorothy and landing somewhere far away, except this land she was passing through was so wild and wide she'd probably end up in another canyon and look vainly for the Wizard. This country demanded respect, and she hadn't caught that in Frida's tone. She and Joe lived in an Orange County suburb and Joe, who was more ironic and acerbic than his wife, said they'd go off on backpacking trips if only to "arrest the brain shrinkage" brought on by the day-after-day sameness of car, dishwasher and dog walks.

Rachel hadn't expected that from Joe, but she was hoping and expecting for surprises, large and small.

"There it is."

Joe meant a dirt road intersecting the main highway they were traveling. It was hardly marked, just a battered tin marker on a wood pole with the number of the turnoff. Joe turned left onto a road that gave new meaning to the word washboard, a dirt and gravel route baked by years of sun into a hard-as-stone surface. For a few moments Joe slowed, letting the bumps and bounces rattle his passengers.

"See," he said, "you go slow you end up with scrambled brains."

"How long before we get there?" Rachel wondered.

"Longer than you'd want like this," Joe replied, and he hit the gas pedal. They speeded up toward 50 mph. Against logic, the going smoothed out and became tolerable.

"Only way to drive something like this," he said.

They had no oncoming traffic to worry about and no luckless vehicles behind to eat the mountain of dust kicked up. But about fifteen minutes into their journey, the last leg before arriving at the rendezvous point with the other hikers, "the old Rainbow Lodge" according to Joe, they passed a vintage Buick whose driver apparently hadn't learned what Joe had. It was going slowly and the female passenger looked like a bobbing cork.

Joe didn't slow and passed them. Rachel couldn't even see them in the dust cloud they raised.

"If he's got any sense he'll learn from watching me. Otherwise we won't see 'em till next week."

"That far? Navajo Mountain looks like it's five minutes away now."

"Multiply that by ten and you'll be about right," Joe calculated.

Rachel looked behind, trying to spot what could only be fellow hikers headed to the same rendezvous as they. She wondered who was in the car and what kind of people they were.

She hoped she'd find someone attractive among the bunch. This was a new world and she wanted to explore it with someone or someones who'd make it even more than an adventure, a pleasure. She was 27 now and the clock was ticking, though she'd already realized that out here she didn't need a clock—she had the sun and light and shadows that reflected the movement of time, and she got the feeling she might soon start thinking about them like the Navajo.

#

Matt did have the sense to speed up his Buick, taking the cue from Joe's example, and as the going got smoother his passenger Roberta said, "This is darn easier on the old noggin."

Matt had a quip but held off. He'd learned in just one day of Roberta's company that though she recognized humor for what it was, how it was generated and how to appreciate it weren't part of her immediate skill set.

"Sure is rocky country," Roberta said, for the third time since they'd made the turnoff, but this time she added a speculation: "Wonder if the trail's going to be like this."

"I don't think so. It's dirt and rock but this is what I'd call a road."

"Yessir, I guess you're right."

#

"Did everybody bring two quarts of water?"

The backpack trip leader, Thomasin, in her '60s but lean and fit as a woman 20 years younger, posed this question after dinner, which had been served around a campfire--the only one they'd be allowed the next six days. This one was permitted because the group had camped around the crumbling brick ruins of Rainbow Lodge, a resort in its day fifty or more years before, that hoped to cater to rich Easterners looking to get way way away from it all. The few who came did, but Rachel rather thought that they'd been so overwhelmed by the wide emptiness of desert and silence, if not the heat and dust, they felt that once done, once done.

The few reduced to none, and the Lodge closed. After time, erosion, winds and perhaps Navajo youths having fun tearing down a dominant-culture structure, only a few low walls remained, and the Lodge now served only as a marker for the Rainbow Bridge trailhead and zone for pit campfires.

Rachel found it hard to imagine that in a few hours she'd be sleeping on the ground, far away from New York's habitual bleating traffic. She wondered how she would deal with it, and the sound of silence. She'd brought two quarts of mineral water from the Catskills.

"This is a desert," Thomasin continued, "and you can get dehydrated before you realize it. Drink water in small doses continuously, not all at once when you feel thirsty. Thirst is a warning sign that it's almost too late.

"Tomorrow we won't find water till the campsite, and that's nine miles around Navajo Mountain. Did everyone try to get in shape before the trip?"

Rachel had, on her bicycle, but she knew that wasn't the same as lugging a 45-pound backpack. She looked around and got comfort from more than one guilty expression and gaze-avoiding down-turned face.

She'd met most of them as they supped around the campfire. Frank, a white-haired man and clearly the elder statesman of the bunch, had been greeted by Thomasin and her co-leader Jo as a celebrity, and it turned out he'd written a series of chapbooks called "The West's Canyons," whose eventual goal was to catalogue and describe every canyon system the West could offer.

"That's a lot," he admitted, "and Father Time may not let me get to them all."

He said it without sadness, just realism. In fact he'd already written about the canyons they'd be traversing, and he talked intimately about Forbidden and Bridge Canyons.

Frank looked as if he'd been nailed to his desk for some time, however, and Matt quipped, "Why Forbidden, Frank? Is that why we had to get a permit?" He said it with a measure of respect, which he later said was genuinely felt. "You've got to admire someone who catalogues canyons. You could throw a rock in a thousand crowds and never hit anyone doing that."

Matt followed up: "Are we going to run across some Keep Out signs?"

Frank chuckled. "I kind of doubt we'll be running. At least not tomorrow. Good thing too because you'll have time to look and appreciate. These canyons are special. You'll see."

"Real glad to have you along, Frank," Matt said sincerely. Later he ordered a few of the books from Frank, who ran his own mail order business. Matt said the writing style would never let anyone forget someone like Robert Louis Stevenson or even Marco Polo, but they filled a need and moreover, Frank had no intention whatsoever of commercializing his little tomes for a wider audience.

"We don't want too many people to come. Then they'll start building roads. Let's keep these canyons for the folks willing to sweat."

Matt said later that was the most eloquent thing he ever heard Frank say, and he'd told him in a note when he ordered that he'd love to see him put it in one of his future books.

Frank wrote back that he intended to do just that if Father Time let him, and in his autographed dedication on the frontispiece Matt noticed a moist stain that he thought might have come from a tear.

"I was so happy that he considered me worthy of the canyons."

Rachel had noticed Matt as soon as he'd rolled up in his vintage Buick, got out and donned his Stetson and started joking about the zillion ruts and bumps they'd just rattled over.

"Anybody have a toothpick to clean the dust out of my teeth?"

"That was funny," Rachel would say later to Karen, "and I said to myself, I can count on this guy for some laughs, assuming he can catch his breath on the trail. But what really got my attention was his butt, which was--is--so cute."

"And people call you an intellectual," Karen laughed.

"I put him first on my list of targets."

He'd arrived with Roberta, and Rachel wondered about their relation. Roberta didn't seem to get the toothpick joke, and didn't manage a supportive smile, which Rachel thought a wife or lover would.

Despite his age, Frank made #2 on her list. Rachel admired people who did wild and crazy things, as she saw very little of these in her ideal future.

When Thomasin wrapped up she turned the discourse over to her co-leader Jo, who repeated the need to have the 10 essentials such as flashlight, matches and sun hat, then segued into the mechanism of a backcountry potty--a hole in the ground that could be covered up after carefully burning one's TP.

Yep, Rachel thought, a long way from Manhattan.

The sun was setting when Jo finished, and Rachel appreciated her non-nonsense factual spiel but regretted a little that she hadn't gone into the history of Rainbow Bridge and the illustrious visitors like Theodore Roosevelt who'd trekked the route they'd be taking-- albeit, on horseback.

Only recently had souls willing to sweat and stumble over rock and sand begun to make the arduous hike to the Bridge. These souls had come from all over the lower 48 and ranged in age up to 70.

Rachel suspected she was the youngest. She felt excited, thrilled, happy even, and took some time before joining a group kibitzing around the remains of the fire to admire the golden sunset, marveling how the desert sandstone magnified and reflected deep colors of orange and yellow.

She noticed Matt doing the same, his back turned to the Lodge and everyone else, as if he wanted to commune with the sun and desert, and just the thought made her happy somehow.

As she watched, a very bright band of sunlight, the last before darkness started to fall, enveloped him and half-blinded her, so he was momentarily lost from her view. She vowed that unless her instincts proved wrong about him, she wouldn't let that happen again.

#

Rachel perused the chitchatting subgroups that had formed around the various Lodge wall remains, almost as if they still served as bedrooms for the night, and she made sure she joined Matt's, the younger crowd.

Roberta was there--though Rachel a bit cattily found her age indeterminate--the two sons of Sven, he originally from Switzerland--all of whom looked like they could scale the Matterhorn before lunch--Suzy, a petite Californian who spoke very little, another Californian named Randi, tall and dark-haired and back from the Yukon where she'd hiked all over and maybe stared down grizzlies--and Jeff, a '40ish guy who resembled the Marlboro man and had the same clean unlinted appearance as the latter--Rachel wondered if dust could ever cling to him.

Jeff was model handsome but Rachel thought he had little interesting or original to say, other than it was important to munch granola bars on the trail from time to time.

"And beef jerky? I brought along a packet," Matt said.

"Well, if it's not too salty. Now granola bars--" And Jeff went into a riff about their superiority to other snack foods, which Rachel immediately tuned out. Her focus came back only when Matt launched into a thread about Los Angeles and the film business, of which he was an aspiring member as he'd just finished directing a low budget film about a teenage prom.

"Oscar won't come to this dance, I assure you. I told my Mom, 'It's a start.' She had a hard time when I changed careers. I'd been studying literature at UCLA and when she asked what I was doing, I'd say something like, 'writing about the idea of imagination in the works of Wordsworth and Coleridge.' Then all of a sudden I was saying, 'Writing a comedy about a talking dog. And getting paid for it.'"

Rachel laughed and said, "You've got to start somewhere. Dogs and proms I mean."

She thought that with this he noticed her for the first time, but it could just have been a cineaste looking for a fan, no matter who or where. It came out that Matt had driven to Las Vegas from LA and picked up Roberta at the airport, where she'd flown in from Wisconsin. They'd spent the night there, then camped at Zion National Park after a dayhike on the East Rim Trail.

"That was my training," Matt confessed.

"Yessir," Roberta added, "it was steep at times. But one step after another, that's what you have to do, and we made it."

Matt elaborated, "There's one stretch where you're looking out over the abyss, one thousand feet down, just this narrow trail where one slip means goodbye. I'm heading up with my heart in my throat praying for us to top out on a wider section, and this guy comes down the trail, stops and starts a conversation!"

"He was a claims adjuster, like me," Roberta added, "pretty interesting fella."

Rachel could picture the scene, with Roberta clueless and Matt on the edge, literally and figuratively, while the two rattled on. She interjected, "If you ask me, he needed his claim adjusted."

Matt smiled wide, the first time she'd seen him do that, and knew he appreciated her wit and understanding. He asked her the proverbial innocuous question, where was she from.

"Med school. New York."

"Oh God, don't tell me we're going to spend the whole hike comparing LA and New York. I came here to get away from all that."

Rachel was confident she could turn his mind to other things if she got the chance.

He'd let slip that the Buick was a hand-me-down from his wife's departed grandmother. He'd also added right away that he and said wife were separated.

In fact this made it easier for Rachel. If he'd heard a thousand conversations about LA vs. New York, she'd heard a thousand about fear of commitment and how dating married men had many drawbacks, but it definitely dampened commitment phobias. Anyway she wasn't looking for a husband on this trip. "When you're rolling in the hay, you don't notice ring fingers, no?" she said to Karen, once again surprising her friend who'd never seen her so down and dirty.

It was getting quite cool this late spring evening, and Rachel experienced the phenomenon of desert extremes. She noticed that Matt went into Roberta's tent to spend the night there. The jury was still out on him and she reminded herself that Frank, who was snoring loudly on his camp mattress pitched a stone's throw away from the camp commissary, remained a viable second choice and she seriously doubted that Suzy would target him, or Randi either-- who she noticed had rolled up in her sleeping bag in no time and placed flashlight and Swiss Army knife at the ready beside her shoulder. She'd done this before, clearly.

Rachel had brought a small tent, as the leaders requested in the event of rain, but tonight she saw nothing but stars, and she decided to roll out her mattress and sleeping bag on the ground, not far from Roberta's tent. She said to herself, "That's strange, I have no fear of creepy crawlers." But then she remembered, "I live side by side with the little beasties in Manhattan."

She was shaking a bit from the cold, but once in her sleeping bag she warmed up and listened to the silence.

It was so profound she felt a sort of vibration in her ears, like they were cleaning themselves inside and shuffling out the noise and clatter of civilization. It was a new moon. Countless thousands of stars festooned the deep dark night sky.

"Out there in the silence and night winds," she said to Karen, "you don't battle insomnia very often, I can tell you that. They rock you to sleep without rocking, but I was so excited at being out there and the adventure and all, I stayed awake for a while. It was a new moon and I saw like a million stars spread all across the sky. About a million more than I normally see. And then one of them fell. I tracked it all the way down and I swear it landed not more than a mile away. I looked up and said out loud, 'Next time, land on me. Go ahead, here I am, hit me. Please, I'm ready. I've been wait-ing for stardust so long.'"

#

Day 1 was a mix of the mundane and sublime.

The mundane began after a "desert continental" breakfast, per Thomasin--no milk, no ham and eggs, just dry bread and pastries and dehydrated cereal--and blessedly, coffee which tasted extra good after a night of sleep in the open air. Rachel's air mattress had been comfortable enough and her sleeping bag warm.

Frank launched into an oral thesis about the effects of wind and water on sandstone, but all she noted were his comments that rainwater made even the largest boulder turn back into its primary material of sand and became quite treacherous afoot, and second that sandstone retained heat for a long time. When she'd remarked that a hot plate or coaster fabricated from it would make superb natural products, he looked at her as if she'd shown her true colors as barbarian despoiler.

"Not that I'd ever want to pillage these canyons. Ever," she hastily added.

To which Frank: "If you did I'd write a whole chapter about you. But it wouldn't be flattering." She decided to make tracks figu-ratively as she'd soon be doing literally, and scooted off to prepare her pack for the jaunt.

She'd noticed that Matt had left right away after breakfast to help Roberta take down her big canvas tent. She doubted they would want to lug it along, but no, Matt tied the rainfly and metal poles to his pack. When she saw him heft it onto his back for the first time, he resembled a beast with a heavier than fair burden. She thought him gallant for helping Roberta, but hoped this wasn't a sign of a relationship.

She'd noticed Matt chatting with Randi over coffee, and hoped ditto. Before they all hit the trail, Thomasin parceled out the com-missary into equal shares. This added 4-8 pounds and when she strapped on the pack, she could feel every ounce.

"Anybody feel hungry?" she heard Matt jest, "Not get enough at breakfast?" He swayed a little as he tried to balance the weight on his back. "Let's eat an early lunch--and pig out."

Rachel laughed.

They hit the trail.

It wound up and down and around the flank of Navajo Mountain and leveled off only at short intervals. The trail according to Thomasin had clearly been used by mountain sheep and deer who'd done the initial blazing, and at some point it seemed men or horses had widened it somewhat for humans. Rachel wondered who they were. In the 1930s the Civilian Conservation Corps had created some of the Western trails used nowadays, but doubted they had come to such a remote area on the Navajo Nation. Perhaps men associated with the Rainbow Lodge during its brief heyday.

At any rate, she thought, they couldn't have been too satisfied with their work, because they'd scarcely made a dent in the thousands of hard rocks and mini-boulders that comprised the path they were trudging over--trudging because it was impossible to get a good smooth rhythm going.

Rachel found she had two main concentrations: lugging the heavy pack, and taking great care not to twist an ankle. Thomasin had emphasized that contrary to some other wilderness backpack trips, they had an escape route at the Colorado River. Tourist boats visited Rainbow Bridge every day from Page, and could serve as rescue in the event of injury or sickness.

Rachel wondered if Matt would accompany her back to civilization if she couldn't handle the rigors of the hike. She doubted very much that Joe and Frida would. They'd made their plans, by golly.

She saw Matt trudging slowly up the trail, weighed down by what was clearly a very heavy pack piled over his head by sleeping pad and a bundle that could only be Roberta's tent, and wondered if she herself would forsake the pleasures of the backpack trip to accompany him to a medical facility.

Yep.

For over three hours they traversed the mountain's flank. Sooner or later they'd have to descend. But when?

Rachel found out at Yabut Pass. Someone had kindly set up a trail marker at the pass--the only human signs they'd seen. The wind blew briskly here and made her shiver.

They were in the shade from the mountain that rose behind them. Below high sandstone cliffs framed a defile through which the trail wound downward into Cliff Canyon. Through the slot formed by the cliff walls she saw their destination for the evening-- a maze of canyons gloriously lit by the sun, stretching north toward where, somewhere in the vast network, the Colorado River ran.

The wealth of golden color and canyons would have taken her breath away in any event, but the final climb to the pass had already done that, and she couldn't immediately say something to Matt, who had come up beside her and gratefully doffed his pack. Just getting it off, she noted, took some care--a broken back at this stage would not be fun.

He found enough breath to marvel, "The Western writers I've read are always talking about the 'call of the canyons.' Once you see them they get in your blood and you don't want to get them out. Ever. Now I see what they mean."

Matt moved away from her without further comment and joined the group around Thomasin who were admiring the panorama from the promontory where the best view could be had. Rachel saw that he took up a place beside Randi and began a conversation. She ambled over and overheard Matt explaining, "It's way down yonder, the Rainbow Bridge."

Rachel was grateful he'd saved the poetry for her, but then again, maybe he thought Randi would appreciate vernacular, and she seized the chance to butt in.

"Yonder?"

"Cowboy talk," Matt explained, turning to her.

Randi said to him, "You look like a cowboy, with that hat."

Rachel thought this revealed Randi to be a few bricks shy of a backpack load, but Matt seemed to appreciate it, and she sensed the threat.

"I thought you'd lead the way out front," she said pointedly to Randi, "having trekked all around the Yukon and all."

She felt proud of herself, the remark being both a putdown and a hint--whichever worked and got Randi off the grid was just fine.

"Boot problem," she replied, looking sheepish.

"Careful not to work up any blisters," Matt said, a little too solicitously for Rachel's taste.

"I'll be all right." And smiled.

Rachel was glad when Thomasin passed them with pack back on, meaning their pause was over.

"Down yonder?" Rachel smiled at Matt.

He smiled back, appreciating the humor, and as he hefted his heavy pack, "If I collapse just roll me downhill."

\#

They stopped for lunch a short time later in a grove of cotton-wood trees.

Thomasin and Jo said they wanted to cut the descent into halves, to cushion a bit the wear and tear on knees and ankles.

As Rachel sat on a boulder taking in the sun, Matt snapped a picture of her, and before she could thank him in a way that meant extra thankful, he said, "Got to take pictures of everyone on the trip--for me and posterity."

"Send me a copy of that one--in case I have posterity." He smiled again and said, "Grandkids are always surprised to see their grandmothers were ever young."

"Maybe I'll be too, in fifty or sixty years. To see that I was young once."

"Let's hope you're still able to remember where you were when you see the picture."

"What about the photographer?"

"I'll write my name on the back."

Once again Thomasin passed by, at just the wrong time for Rachel, and the rest of the afternoon passed in a sunbaked slog, which Jo said on the contrary had ideal temps and they were lucky it wasn't truly hot.

Rachel found it exciting to leave the mountain flank and plunge into the first canyon, with its beautiful fluted and curved sandstone walls.

"Welcome to canyon country!" she heard Matt exclaim to any-one and everyone, not least himself. She said to herself, glad to be here.

They arrived at their camp beside a small stream of running wa-ter and everyone chose a camp spot. Rachel noticed that Matt helped Roberta erect her tent but laid out his mattress and sleeping bag on the ground some distance away.

Randi looked pained and removed her boots as if they were tor-ture devices. When Thomasin called Rachel over to administer care she saw that in fact they were, as 2 large blisters had formed on Randi's soles from the boots that hadn't been broken in properly before the hike.

"Too confident I guess," Randi allowed, and Rachel could have made an "and how" comment, but satisfied herself that for all prac-tical purposes, Randi had rendered herself *hors de combat*. She'd be hobbling behind one and all, sucking the others' trail dust. Matt's included.

"I'll need the First Aid kit," Rachel said.

\#

Thomasin had scheduled Day \#2 as a layover for anyone who had sore feet, knees, fatigue or blisters. For the hardy she would lead a dayhike.

"'Aztec Creek flows through Forbidden Canyon, a canyon of rare beauty. Sandstone walls that climb higher and higher toward the sun, dwarfing puny hikers.' That's how I wrote it," Frank said to the hardy and energetic group that included Sven and his sons--naturally--and a few others including Joe and Frida and Matt. Hence Rachel.

"Sounds like good material for a docu-drama, Frank," Matt offered.

"What's that?" Frank was staying in camp. On Day 1 he'd struggled mightily until several others proposed sharing his load and partitioned. After a good night's rest he'd recovered somewhat, but "not enough to join the crowd. I'll meet you later at the swimming hole. You'll see it about a mile in."

It was a depression under a tall cliff where enough rainwater had collected to form a long plunge pool. It looked wonderfully clean and cool to Rachel as they passed by, encumbered only by their water bottles and group lunch, but Thomasin said another one lay farther down the canyon.

"This one's for the boys."

"We're not going coed?" Rachel asked.

Matt countered, "With this bunch? No woman would be safe."

"Or men," Rachel added, hoping he'd get the subtext. He laughed, but didn't give any clue that he had. Maybe he's all text, Rachel wondered.

Rachel had slept soundly throughout the night and hadn't been awakened by a thunderstorm that passed near them--though Matt had, "briefly," he said. He said he'd been sleeping "like a cottonwood log" after the nosebleed exertions of yesterday.

"Nosebleed?" Rachel asked.

"I wasn't sick or injured. I think after the nine-mile hike with all the gear and food and Roberta's tent I just started literally sweating blood."

Then he paused and said, "I was about to whine to Sven when he said very seriously, 'We're not getting enough hiking.' That shut me up right quick."

Rachel hadn't found the day exhausting, a testimony to her get-in-shape routine on her bicycle. She no longer feared she'd have to be evacuated by boat when they reached the Rainbow Bridge marina. And anyway, evacuation was the very last thing she wanted at present.

Matt had checked with Suzy, who confirmed there had been loud blasts of thunder the night before. They'd woken her up, and that, together with other little phobias that had cropped up, led her to trip co-leader Jo, who decided the best thing to do was take Suzy and her sleeping gear down to where the main group of campers had gathered.

Matt was in the group and groggily noted their arrival. "But I'd been woken up just before, more or less, 'cause I kept hearing some loud booms. I opened my eyes and looked up at the sky and saw nary a cloud. So if not a thunderstorm, I said to myself, what else could it be but— "

"The cops, blowing away some bad people who had it coming."

He stared at Rachel.

"I'm from New York, remember."

"Much more obvious solution. Nuclear war. Our leaders had fucked up again, pardon my French, and there went the civilized world. But I said very logically, what could I do? I'm here in the wilds of Utah. Sad for civilization, but we were safe. Me, Suzy and Jo at least. So I rolled over and went back to sleep."

"I'm glad you gave at least a passing thought to the loss of the civilized world," Rachel quipped.

\#

Forbidden Canyon was hard going, even without packs. When they weren't trudging through dry sand deep enough to override bootstraps--more than once Rachel had to stop, remove her boot and pour out the accumulation--they were thrashing through shoulder-high reeds or stumbling over rock scree. All the while keeping an eye out for "sunbathing rattlers," as the phlegmatic Thomasin chuckled.

The sun broiled this day, and they had little shade. Lunch in the shade of a cliff grove gave some relief, but the group had little zeal for chitchat. Only Sven and his 2 mountain goat sons had energy to spare, and they'd clambered up the sandstone cliff searching for petroglyphs or other signs of the Anasazi.

Noting Rachel's puzzlement, Matt said, "The Ancient Ones. They populated this area for hundreds of years and you can find granaries and cliff dwellings all over. There's a cliff painting over near Moab in color. The figure looks like a rainbow man."

"How do you know all this?"

"National Geographic Magazine." He was pouring some sand out of his boot and noticed her smiling at him. "Go slowly, sands of time," he said.

That was subtext, she hoped.

#

As they moved deeper into Forbidden Canyon, Rachel thought Frank's purple prose had not been purple enough to do justice to the immense sandstone wonderland they explored in the afternoon.

Water had cut through the rock, and wind over time had sculpted and hardened the channel sand into high cliffbanks and rounded domes whose tops they could not see. They loomed higher and higher as the group hiked toward the Colorado River.

They would not reach it. Thomasin halted where the canyon opened up.

Ringed by sandstone cliffs that lay all around, the group leader opted for a leisurely stroll around the amphitheater--"like she's admiring the Sistine Chapel," Matt said--and left it to the others to explore as they wanted, within natural limits. "If you reach the river, don't," she said firmly, a sentence difficult to parse but very plain to understand.

"I'll be here like a desert hen."

Matt set off immediately for a small pour-off that flowed out from a slot in the sandstone high up where a canyon boxed in. The fall looked reachable, and if not, at least "a man's reach should exceed his grasp," Matt chuckled.

Rachel remembered the line from Browning. She hadn't studied literature but she'd read extensively, and she told herself to be sure and point out this fact if he ever tossed off a favorite quote like that one. If he meant to impress, he had, but she could keep up, and thought again that she'd gauged her reach just fine.

#

She caught up to him at canyon's end where the walls came together, leaving a narrow slot where the small stream poured off and down to the sandy desert floor. It was possible to climb up the sandstone and peer through the slot up toward the sky--or whatever was cached there. Sven and his sons were already scrambling up, and Rachel and Matt had to wait till they finished.

In the distance they could see another canyon branching off, but Thomasin had asked them not to stray too far.

"Bridge Canyon," Matt said. "If we follow it, we'll end up where we'll be tomorrow, at the Rainbow Bridge. It's called Nonnezoshe by the Navajo. I read that in the only book I could find about it."

He explained that The Rainbow Trail was a sequel to Zane Grey's famous Riders of the Purple Sage, and the trail to the Bridge enables Lassiter and Jane, who were lost in a canyon called Surprise Valley many years before, to arrive back in civilization. "Lassiter is a gunfighter with a blood grudge against certain elders of the Mormon religion. He's known as the Mormon Killer."

"What a thing to put on your resume!" He laughed and she could see he appreciated the wit of her remark.

They lay against the cliff wall in the shade. Matt eyed the aperture where Sven was trying to scrunch his shoulders through so he can reach a higher level.

"What if he gets stuck there?" Rachel said.

"He'll have to wait for erosion to wear away the stone. Couple hundred years or so."

The Swedes descended and Matt and Rachel went up toward the slot canyon.

Matt continued, "When Lassiter and Jane catch first sight of the Bridge, their Navajo guide yells out, 'Nonnezoshe!' Stone rainbow. Maybe I'll do that tomorrow."

"I wish you would."

"I've always been fascinated by Nonnezoshe. Maybe I just want to escape civilization."

"First you ought to find your Jane." As soon as the words left her mouth Rachel regretted them. What if he said he already had, his wife?

"Yeah," Matt agreed.

"Nothing up there," Sven said in passing. "Don't bother." Matt looked at Rachel. "Oh but I will."

They were able to clamber up the smooth sandstone fairly easily until they reached the sandstone shelf where the small stream of water landed after plunging from its source high above. They were just able to squat on both sides, lean to the side and peer up into the slot. The cliffs rose high and smooth and even narrower, very high toward a window of light through which they could see sky and a few wisps of clouds streaming across the deep blue.

"What do you think is up there?" Rachel asked.

"Beautiful sculptured sandstone and a view that climbs to heaven. Wish I could make it up."

Once more Rachel thought, he's got some poetry in him. What kind of dialogue did his talking dog spout?

"If you find a way, I'll come along," she said.

He looked at her again, like he'd done on the first night they'd met, "a look that was more than a look," she said later to Karen, "but not romantic. More like, this girl's got some spark to her. Maybe she'd do all right driving a covered wagon."

When they got down some others in their party, Jim and Frida among them, were staring upward, and Jim was saying, "I don't think it's worth it, no? I mean, what can you see? "

The question was meant for Rachel. "Rock sculpture and water."

"That's all?"

Rachel looked at Matt, and he gave her look that she thought meant, even if they make it up they won't appreciate what they see. Like we did.

Matt said, "It's reserved for birds and God."

"I ain't neither," Jim laughed, and they all turned around to head back down the canyon.

Rachel thought, well. She had always dreamed about marrying an artist. Directing a dumb teen film and writing about a talking dog didn't rank up there, but he had time and his career was just beginning, like he said.

They had no room for conversation after that. She wondered about his religion and had a sneaky feeling that if he had one, it might be the kind that spanned a creek in the heart of a sinuous canyon below high-arching sandstone cliffs.

#

On the way back Thomasin stopped the group at one of the pothole pools they'd passed. The ladies who wanted could use this for a refreshing plunge after all the heat, sand and dust of the last two days.

The men would use the pool further up the canyon, which presented a logistics problem in Rachel's mind.

"So if we finish early and pass by, we don't look?" Rachel asked.

"Just stare at your feet," Thomasin laughed.

Matt added, "Or my feet. That'll send you off screaming in horror. "

Rachel laughed along with the others, but as she would say to Karen, "His feet weren't what I had in mind." Wilderness etiquette did not call for swimsuits other than birthday, and the water in the pool was cold enough that it wasn't very long before Rachel was stretched out on her stomach warming up in the sun.

"I figure this pool fills up even in dry years," Thomasin said. "The drainage troughs off the cliffs are just right."

Rachel was thinking about what it would be like to be alone with Matt at this pool, just the two of them deep in the canyon's heart, on this warm spring afternoon, making love and enjoying sun and water.

"Weren't you getting ahead of yourself, way way ahead?" Karen asked when Rachel recounted her trip.

Rachel explained, "The sun lights up the trail real clear and bright out there in the West, and all you've got to do is decide to take it. And listen, it's called Wild for a reason."

After a time, when the sun passed over the canyon cliff and the pool fell into shade, Thomasin dressed and they all went back up the canyon, heading toward camp. When they reached the men's pool Rachel yelled over, "I'm just looking at my feet, gentlemen. They're so nice and clean now."

Jim yelled back, "And we really believe you, Rachel." They all shared a laugh. Rachel looked enough to notice that Matt did not raise his head.

Rachel to Karen, chuckling: "If that boy thought that a little indifference was going to stop me, he didn't know how determined a nice Jewish girl from New York could be." Five minutes later, after all the women had passed toward camp, Rachel came walking alone, back down the canyon.

"Don't get excited, boys. I forgot my hat."

This provided great fodder.

"Yeah, right," Jim said. "Accidentally on purpose. You don't even have a hat, do you? You could have just come over and taken a look. We're not going anywhere."

Rachel laughed.

A few minutes later she passed on the way back. She did have a hat in hand.

Sven yelled over, "Don't let it block your eyesight."

She smiled and said, "I hope I haven't forgot anything else."

Jeff piped up, surprisingly, "Who cares? You've already seen everything."

Rachel had already seen what she came to see, Matt lying on his stomach in the afternoon sun in the suit he was born in. She liked what she saw and if he had only turned around to look at her, she'd have been the happiest nice New York girl in Utah, but he didn't and he hadn't said a word, so she still wondered if he at all cared whether she'd forgot her hat on purpose.

NONNEZOSHE

Day 3 began early as Thomasin wanted to spend some time at the Rainbow Bridge.

After a quick breakfast the group headed out with packs somewhat lighter after two days of eating their way through the commissary.

In about an hour they climbed one by one up Redbud Pass, a narrow defile in the rock partially blasted out by the first travelers to the Bridge to make it easier for their horses.

Another hour or so of hiking and they arrived at their camp for the night at Echo Canyon. They lunched there, and Rachel became more and more impatient to head downcanyon.

"Bridge Canyon," Thomasin said, "and it's a treat in itself."

So it was. They'd left their packs and taken just cameras and water bottles and some, a daypack with snacks. An easy path followed the streambed canyon and they wound in and out as the stream, dry here, curlicued.

Rachel had no more concerns about appearing too obvious and hiked behind Matt. The trail was narrow and single file but they managed to converse.

Matt looked contemplative. "I've waited years to see Rainbow Bridge," he said. "I can't say exactly why. Most Native American Indians say there are spirits in nature and some places speak to you, where you feel, this is home. Maybe it will feel like home."

"You're about to find out," Rachel said.

Matt nodded. "Riders of the Purple Sage ends with Lassiter next to a big boulder with Jane and her adopted daughter Fay. They're being chased by some very bad Mormon guys who don't care that Jane's a Mormon too. She's with Lassiter and that skews everything."

"If they believe that, they're not really religious."

"They're high up on a sandstone cliff. Lassiter's used up all his bullets and their only hope is for him to roll the boulder down and crush the bad guys. But if he does it he'll imprison the three of them in Surprise Valley down below. For the rest of their lives. So he hesitates. And hesitates. Maybe he thinks even if they survive, it's not a life, especially for the little girl. He doesn't say. It's not like he's got a lot of time. "

"So does he roll it or not?"

"Only after Jane shouts at him to roll the rock. The clincher is when she says, 'I love you.' "

"She hadn't said it before?"

"To a gunfighter with a price on his head? No."

"But did she say it because she really did love him or because she wanted to save him and Fay? And herself?"

"Well, they had a lot of years to find out."

"But they got rescued?"

"Yes."

"And did they look like they'd been happy together?"

"Very. And then they all leave the valley and pass under Rainbow Bridge. Nonnezoshe."

They kept walking, alongside the dry streambed. Forbidden Canyon's walls rose far up toward the sky. The afternoon had turned warmer after a slight chill in the morning, but not hot. Rachel thought it was perfect weather and had the strange feeling that the gods had arranged it just for them.

"I have had a kind of strange feeling that the rainbow god has something special waiting for me," Matt continued.

"Like what?"

"I don't know. The god hasn't said."

"Gods can be like that," Rachel said. "You just have to trust them."

He had half-turned back to smile at her. So Rachel saw before he did in the near distance a majestic sandstone arch spanning the stream from one canyon wall to the other.

"Nonnezoshe!" she called out.

A few minutes later they were all milling about under the great stone rainbow. Its contours were smooth and the arch as perfect as the rainbow for which it had been named

Rachel took myriad pictures, of the Bridge and all her companions, one in particular, figuring this was as good a moment as any for pictorial souvenirs of these people who had grown close through their shared experience, but whom she knew she probably would not see again any time soon or ever.

All of the backpackers had the same reaction to the clean, well dressed and platitude-popping tourists who arrived from the boats to take a cursory picture before hurrying back for the return to Page: "Amateurs who haven't earned the right to be here," Matt scowled. "And since I did it once, I include myself in that category."

"But not now," Rachel interjected. "No siree," Roberta chimed in. She'd overheard. "You got here on your two feet over a lot of rock. Sweatin' and chuggin'."

It was the most eloquent comment Rachel had heard from Roberta, and she wondered if there were layers there unbeknownst to casual observation.

"You said it. 'Chuggin'." Matt responded, looking as surprised as Rachel.

Thankfully, the boat was leaving to head back to Page and the tourists who'd paid a chunk of money for the two-hour ride and 10-minute photo opportunity were hurrying back for the return trip.

She wondered how one of them might react if the boat left without him, condemning him to three or four hours of wait time and canyon silence before the next arrival. Probably he would not have brought water or snacks and the wait may have appeared a savage ordeal in the wilderness, a personal vision trek needing strength and perseverance to survive.

It was a glorious spring afternoon and Thomasin was in no hurry to leave the bridge and get back to camp. They lolled, sitting on rock benches or above the stream, legs dangling over the water that here lay several feet deep. Matt had joined in on the small talk and photo opportunities but abruptly he moved away from the group and walked back up the trail.

Rachel had just enough time to regret that he had not asked her to join him when a loud twangy voice from behind said, "Excuse me, could you take my picture?"

A tourist, in shorts and an LA Lakers t-shirt over an expanding belly, with designer sunglasses and sweat pouring under them.

"Sure," Rachel said, figuring this was the fastest way to get rid of him.

"You just touch this little button here after you've lined it up, the shot I mean. I want to be right in the middle, like I'm under it, you know?"

"I get it." She waited as he took up position very carefully at the bank edge.

"Don't fall. You'll end up looking as dirty as me." He looked a little puzzled.

"We backpacked here from the other side of the mountain."

"Jesus H. Christ! I wouldn't do that if you paid me."

"Smile and say fromage." He did smile and she snapped a picture, then another "to make sure they know you made it." He thanked her profusely, then "Fromage means cheese, doesn't it?"

She nodded. "Where you from?" he asked her.

"New York."

"I go there a lot on business. Got my own consulting company, how to boost worker performance. Maybe..." he reached for his business card but realized he hadn't put one in his shorts pockets. Before he could expatiate further Rachel cut him off at the pass--"Better get back, boat's leaving." They could see the boat captain waving energetically.

Rachel added, "I've got to go join my boy friend. He's that guy over there"--Matt had come into view on the other side of the stream, next to the buttress of the Rainbow Bridge difficult to access. He had found a way to get across the stream and rough it back.

"He's going to climb up with his bare hands."

"Yeah...isn't that against the rules?"

"He's part Navajo and anyway, he doesn't care about rules. He's pretty wild. A little scary sometimes."

"Yeah, well, good luck. Nice meeting you."

"Have a good boat ride."

"Yeah, I almost got seasick." Rachel didn't bother watching him leave.

Matt was just standing in place, staring upward at the majestic curve of sandstone.

Rachel imagined he was thinking of many things having to do with the Navajos and their sacred Nonnezoshe and maybe, just maybe, what it would be like to be lost in these canyons like Lassiter and Jane.

Thomasin was saying to the others that Matt liked to march to a different drummer and she hoped he wouldn't attempt to climb the arch.

Rachel assured them, "He has too much respect to do that. For the Navajo tribe and all." Thomasin and the others looked at her and she imagined them wondering how she pretended to know Matt so intimately.

But luckily or not, Frank chose the moment to launch into another lesson from his experience:

"It's the natural bridge with the widest span, but it's not the longest one--that's in Arches Natural Park. Now that's a park you've got to see. It took me three books to cover it all and I kind of think there's one or two hiding out there someplace. They can form any day, you know. Nature doesn't sleep."

On a whim, Rachel interrupted and asked, "Do you know where Surprise Valley is?"

Frank looked surprised himself. "You're a tenderfoot from New York and you know Surprise Valley? No offense. "

"I'm not as provincial as I look."

He nodded toward the east and said, "It's over yonder, above those buttes. When we start to climb out tomorrow we'll be looking over it, kind of straddling the crest. Real hard to get down into it. I tried once and didn't make it. And if I had, who's to tell if I could have gotten out. Don't think there's anything for me down there. To write about, I mean."

"Sounds like a lost world."

"Yeah, kinda I guess."

Rachel noticed Thomasin getting up and heading back toward their camp at Echo Canyon. Her leadership style, Rachel and the others had noticed, was like that. No verbal orders or orders of any kind, just "Well, follow the leader," Frank interjected. Rachel saw he evidently meant to accompany her back. She looked up and saw that Matt had already started back himself, further down the canyon.

She was disappointed that she hadn't been able to share his thoughts, and even more that he hadn't waited for her.

She marched up the trail with Frank, who in just two days had regained a lot of the spunk he'd probably had in full supply before jockeying his desk the last few months, and of course, advancing in years faster than his footpace.

The great bridge loomed high above as they passed, a couple of stray clouds scudding across the sky this late afternoon. As she crossed under it, Rachel felt a sting of sadness. She would have liked to stay longer, and with Matt, but he had left.

Frank had launched into a history of Rainbow Bridge and how conservationists in the 1960s had fought to prevent water from newly formed Lake Powell advancing too far upstream and undercutting the bridge's foundations.

It was an essential part of history but Rachel found that mundane human politics could take a rest this day when nature showed forth at its most splendid, and she was only half listening when they rounded a curve--the bridge had been lost from sight--and found Matt, alone, just lounging on the rocks in a small alcove at trailside.

"Meditating?" Rachel asked.

"Kind of. I'm in no rush."

"I'm not either." She abruptly stepped down off the trail and leaned on a rock bench near him.

Frank to his credit didn't need a picture drawn to realize that he'd better continue his history lesson some other time.

"Well, don't get lost on the way back. You just follow this trail."

Matt and Rachel nodded indulgently at Frank's kind advice illustrating the obvious. He walked on.

"Frank told me how to find Surprise Valley."

"Where?"

"Over yonder." He looked in the direction she was pointing.

"Too bad we don't have time to go exploring."

"I'll go if you will." She meant it but as the words came out she realized that she'd told him she'd gladly follow him on an adventure and if he didn't get the implications, he wasn't as acute as she thought he was.

Roberta passed by along with one of Sven's sons--Rachel still hadn't got their names firmly identified to faces, maybe because they usually moved in a rapid blur on the trail.

This time he'd slowed down to accompany Roberta, who said to Matt, "Hey, don't forget, it's our time in the commissary."

Each night a group of 3 or 4 prepared the evening meals, and Roberta and Matt's last names ranged close in the alphabet. "Get the soup ready. I'll be along directly."

Roberta nodded, reassured, and headed away with her escort.

Matt remarked, "That's what the cowboys always said, I'll be along. And 'I'm a-comin'. That's pretty standard."

"Don't say that in New York. They'll take you for a hick."

"Won't they anyway?" She laughed.

Jeff came along, alone, and answered before their asking.

"I'm the last."

Rachel said, "We'll be along directly." He gave them a look, then nodded and headed away. Now they knew they were alone.

"You learned how to talk cowgirl right quick."

"There's sides to me you don't know." He looked closely at her for a moment and she let him. She had made sure to take a seat on the rock ledge not elbow to elbow, but within striking distance. Now she thought he might be deciding whether to strike.

"Did the rainbow gods speak to you under the bridge?"

"Not being a prophet, no. Probably they didn't want to waste words on me. But I felt something. Kind of spiritual. Hard to describe. "

"If you could describe it, it wouldn't be so spiritual."

He leaned close and kissed her. The kiss went on and was followed by another, and another, and they went as far as they could, knowing it wouldn't do to doff their clothes and make love on the sandstone.

"Though I thought about it," Matt said to her later. "That sandstone was like a warm blanket after the day's sun," adding, "and so were you."

Rachel would say to Karen, "I'd been dreaming after him and boom, here he was. I was going to enjoy him as long as I could."

She realized she'd been talking about him like a pleasure object, as men often did about women--"but that's kind of what I felt at the time. Him too, I'm sure of it."

As it was, they went on until Matt noticed out of the corner of his eye that the whole canyon lay in steep shade. They had no more than 30 minutes of daylight left, and neither he nor Rachel could remember how long it had taken them to arrive from the camp to the Bridge.

"I hate to stop," he said.

Rachel added, "Don't let me stop you from stopping." And this pleased him so much they spent several more minutes of daylight wholly and solely with each other, oblivious to night and day, before reluctantly gathering themselves together and hitting the trail.

Neither said much as neither was sure how to articulate what had just happened, but it became easier when they saw Thomasin and Jeff coming to meet them. Rachel said, "It's like we played hooky. We're in trouble now."

Jeff and Thomasin, reassured, just turned back and led them into camp like wayward sheep.

"We been bad," Matt laughed. No one among their brethren said anything about hanky-panky, but everyone knew it had occurred. Their attitude seemed to be, just another fork on the trail.

For Rachel it had been great fun and satisfying to know she'd bagged her quarry, as it were. She moved her camp site to a spot near his, and got double satisfaction to see Randi displace hers in a huff. She'd been right, the "girl had put him in her sights," but blisters and a determined rival had outflanked her.

Rachel thanked her lucky stars, maybe the ones she'd seen that first night, that Matt had decided to take a break in that rock alcove.

\#

In fact, there was no luck involved at all. Matt had stopped on purpose, to see if she'd do the same.

He'd noticed from the beginning of the trip that she seemed to have her eye on him. At first he hadn't reciprocated, or at least, did not jump at the bait right away. He'd been more drawn to Randi, the kind of lithe, raven-haired beauty he found very attractive. She was not shy but not forward either, and he had some difficulty finding moments on trail and in camp where he could get to know and charm her. Plus he had the added complication that Rachel was usually hanging around in his orbit.

He'd made some headway though, and thought it was a good sign when Randi had chosen a spot near his to lay down her bedroll for the night.

But that was on the morning of the trek to Rainbow Bridge. When he returned from his consort with Rachel, Randi lost no time in packing up and moving away from his vicinity. Rachel had been forward and knew what she wanted, and went after him. He appreciated it.

When Matt thought of his love life to the present, he often made reference to the famous image of Laocoon wrapped in the coils of serpents, agonizing and unable to break free.

He'd married young and in haste. He'd come to Los Angeles from Mississippi after a heartwrenching breakup with his first serious girl friend. His wrenched heart, not hers, as she had jilted him for someone else and this had shocked him to the core. He decided it was because he'd had his eyes set on far horizons and she rightfully sensed his lack of full commitment.

So when he came West, a year later, he brought along a trunkful of regrets and determination that the next time he got seriously involved, he would not let it fall apart through his lack of commitment.

He met Lynn, with whom he had a great rapport. She was very lovely and witty and funny and they had great discussions about life and the world, with a bottle of wine or without.

He would often share confidences with his friend Walt, who even though some other friends swore had "a wire loose," nevertheless gave him a perspective on things others couldn't. Walt said, "She seems a little brittle, but other than that, she probably asks herself every day why she's with you."

True or not, Matt found that he had only, say, to glance off at the sunset for a couple of minutes before Lynn had another suitor moving in. So he was both glad and surprised when she agreed to get an apartment together.

Matt found this gave him some assurance that she wouldn't head off for a drink or movie with someone else at the first opportunity. Later he would think, "Being grateful for small favors can lead to big mistakes."

They discussed her future over a second bottle of wine one night and Matt found himself overtaken by his vow not to show a lack of commitment.

Somewhat offhandedly, he proposed marriage, in the style, "Well if we get married we can make plans together."

Lynn bit her nails and smiled. "Yes, we could."

They got married six months later and both immediately felt trapped. They lumbered along for four years until she found a well-paying job in San Diego. For a year they commuted back and forth on weekends and felt so much happier knowing that the good times on Saturday and Sunday wouldn't be spoiled by the proximity of the mundane every day.

Matt learned to surf, and she learned to scuba and they reveled in San Diego's beaches, a stone's throw from Lynn's apartment. Matt wondered if paradise was like this, and wondered what the future held. He had a strong sense of fidelity and honor and the aforementioned sense of commitment, and held off for a long time having an affair, even when she had had a fling while they lived to-gether.

When he finally did, Lynn found out immediately, with unerring psychology and the instincts of a master spy, and asked for a di-vorce. He did not object, but neither of them up to now had been able to take the step of actually filing.

They would see each other from time to time, for a wine tasting or weekend at the beach or short excursion into Mexico, and always had the same rapport in each other's company.

Matt decided to live for the present, and act as if he were indeed and truly single, and began dating as often as he could, with one resolution in mind: not to get serious. If before he had faked commitment for some sense of righteousness and honor, now he had no intention of making the same mistake, and no intention of settling down to one person. He'd been there, done that.

"I'm going to sow wild oats," he told Walt, "make up for lost time."

"I hear you," Walt said, "and if you do, I'll really hear you. Liter-ally." Walt had found an apartment right next to Matt's, and sound carried well through the walls. He added, "I'll keep an intensity scale for you. You probably don't know it but you can measure sexual satisfaction and that's a necessary step toward true love."

"You're telling me that orgasms lead to love?"

"Where else?"

Matt tried to socialize as much as he could despite the 24/24 freelance pursuit of cinema jobs, always stressful and frequently desperate for everyone in LA who wanted to be somebody, i.e., vir-tually everybody.

He joined groups like the Sierra Club, and when he saw an an-nouncement for the Rainbow Bridge backpack trip, he didn't even wait to read the full trip description. Come hell or high water, he was going to earn his right to see the Bridge, as men before him had done, like Theodore Roosevelt and John Wetherill and Nasja Begay, their Navajo guide. And Zane Grey, one of the Western writers who had marked his youthful reading.

He was very busy finishing the editing on his film, and though he bought backpack and sleeping bag and all the equipment neces-sary, he had no time to use them or do any practice hikes. He placed trust in his adrenaline, the sheer pleasure and excitement of being in the canyons he'd dreamed about.

When Roberta wrote and asked to share a ride from Las Vegas, he'd already made plans and booked a room in Page the night before the trip rendezvous, which to others might have seemed to be in the middle of nowhere on Navajo nation land, but he'd read about Navajo Mountain many times and knew Rainbow Bridge lay deep down in one of the canyons flanking it.

For the trip back, he'd rented a room on the rim of the Grand Canyon at the El Tovar Lodge, the most beautiful and historic hotel in the national park, which he'd only seen in passing on one of his car trips west. He thought it would be a nice way to cap off the hike which no doubt would prove to be strenuous, and he thought he might merit some Old West luxury.

He left behind a cadre of lovers or could-bes: his wife who, though estranged, made him swear to call from the hotel as soon as he got back from the hike. His current girl friend about whom he was lukewarm even though she claimed to love him, and his housesitter for the week, a young film student he'd met and who had caught his eye and needed a place to stay after moving out from New Jersey--their relationship hadn't gone very far, but they had time.

Walt promised to keep an eye on her while he was gone, and Matt knew what that could mean, but it was not like he was in love. Deep down he still felt alone in the world, but no longer so lonely because he had "celestial bodies circling in orbit around me," a metaphor Walt thought ridiculous but he had to concede the word celestial applied to the film student. Thus comforted knowing he had hearts to return to, Matt drove to Las Vegas and met Roberta, who evinced no interest in him, nor he her. That made the travel smoother, if not the small talk.

They had decided to take an extra day and camp at Zion National Park, because Roberta hadn't done much training either and thought a healthy day hike could at least get their hiking muscles warmed up.

They marched slowly but surely up to Zion's East Rim overlook above the valley, with just the one stretch of insurance adjustment to make Matt uncomfortable. He made it without getting excessively winded, and got some encouragement, though Roberta, who he'd quickly learned defined no nonsense, qualified with, "We didn't carry the heavy packs."

"Well, better than nothing, which is what I've been doing."

"Yep, you're right there."

Roberta's tent was huge, the kind of car camp tent one would not want to lug on a backpack trip, with enough space between them to reassure Roberta. As Matt settled in for the night, he remembered how he and his new wife had camped at Zion on their honeymoon trip West, and the realization hit him hard that they would never be here together again, beside the rippling Virgin River, and despite the doubts he'd felt about the marriage even then, and the unhappiness that had followed, he felt a pang of regret. For the past, for time passing, for his future that would not include her.

The next day Matt drove out of Zion on the spectacular highway that had been blasted out of rock walls, enjoying seeing again the whorled mounds of sandstone rock where he'd picnicked years before. In Page at the motel, Roberta insisted on sleeping on the floor on her camp mattress, and that was just fine with Matt.

When they arrived at the ruined Rainbow Lodge, Matt took some comfort seeing that with the exception of Sven and his sons, none of his fellow trip members seemed the types who could outrun jackrabbits without getting winded. Randi might--she was in great shape and Matt vowed to turn on as much seductive charm as he could, but she seemed shy.

Matt noticed right away that Rachel interjected herself into the conversation most often when he was taking part in it. He found her attractive, but she did not turn his head. Matt slept in Roberta's tent that first night, but he noticed how Randi settled in on her camp mattress under the stars and decided to do the same next night and thereafter if it did not rain.

Roberta could not and would not part with her tent and was determined to lug it along.

"It weighs a ton," Matt warned.

"Yes but it's so darn comfortable."

Matt gallantly offered to share the load, and she didn't object. He'd read that one shouldn't pack more than a certain percentage of body weight, and when Thomasin and Jo allocated equal shares of the commissary to each participant, with the tentpoles and rain cover for the tent, his load rose off the charts.

It was all he could do to lift the pack onto his back.

For the first hour of the hike Matt had serious doubts he could make it. The pack weighed a ton and the hard rock trail never let him get a rhythm--any minute he thought he might tear a muscle or twist an ankle or plain and simple just topple down the steep mountain slope. "I'll know how Humpty Dumpty felt. What they don't tell you is he was carrying a pack like this."

Maybe someone chuckled at this, he didn't know--he was too busy sweating and struggling.

After the first hour though he noticed he'd found an equilibrium. His back and ankles were holding up and he'd gotten used to the weight.

After several hours of hard hiking, when they topped out at Yabut Pass, he realized the worst slog was over. They would be heading downhill, deep into the magnificent canyons where the Rainbow Bridge would lie, and a surge of excitement gave him extra adrenaline. The 9 miles did not go fast, but they did go and when the hikers reached camp late that afternoon, he was not the last to arrive.

Matt had not found a moment to charm Randi, and in camp he discovered that she'd worn blisters on her feet from her new hiking boots and was being attended to by Rachel. He decided that with aching feet she'd be in no mood to listen to his bon mots, and put off flirtation for another day. In any event, he worried he might fall asleep between the bon and mot after the strenuous day, and discovered what all of the novices along on their first extended backpack had.

"Out here there's no electricity," Roberta said, and truer words weren't spoken that evening. After dinner and when night fell, sleep beckoned to one and all.

"No one's in their tent reading War and Peace," Matt said to himself. He'd rolled out his mattress and blanket on the ground and got into his sleeping bag.

"You're not afraid of rattlers?" Roberta asked. "I wouldn't want one of those in my sleeping bag, no siree bob."

Matt was, but he wasn't about to chicken out when Randi had already turned in for the night under the stars, and was sleeping soundly.

He noticed that Rachel too was bunked down not far away in the sagebrush, and the thought occurred to him again that she might be attracted to him and wanted him to know it.

The next day on the long dayhike Randi stayed in camp, nursing her sore feet. Rachel came along and more than once she marched near him and missed no occasion to converse. He appreciated when she'd shown herself interested in his stories of Rainbow Bridge and the West. No one else ever had. He knew there were people out there in the world who shared his passion for the Old West and its mythos, as the intellectuals called it, but he hadn't crossed their paths. Maybe because they were out here, as Rachel was now.

His wife had never cottoned to westerns and thought they'd transformed him, the strong silent type, into a speech-challenged type incapable of expressing romantic feelings. He felt that might be true to an extent, but then again, if he didn't have romantic feelings for her, he had nothing to express. But being the strong silent type, he didn't want to hurt her by saying this so bluntly.

He liked it that Rachel was so quickwitted, and he thought she had the very pleasant laugh that some people had where her whole personality transformed. Not so much "infectious" as "radiant," but that didn't do it or her justice either. It was nice to hear, and since he liked hearing it, he tried his best to coax it out with wisecracks.

That late afternoon when the two single-sex groups had pool dipped, he hadn't joined in the raillery when Rachel came and went two times past them. It wasn't his style. He did think though that she'd left the hat accidentally on purpose, as Sven had claimed, and flattered himself that she'd wanted to take a look at him. If so, he admired her straightforward tactics. He decided, if she does want me that bad, she can get me.

So it was that on the signal day when he saw the Rainbow Bridge and really saw it, having earned the right by trekking overland through sinuous sandstone canyons, braving heat and sand and leg-jarring rock, he decided to wait for Rachel.

#

Out here in the Utah desert Rachel slept well, with the quiet night cradling her dreams, and the stars and a waxing moon overhead to give her enough light if she woke up to see "what was not stirring," she told Karen. "Animals were out there but they knew better than to come near a bunch of smelly hikers like us."

So then she would beam her gaze upward toward the new moon and stars. She found she could relax and unwind from her usual frenetic pace of work and study and anxiety about age and future. Out here she was living to the rhythms of sun and earth, weather and water, putting one foot in front of the other and burdening the pack. In a matter of a few minutes she would fall back asleep.

This night though she looked over toward where Matt slept, on a slight embankment. She was glad to see him there.

And this time before she fell back asleep, she hatched a plan.

#

She woke early the next morning and noticed for the first time how pungent and lovely were the pinyon pine trees and junipers at dawn, and how the morning light changed shades on the cliff walls all around.

She took her time packing up and had the pleasure of Matt's conversation as he was engaged in same, though Frank came up and discoursed on the intricacies of Cha Canyon, where they would make their penultimate camp. "There's a bridge down there, not easy to get to and not so impressive but it's a bridge and I spent a couple of days trying to find it."

Luckily Frank hadn't forgotten her query, and as the group expended much breath and energy climbing a somewhat featureless--compared to where they'd been--slope eastward, he waited for Rachel and pointed north toward a gap in the sandstone walls that seemed to widen out to the north.

"That's Surprise Valley. Hard to get to, I'll tell you that. You might make it in, but you might not make it out."

"Could you live down there?" Matt had come up.

"Maybe. If you had to. But who would want to?"

"Lovers."

"You can't live on love," Frank rejoined, rather emphatically. "Hard thing to say, isn't it?"

He turned and headed up the trail with the others. Rachel seized the moment and said to Matt: "I'm thinking of coming with you to the Grand Canyon. You're taking Roberta back to Las Vegas and I can change my flight to fly out of there."

Thus said, it sounded like a private thought. Certainly he was free to not accommodate her thoughts, not to mention plans.

He smiled and said," Hitch up your wagon, pardner."

#

The next and last day was a chug, and they did not arrive at their last campsite before late afternoon. Rachel pitched her mattress and sleeping bag near Matt's, as before, and somehow or other--she could never remember how--launched into a panegyric about opera.

It turned out that Jo had lived for many years in Manhattan before retiring to Arizona, and loved the Met.

"What are your favorites?" Rachel asked.

"I'll tell you on the way, if you two are up for it." She meant Rachel and Matt. No one had said a peep about what they might have been doing when playing hooky the other afternoon, but one mattress led to another side by side and conclusions could be drawn.

"Up for what?" Matt logically asked.

Thomasin chimed in: "The Dome."

She meant a huge pile of sandstone not far from the campsite that whorled its way toward the sky, not so high as to frighten faint hearts, but a pull nevertheless.

"Mine are Verdi and Mozart, any and all"--Rachel said as she picked up her water bottle and looked more than game for the Dome. She said to Karen, "I was getting him back for Browning, but I also was testing to see if he turned down his nose at my other true love."

He didn't, and his water bottle was already strapped to his side as Thomasin and Jo led them and other hikers who joined in along the way. Matt averred with some regret that he'd like nothing better than to hear a Verdi opera--"or Mozart," he hastily added, mindful of Rachel's sensibilities--and she laughed and liked this--but none ever got staged in the heart of the heart of the country where he came from, and he looked forward to a trip maybe someday soon to the Big Apple where he might initiate himself.

Rachel said, "You need a guide."

"Well, maybe I'll find one. Somebody who lives in Manhattan and loves opera and knows one or two things about it."

She read that as a humorous challenge and all the way to the dome waxed on and on with Thomasin and Jo about various operas, in between a few pauses to catch breath.

Matt said later, "I didn't expect to get an opera lesson in the desert. It was a crash course without the crash, except for Wagner who got left out."

"He deserved to be, " Rachel said acidly.

Though it was easy hiking to scale the Dome, it did mount steadily and "it's no picnic," Suzy gasped. Matt remarked later that this was about the only thing he'd heard her say on the trip. She rivaled Randi for laconic. The latter again watched the group from below. She would hobble toward the end, but only when necessary, as Rachel duly counseled every day.

When they all reached the top, the group spread out. The dome had more than enough space for all and its curls and dips merited exploration.

Rachel and Matt left off opera and enjoyed the moment. "And some moment it was," Rachel told Karen, who actually thought she saw tears in her friend's eyes.

"It was so beautiful, and he kept saying such beautiful things. The sun was going down and it was like we lived in a world of gold and orange. Plus the sandstone holds heat for a long time and the warmth just went right through us."

"It's like we're glowing," Rachel said to Matt, "lit up from inside."

"I already am," he said, looking at her. Rachel searched for a rejoinder and could find none. For a long moment she was speechless.

Karen would say, "I don't believe it. You speechless?"

"Part of it was, I wasn't sure he was talking about me. The other part was, if he was, my little heart was going to go up in flames. "

"So what did you finally say?"

"Something logical and completely banal."

She turned to Matt and said, "Did Jane and Lassiter have sunsets like this?"

"I'm sure they did. A lot." She thought a moment.

"How could they not have been happy?" She knew that she was, right now, there in the warm golden sun.

They stayed there until the sun headed down, happy to be with each other. Jo took their picture and as she was focusing the viewfinder said, "I don't know which is brighter, the sun or your smiles." And for the second time this incandescent afternoon, Rachel was rendered speechless.

#

Matt had lost a girl friend and a wife and he knew very well that feelings were ephemeral and the grand moments just that, moments.

On the sandstone dome he reveled, but the thought wouldn't leave, no matter how hard he fought it, that all this, the glorious canyons and sunset and most of all, Rachel, wouldn't last. It was too much happiness, and he'd never had much of that, even if his life hadn't been marked by death or tragedy. He'd been cool, and life had been cool.

So no matter how much pleasure he took that last evening of the backpack trip, he knew it was finite--a couple days more and it would be all over. The sun would set, they'd have a nice time at the Grand Canyon, then Rachel would go back to New York and he to LA and the twain wouldn't cross the continent.

Tomorrow would come and would surely not end with another sunset like this one, and they wouldn't be there like Jane and Lassiter to enjoy it.

Still, it was he who he made sure to ask Jo to take some pictures of them arm in arm on the dome, smiling as if tomorrow would bring the same sunshine as today.

#

Rachel had done what she had asserted to Karen, take the bull by the horns. Matt was driving, and on the long road back from trail's end to the Grand Canyon, while the three now well broken-in hikers replayed their hike in anecdotes and gossip, she strategized.

Phoenix was a no-brainer. She could get by with "my plans have changed," and she doubted very much that Jim would press the case.

Roberta was another story. Matt had rented only one room at the El Tovar, and Rachel wasn't about to share the room floor beside Roberta. She'd had enough of her sleeping bag. A nightmare vision came to her of Roberta setting up her tent at bedside.

They stopped in the first big town for lunch, Tuba City. "Where are the tubas?" Rachel asked.

They were not to be found, but sandwiches were, and they downed them quickly and hit the road again. They stopped once, at the first overlook into the giant Canyon. The sun had descended just enough to highlight the immensity of the canyon's mile-deep plunge to the Colorado, which from this height resembled a thin brown ribbon.

Matt said, "I'd like to hike some of the Bright Angel trail tomorrow. You guys up for that?"

"You betcha," Roberta chimed.

"I'll go where you go," Rachel said to Matt, for Roberta's benefit as well, as she couldn't be so naive and/or thick to miss this flashing neon.

They arrived just before sunset at the El Tovar, and Rachel, who'd seen some of the historic hotels of Europe, loved its huge wooden beams and rustic Old West charm. "Teddy Roosevelt stayed here after seeing the Rainbow Bridge, or before, I can't remember which," Matt informed.

"It's magnificent," Rachel seconded.

"Look at all those stuffed animals on the walls," Roberta gaped.

"I'll get the room keys," Matt said, and while he did this at reception, Rachel seized the moment.

"I really like him, I mean really," she said to Roberta.

"Yeah, I kinda saw that."

"Could we have a little girl talk?"

"I don't getcha," and she looked genuinely puzzled.

Matt came up to them with the keys. "Room 406, right on the rim, like I asked for."

Rachel said, "Why don't you go on up and we'll reserve the restaurant. We don't want to miss out on a table and have to eat freeze-dried food again, no?"

"Yeah, all I could think about at the end of the hike was a steak and a bottle of wine."

"We'll make sure you get that, " Rachel said, thinking, "Before the night's over we'll give you something else to think about, pardner."

He smiled, with a slight expression that suggested he knew something else was afoot, but as a man caught between two women, realized he'd better leave the situation in their much more delicate hands.

Rachel's girl talk got right to the point: she offered to pay Roberta for a separate room, all to and for herself. She clinched the argument with a practical consideration that she knew would work, that their room only had one shower and they had limited time before their restaurant reservation.

"Right you are," Roberta agreed, and accepted a room that overlooked the parking lot.

Rachel headed upstairs to join Matt. "A gal's got to do what a gal's got to do," she told her very impressed and pleased man.

They were not yet fully alone together and had to get through a copious Western dinner in the historic dining room, also overlooking the Canyon—"Gonna be a lot of wind tonight," Roberta observed.

Matt had a steak "big enough to fill a chuck wagon," and offered dessert for everyone, but the wine had gone to Roberta's head and she unaccountably turned on the blarney to revive a gent at the next table who looked like he'd fall out of his chair any minute—"a pseudo-Western coot on the make," Matt uncharitably described.

It took some very long minutes of tedious conversation before they could send the coot stumbling back to his lair, and after all Roberta had lost interest in him very quickly. "I think he was drunk. He talked like he'd had one too many, if you know what I mean."

"Bottles, you mean," Rachel added somewhat acerbically. She and Matt accompanied Roberta to her room and left her there with multiple sincere "good nights," then headed off to at last indulge their fling.

#

"Except something happened," Rachel confided to Karen.

It was only a few days later, but it seemed so much longer, as any time when an experience changes a life.

"Something really really surprising. He said he was as much surprised as I was. "

"What?" Karen asked.

"It's hard to explain in words."

"Come on, I'm suffering here."

Rachel reflected a long moment. Then said simply, "We started out having sex, and ended up making love."

#

"It was something I'd never felt before. Just this physical emotional force I couldn't control, even if I wanted to. Which I didn't."

Rachel laughed, that infectious laugh that captivated everyone.

"Let me set the scene. A most amazing scene.

"Matt had reserved a room right on the canyon rim. It was cosy and Western and warm, like sandstone. We could look out and down and see all the layers of rock the river had sculpted for eons, even when night fell, because it was a full moon night. But that wasn't all the moon did.

"Trees are tenacious, you know, and this pinyon pine had managed to take root right there on the rim edge. A big wind came up and the branches started striking our window. Clack clack clack. The moonlight shone into our room like a big soft beacon and the shadows of the branches hit the wall in front of our bed. 'They're like little tree elves,' I said. And they were.

"They never had the same pattern, my tree elves. Dancing in the wind nonstop. Just one leap and spin after another, and the sound of branches hitting the window making a kind of music. Nature's music. Matt called it our magic lantern. A show just for us, in our cosy little room at the Grand Canyon.

"And while we were watching the show, and I was wondering whether he felt the same magic I was, he told me his story."

#

When his wife's grandmother passed away, Matt had gone back to the Midwest for the funeral and promised to drive her car solo back to Los Angeles. It was specially made by Buick and though absolutely not the style he or his wife would have chosen, it had hardly been driven and they did not want to refuse a gift from the late grandmother, who had insisted as if the car were a rare jewel.

En route across New Mexico and Arizona, Matt noticed it was only a short detour to Page where he could take a boatride to the Rainbow Bridge, and even though he detested the idea of going by boat for a 10-minute looksee, he couldn't resist the desire to see up close the Monument he had read and fantasized about since youth.

So after a night at a Page motel, he left early, first calling his wife to tell her his whereabouts. She didn't answer, at 7 in the morning.

"That told me a lot," he said. "But I wasn't going to mope around and keep calling."

He had felt alone before and for a long time during the marriage, and now he knew he was alone. If he fell into Lake Powell and drowned, authorities would fish him out and a ceremony would be held somewhere--probably LA--and that would be that. A few crocodile tears from the spouse, but very soon after, back to the daily routine of life, slightly altered because "she would have to do something about the car."

When he did at last stand before the magnificent stone arch after two hours of boat motor fuel spewed into lake and Utah sky, the thought flashed across his mind that he could do worse than hide behind it and wait for the other tourists to leave, then wander off into the canyons. Maybe he could live and sustain himself, maybe not. Anyway who would care?

But something about the Bridge gave him hope. He had never been able to explain what fascinated him about it, or why he wanted so much to see it and earn the right to do so.

"I just somehow, always felt something wonderful was waiting for me there."

In the weeks leading up to the hike, from time to time and at any hour of the day for no rhyme or reason, a flash of intense wellbeing would come over him, as if something good was about to happen. He couldn't say what it was or what it meant, but it was real. He thought it might be linked to his longtime desire to see Rainbow Bridge.

Walt was no help: "Some kind of psychological hot flash," he opined.

"But good or bad?" Walt didn't have a clue.

#

Rachel said, "So there we were, watching our elves dance on the walls, and Matt said, 'Now I know. I found it, that something wonderful. Its lying here right beside me. You.' "

Karen said, "That is so sweet. And romantic." And added, "I am so goddamn jealous."

Rachel said, "And it was like all these emotions bottled up and dormant for 27 years sprang up and completely changed me and everything I'd been."

#

Before leaving for Las Vegas the next afternoon, they hiked down the Grand Canyon's Bright Angel Trail. "Named after the faithful mule who carried travelers years and years down to the canyon floor," Matt said.

"He's passed on to mule heaven?"

"Yep, probably carrying people around to the sights up there."

"Bless him," Rachel added. "Guess you'll have to be my bright angel today." He liked that.

They hadn't gotten much sleep, and they were shy about the night before, still not sure what had happened to them. They carried on as if they were still on the Bridge hike.

Roberta had decided to hang around the lodge. They hiked quickly down the trail about two miles, then picnicked. Matt had to beat off a couple of the aggressive canyon squirrels who wanted to pilfer their picnic, and vaunted his prowess.

"I'll protect you from these beasts," he affirmed boldly.

"You sure you weren't protecting the sandwiches?" She quipped.

He got back at her on the way back--and up. Even though they'd just done an arduous backpack, they found it no easy thing to trek back up the steep trail in the midday heat.

Rachel said, puffing, "I'd give my soul for a coke."

Matt quipped, "Are you sure your soul would fetch a coke?"-- and was rewarded with one of her delighted laughs.

They'd decided to prolong their time together in Las Vegas, where Rachel had adjusted her plane flight.

Late that afternoon they arrived at the Vegas airport and saw Roberta off, with vows to meet again somewhere sometime.

"Think about getting a lighter tent," Matt said.

"I sure do appreciate you helping me carry it," Roberta said, sincerely as always.

#

Matt found a motel further down the Strip from the giant hotel casinos. It had a pool and most usefully, a laundromat next door where they could wash the dirt and dust from clothes seasoned by a week of Utah canyons.

With clothes washed and them both luxuriously showered--Vegas had nothing if not amenities--they became "dudes with duds," Matt said, making his lover laugh.

That they were, lovers, for the next day and a half, not coming up for air till their last night together when they took a stroll down the Strip, all lit up with neon blazing and obliterating the clear desert night sky.

Rachel quickly saw enough, people and places, to proclaim, "Vegas is not us. We're maybe the only couples around who can resist the slots."

"I've already won big, " Matt said.

He wasn't given to gushing, Rachel knew very well, so when something like this came out "I bathed in it," she said to Karen. "Las Vegas is a desert, you know."

"No wonder he's in the movies," Karen said. "How can he keep saying things like that? You must have made his head spin like a top."

They went into a casino that offered a lobster dinner roughly 80% cheaper than anywhere else in the world.

"They take a loss," Matt said, "so the suckers come in, eat high on the lobster and get stoked on wine--"

"And those 99-cent margaritas," Rachel added.

"--right, and then what else is there to do but hit the bandits and lose all your hard-earned money."

"Like you just did. But you stopped at 20. How could you resist temptation?"

"I have something else to do." And he did, with her, after a stroll through some of the casino's upscale boutiques, where Rachel delighted in a music box store that alternated tunes from pop hits to Debussy. The latter graced a magnificent box that to purchase, Rachel lamented, "would oblige you to write a hit movie, honey."

"Or two."

They got little sleep that night and lingered in bed till the last moment before heading for the airport. Rachel was the last passenger to board.

"They look impatient," she said, meaning the flight attendants waiting for her boarding pass.

"No, that's jealousy."

"Let's give them more green eyes." She kissed him so long and hard he really did think she'd decided to miss the plane, and only when they saw the attendants entering the plane and preparing to close the door did Rachel take off running and just manage to squeeze into the aircraft.

Much later Matt thought it would be a terrific scene for a movie script, and at that moment, he told Walt, "I was rooting for the door."

But no--she made it, and "regretted every single mile of distance between Vegas and New York," she told Karen. "I thought they'd have to mop up my tears."

No man had ever loved her like that, and she had never felt so much like giving it back.

\#

Matt waited at the departure lounge. He'd noticed that outbound planes were using the front runway and he could follow her plane from access to takeoff.

It lingered an inordinately long time, it seemed to him, poised and waiting, and he imagined Rachel haranguing the pilot to let her off. Any second he would see the door open and her racing down the stairsteps and across the tarmac toward him--where he'd be rushing down to meet her halfway.

But this wasn't the movies and he wasn't writing a script.

The plane roared past him in full view, and he tried and failed to catch sight of her at a window. He watched until the plane passed the limits of his sight on the horizon in the bright desert sky. He wondered if he'd ever see her again. He knew what he felt, but it seemed so much like a miracle and he knew from his Catholic upbringing that those didn't come in bunches and he'd read the New Testament and never saw the Christ repeating one.

Thinking only fling, neither had planned for the future.

Matt left the airport, made one stop along the way, then hit the Interstate for the trip back to LA. He couldn't bear to stay in Las Vegas a minute longer without her.

The sky was clear and blue and the air too, as a wind the night before had swept most of the pollution from the air, but Matt told Walt he drove every mile in "your classic daze. You're moving through this cloud and you've not sure where you've been or where you're going."

"Thank God for Interstate 40 and one-way traffic. Sounds like serious impairment to me. Dean Martin said it first. That's amore. Surprised you made it back in one piece."

"I didn't. Part of me landed in New York."

The next day he went to the Post Office and packaged what he'd bought on his stop in Vegas, the most expensive and beautiful music box they'd seen, that serenaded Debussy's Clair de Lune. Matt told himself, if we never see each other again, whenever she opens the box and hears the music she'll think of me and how the moonlight danced that night at the Grand Canyon.

3. LET THE BELL RING

For good and true friends at orange blossom time.

One ferociously suffocating day many years ago, an August
after my friend Jeff's senior year at University and mine mark-
ing time, we escaped the boredom of a Mississippi Sunday
and took a ride into the countryside. No destination. Just driving. We had no plans, no ideas for plans, and no girls waiting
breathlessly for us to come calling. Jeff's girl friend Beth had
been obliged to submit to a weekend family outing on some
lake across the border in Arkansas, and Jeff said, "I'm not
crossing that State line, no way. They use convicts as prison
guards and all the bodies haven't been found yet."

A scandal had erupted at the Arkansas prisons a few years
ago, having to do with cadavers and summary justice and
overall, what one could call at minimum unsafe conditions. It
later became a film starring Robert Redford, who was not a
native southerner but roughly 0 persons in the cinemagoing
universe objected at that time to his casting, and it succeeded
both commercially and artistically. I didn't have the sense
then, or ever, to lock up the rights, and thus went the way of
my world.

"What do her parents have to do with prison?" I asked.

"They don't. I do. Instead of locking up her daughter. Get
the picture?"

I did. It stunned me that they'd disapprove of Jeff, a great
guy who'd become a good friend, an all around solid person
who radiated confidence like a saint's neon halo.

"I'm heading out of state which is just fine with them, but
Beth's going to follow and they know that. Can't forgive me
and can't let her leave their coattails. She's going to get both
earfuls all weekend."

Jeff had moved south with his family, something to do with
his father and greener business pastures, and even though at
22 he could have moved on to brighter lights and bigger cities,

he'd chosen to use some of his GI bill money to come along with them and share their huge house while he finished college. He bought a VW bug for postclass fun and bided his time till graduation, when he intended to move to Arizona, where he'd been stationed in the military.

"Phoenix is hot as hell, maybe even hotter," he told me, "but once you smell the orange blossoms in spring, I swear you'll fall in love with the first woman you see. And not stop there."

He meant it not in a salacious hound dog way—though I imagined Beth's parents would have thought so—but like a kind of troubadour, singing of medieval romantic love, where the senses came together and found the joy of life and romance.

He was no literary guy, far from it, but he loved a good time and knew how to find it. Often in the most unlikely ways and byways.

Having taken some years from his studies to give to the US, he was older than me and one class behind, but for some reason he'd taken me under his wing. Every true adventurer needs a sidekick, I surmised, and I had no problem playing second banana, especially at that point in my early life. I'd just been dumped bigtime by my first serious girl friend Vicki, and Jeff would call and pick me up from time to time to share whatever pastime he couldn't or wouldn't share with Beth, or as now, when she was *hors de combat*.

We'd met on a double date, Beth and Vicki being the best of friends, and for a while the foursome had functioned like a Swiss clock. We particularly enjoyed our booze evenings. Mississippi at that time being no place to enjoy a convivial glass of wine, i.e., liquor by the glass, Jeff would buy a bottle of whisky or bourbon or very exotica, vodka, a six-pack of Cokes and tons of chips, and off we'd go to the forest. Somehow he'd maneuver his Beetle through the trees, crunching pine needles and fallen branches and big thick cones that seemed like they reached up to door level, until he chose a viable parking space—among the trees and sheltered, far enough away from the gravel road that'd led us there to escape easy detection and out of ear range.

Then we'd settle in for mixed drinks, the only decision being which got poured first, liquor or Coke, chuckles and some making out. We could not go all the way, group etiquette being what it was at the time, but some serious petting got done amid some serious drinking.

I wondered whether Jeff and Beth eased into the same woods and drinks evenings after I became past history and Vicki took up with Carl, but I never dared ask my friend—who'd become just that. He reserved some fun time with me, and once or twice we'd played cards and hung out with a couple of girls he knew, non-sexual events, alas for me, where of course Vicki's name never surfaced in the conversation.

I'd gone through some major soul-searching time after I learned Vicki had two-timed me. Two months of outright obsessing over how and why everything had gone wrong, as during our dating nothing seemed to go wrong. In short, I'd had no clue.

A ton of bricks fell, and I just managed to hold my psyche together. Just. It did not help that during my forty days and nights in the desert of loneliness and rejection, one of the worst heat waves in history hit the state. Day after miserable day of 110 F° temps, no clouds, no rainstorms in the afternoon to give some relief. Hell had come, as if my own were radiating outward and infecting the land.

It was the epoch of the Vietnam War. Rumors floated above the deathly heat that the President had a plan to end it, but no announcements came, except one for me, a summons to a US Army physical. Having just graduated and no longer sheltered from duty by higher learning, I envisioned a destiny where the local paper would proclaim, "Local Youth Becomes Last Casualty of War."

Those age-old twin stresses, love and war, hit me hard. And as always, Jeff came through. He called and said he had a bottle that needed drinking, and what better way to prepare for the physical next day than get roaring drunk.

So we drove out in his Beetle to the woods—thankfully, he'd chosen a different locale from the ones we'd frequented on double dates—and we downed the bottle over laughs and news of the crazy world that we would put to order once we had the chance, very soon in the coming years. The subject of Vicki was skirted. Jeff continued to see Beth, who remained friends with her, and from what I could dare glean from him, the pines surrounding us were nowhere used as a verb in regard to me.

We finished the bottle, and self-absorbed to psychosis as I was, it never occurred to me—before the quantity of bourbon took over and blew clouds into my brain—to thank Jeff for coming to my rescue. For one evening, he'd treated me as a continuing member of the community, who might have some self-worth beyond pathetic cuckold.

I took the physical, among doctors and interns who treated us like future cannon fodder, sailed through the blood test and other more demeaning tests and managed to pee in a bottle when yelled at to do so.

Hungover or not, I saw the rice paddies waiting and wondered if there'd ever be an evening where good buds could share a bottle, and if enough trees could be found in 'Nam to give shelter away from mines and bullets and grenades.

But no. The head doctor gave me a three-month deferment. "You have too much albumen in your urine," he said. "This could be serious for your kidneys." In effect, he said to use the three months to get cured, then come back. At which time, yes, I would be found qualified to fight in the rice paddies against an enemy across the world threatening the vital security of the United States, though at the time I had no idea how and no desire to find out. I was much more concerned, existentially concerned, to find out why Vicki had rejected me.

I did manage to learn that albumen could build up from excess alcohol consumption, and when I saw our family doctor, neither I nor Jeff saw any need to tie one on beforehand. Thus sober, urinalysis came through spotless, as it were. "Still, let's take a blood test to be sure," the doctor said.

While waiting for the results, he examined my pulse, heart and blood pressure while I wrenched brain and soul over Vicki, as I'd been doing for the last two heatwave months.

When I woke up from my blackout, remembering only how I'd vaguely thought that death seemed so peaceful, a relief like sleep, I found an oxygen mask over my nose, and the doctor sweating bullets. He'd clearly worried for my life.

He promptly put me in the hospital for five days of tests, blood, glucose—you name it, including a spinal tap. All came back negative.

I knew very well why I'd fainted, an excess of stress brought on by bitter, misspent love. But I'd gone into convulsions and swallowed my tongue, and based on that alone, was diagnosed as an epileptic and placed on a lifelong regimen of Dilantin.

The doctor gave me a letter for the Draft Board, and though I still hoped Vicki would take me back, not so for the former. Thus armed, and once again not hung over, I sailed through the urinalysis to the satisfaction of one of the two head doctors—a blond young practitioner who reminded me of the German actor Hardy Kruger—and I whipped out my doctor's letter posthaste.

"Humph," he snorted. "Humph. HUMPH!"

Handling the letter like a strip of shit-soiled toilet paper, he got up and charged over to his colleague—the doctor who'd urged me to take care of my albumen problem.

It was a slow day at Uncle Sam's clearing house, and both doctors fell to examining my case. Suddenly what had seemed to me a pro forma exercise turned into a trial I had only a fifty-fifty chance of winning.

Dr. Kruger—his real name blocked from my memory after all these years—sneered, snorted and loudly and emphatically verbally dismissed the contents of my doctor's testimony.

"It was a blood test!" he roared. "The guy flipped out over a blood test!"

"No," his colleague—whose name, Dr. Alberto, I do remember—"convulsions, oxygen, the tongue—I have been three years at Mayo Clinic."

"C'mon Al, I've seen them come out of that room, fall on the floor and shake. Conniption fits, that's what it is, no more and no less."

"No, is serious."

To my everlasting luck, or maybe Jeff's wisdom in getting me drunk that night, Dr. Alberto had seniority and led me into his office where, after various counsels to take very good care of myself—"these kidneys, this is serious"—and repeated validations of his diagnosis by referring to the Mayo Clinic, he signed my get out of jail card.

As I hurried out of purgatory, Dr. Kruger was ranting to one of the interns. "It was just a blood test!" And if looks could kill as well as the Viet Cong...luckily, I told myself, I was well out of spitting range.

It took me a year of hard editing work at the local newspaper to gather the means to leave Mississippi and head west, not stopping till the dreamland called Hollywood, which coincided with Jeff's last year at university. Whenever we got together, I could be sure something fun would happen. He was up for anything of the non-criminal variety, and had imagination for pleasure and mischief in equal measures.

It would never have occurred to me, one night as we walked off an evening of beers and crossed a construction site, to proclaim like him, "I can drive that sucker. Want to ride shotgun?"

That sucker was a bulldozer, parked among the piles of hard wild Mississippi earth dug and cleared for future comforts—in this case a golf course.

Jeff climbed aboard, and me dubiously to the passenger seat. It crossed my mind to wonder why a bulldozer would have one, but the thought vanished in the noise of a John Deere coming to life, there in the dark night.

"Told you!" Jeff crowed, and then off we went, slowly but...not so surely, as in the dark Jeff hadn't noticed a ditch made even more soft and unstable by the recent rains.

Down went the beast, almost guaranteed to crush me under it. Except life was charmed with Jeff along, and I leaped down and far enough away to escape with just a few splashes of mud.

The guck was explainable. Death would not have been, but I had no worries for my friend, and sure enough he appeared, having seen the crash coming and as always, one move ahead.

He eyed the hulk, half submerged almost in the rain-filled ditch.

"They'll have to call in a crane," he concluded matter of factly. "Let's wipe it for prints." He was joking, but for days afterward I worried about strange knocks on my door.

"Time to go west, young man."

And it was. But August had to be endured. Jeff said, "It's dry heat in Phoenix, not like here, but still, if you leave a wrench out in the sun past thirty seconds, I wouldn't advise you to pick it up again without gloves."

That got my attention, as well as his insistence that we take a ride in the heat of a Sunday Mississippi afternoon, for no good reason except "get acclimated, you know."

"I grew up in this," I protested. "Twenty years and still trying to get acclimated."

"Look, when we head out into the world, escapades happen. And besides, what else have we got to do?"

Had me there. So here we were, broiling sans air conditioning in his Bug, heading nowhere fast. For sure, no oncoming traffic, or following traffic for that matter, imperiled navigation.

All around we saw flatland growing corn and cotton and some soybeans, which had become a more popular crop. And then, out of the haze that waved so strongly I thought at first it was a mirage, we saw a ruin.

Jeff slowed. Stopped. We'd reached a stretch of pine woods, but he seemed to be fascinated for some reason by the forlorn country church that fronted them, like an outpost for those entering or leaving the big forest.

"I got religion," I said. "Don't need to put on my Sunday go to meeting clothes."

"For this church, shorts will do."

I didn't understand. It was one of those small churches built Lord knows when, of timber from the surrounding woods, and maybe once it had attracted the local farmers, but now with auto transport more developed and urban growth and whatever other reason to leave the country, it had been abandoned.

The structure still stood, but the interior had been devastated, ripped out almost from its foundations, windows shattered, door open to a jumble of pews and broken chairs. You couldn't save anything worth saving, because nothing was. The souls who might have been, had long gone to the Lord's or greener pastures.

As usual, Jeff saw farther than me.

"Lift up your eyes toward the Lord, Matt."

"Like I said—"

"You don't have to make it to heaven. Not that far."

I looked up, and then saw what he was looking at.

"The Lord's given us something to mark the hours and days of our lives. But we've got to earn it."

I thought a moment. Then, as usual: "If you're thinking what I think you're thinking, I'm with you."

Over fifty years had passed since that broiling afternoon when I got an email from Jeff, so out of the blue it might have come from heaven itself. In these days of instant connection, cyberwise, it's become easier and easier to track down someone among the billions of people inhabiting the planet. They don't have to be alive, of course. Death records are reli able and at hand, humans having eons ago decided that the dead could and should be remembered, at least in their family circles.

Living records too proliferate, and Jeff had taken the time to scroll past my occasional TV movie and two massive feature flops to my part-time gigs at the local desert university outside Palm Springs. My email address there isn't often used except when students have a complaint about a grade or need to submit their latest draft of a script I've busted brain and heart over, trying to find emotion and originality or at least something to hold cynical 21st century viewers' attention, knowing also that however sincere their intentions, roughly 99% if not all of them will have devoted less brain and heart.

But I learned long ago that a gig is a gig, and can lead to others. Even at my age, I still dream of an Oscar, which I only now, half a century later, confessed to Jeff.

I'd made the decision not to that very late, near dawn, snowy evening in New Mexico where we ran out of gas. We'd decided to pass spring break with a scout trip West to Arizona, where Jeff still had a friend from his Air Force days. Every day counted, and we didn't want to waste one en route, so we tagteamed driving and tried to forget sleep. It worked well, and we'd driven all day at top speed and most of the night. At this rate we foresaw arriving in Phoenix just when our eyes could take no more, the evening of our second day—when we could fall into bed exhausted and wake up next morning to "the intoxicating scents of the orange blossoms," Jeff waxed, one of the few times he ever did so poetically. He was earth solid, and so were his dreams, and as time went on they took firm solid root like the orange trees.

Alas, we hadn't counted on the fallibility of our fellow humans who apparently didn't have the same impatience and packed agendas, especially when it came to sleep.

Halfway out of Albuquerque, we discovered that all-night service stations had not yet been invented. Or at least, mass produced and installed in western New Mexico. I was sleeping, having dutifully fulfilled my four hours at the wheel, and then turned it over to my friend.

The slowdown and then crawl to a stop at roadside woke me.

"It's snowing," I said. "Good driving. We don't have chains, right?"

"Or gas. Everything was closed. And we were making choice time."

"So what do we do now? I'm fresh out of ideas before I even had them."

"I'll flag down a car. We're not too far outside Gallup."

"At four in the morning during a snowstorm? You'll freeze out there."

"Well in that case, you'll take over. You should last longer inside the car." So there he went, hitchhiking for cars that might not come till he'd turned into Frosty the Snowman.

I should have been worried, but Jeff's luck always held, and not so many minutes later, a car not only passed, but stopped and picked him up. The second part of his plan had been unsaid, which was that even if he and his benefactor found a station, Jeff would have to find a ride back to our car. And really, how many folks wanted to venture out into a blizzard?

"Find a doofus idiot like us, Jeff, someone who plows ahead through a snowstorm in the middle of the night," I said to myself and future cinema producers, and began thinking about whether I could get a feature film out of this situation. No, I concluded, unless I added kidnappers or a killer—some big action scenes, at minimum.

I wanted to make it in Tinseltown desperately, even if I never mentioned to my friends just how badly. And at rainbow's end, an Oscar. Emmy would be just a steppingstone.

The colder it got—and it did—and as the snow continued to shush down—the warmer became the reception and adulation for my films, and I would have got up to a dozen or so Oscars if Jeff hadn't arrived, just like in cheesy melodramas, as dawn broke and so did the storm, with a gallon can of gas, enough to get us to Gallup.

"Who did you find to bring you back?" I asked.

"Same guy. Guess he enjoyed my conversation."

As well he would. The boy could pour on the charm. Especially under duress, and in theory to save his pal who might freeze along with the Beetle.

The only time I saw it fail was the next day, and the failure was qualified. We found a cheap motel in Gallup, gassed up and hauled ass toward Phoenix. Our asses were pulled over however by a state trooper outside of Payson, in the high green mountains of the Tonto Plateau. Jeff piled on the rap, a combination of good buddy and admission of infraction with accompanying regrets, and subtle flattery for an officer doing

83

his job well. No luck—still got a fine—but the officer reduced it and best of all, didn't throw us in the local hoosegow.

"Payson looks like a nice place," I said as we hauled ass out, albeit less quickly than before.

"Fines aren't fine," Jeff said, "but Arizona's still Old West, you know. It could have been worse."

"Amen."

When we rolled into Phoenix it was night, and gratefully, another motel beckoned. The morning dawned early that fine spring day, and when I awoke I stepped outside into the brisk morning of a desert day, still cool but one could feel the warmth coming along the way.

An intoxicating scent filled the air. I looked around. No orange trees that I could see anywhere. Jeff, reading my mind: "That's just it. They travel, the orange blossoms. Follow you around like a beautiful woman. Enjoy, because they don't last long. The heat takes over. Not to mention, time."

"Good to remember."

"The ideal is to have both. Woman and blossoms."

"Even better."

My prescription of Dilantin pills ran out a couple days later. I junked the bottle and never took another.

Years later we swapped memories. There were lots of them. Nothing so extraordinary as to fill a book or make for a film, TV or otherwise, but fun moments from our lives.

We enjoyed Phoenix, the view from Camelback Mountain at night, the cowboy bars, the Superstition Mountains. The next year, when we drove out together but in separate cars, changing our lives, Jeff had somehow already wangled digs, a cheap house next to a busy road, so your head jangled from the constant traffic, necessitating the mind-enhancing choices of the epoch, beer and pot. But a house was a house, and with it as a base, Beth found it very easy to come out to Phoenix and finish her studies at Arizona State, while Jeff did odd jobs and ruminated on some career path or other.

I moved on to Los Angeles, and again had my way paved thanks to Jeff. We'd zoomed to the City of Angels three days later that first trip, and crashed with his friends from his high school days, now married and well ensconced. They put me up for the time it took, next year, to find an apartment.

Life moved on for both of us then, but we still found time for escapades.

When I passed through on my way back home to Mississippi, I would always spend a few days in Phoenix.

We made excursions. Mountains surround the city, much like Los Angeles, and in those days one was free to drive up South Mountain and find a parking spot from which to see the lights of the city below, enhanced by the properties of a joint, or even two, and a beer to wash it down.

In the afternoons when the desert heat rose—and rose— we could cool off by renting inner tubes and driving to the Verde River. A car shuttle took us to a put-in point and from there, we simply lounged in the tubes and floated down the river to where we'd parked our second car.

The sun dehydrates, and to prevent this health hazard we'd thoughtfully brought along a six-pack. To keep the pack cool, it sufficed simply to drag it along behind in the water. When need arose, a can would be there.

Few things before or since have given me as much pleasure as that, floating along in the open sky under the sun, on the cool river, drifting past tamarisks and cottonwoods, tanning and feeling stress disappear in the tube's wake.

Beth was off at university and found no time for me, and eventually she had none for Jeff either. He'd told me she'd found a circle of school friends, and Jeff, older and past all that, didn't fit in.

She dumped him, much as Vicki had done to me, but Jeff had the distinction of pioneering a phenomenon little current in those days, i.e., being dumped for another lover who happened to be a woman.

As chance would have it, I visited when the dust had hardly settled. Jeff seemed somewhat less imperturbable than usual, but resigned, maybe because "I can't exactly kick the bastard in the balls," meaning the unscrupulous lover.

"Beth always seemed passionate, a really passionate lover," he said, wondering.

I speculated, "That doesn't seem to be all there is."

"Well, I know she, whoever she is, hasn't got what I've got, but what has she got that Beth hasn't got?"

This was too much of an existential question to be solved by guys like us, so we parked our brains outside the local pool hall and proceeded to play. And play. With beer to refresh when the shots weren't falling. For some reason the joint stayed open all night, which we confirmed by doing so.

Home at 10 am, we slept a few hours, then asked ourselves, "What do we do tonight?"

Back to the pool hall. The young night duty counter guy raised eyebrows, motioned toward the same stick rack that had served us so well the night before, and announced to everyone in sight how these maniacs had become addicted or something.

"Bad love affair, that's the reason," I confided to him.

"We let women in here, but reluctantly," he said. "Pool you can understand, it's got rules, but them..."

Jeff liked that, and I could see signs of revival.

"What we really need to do now," he said, "is find the Lost Dutchman gold mine."

We headed east out to Apache Junction, at the time a real Wild West town and gateway to the Superstitions, legendary mountains which have long been said to harbor the Dutchman's gold mine. The Dutchman was never lost—he passed away in civilization—but his mine was, and goldseekers have scoured the range for a century, trying to refind it.

Jeff said we could, and try as I might, I couldn't verify he was kidding. Maybe he'd contracted gold fever. "I've got blankets and we can rustle up some grub"—he fell smoothly into cowboy talk, I thought—"then start looking."

"And what if we don't find it?" I asked.

"Charlie tells me the view's great."

There were bars in Apache Junction that could be mistaken for saloons, and characters who (thankfully) did not have guns strapped to their sides, but talked like they could use them pretty damn well. We took care not to talk contradictory poli-cies to these pardners, just offer 'em another round—which they never refused.

Charlie was chief character, and for all I knew, a former gunfighter. He looked the age and part, told tales as I imag-ined a piece of well-oiled but aged leather would, and in some ways resembled a leather belt come to life, except a belt wouldn't have worn a gen-u-wine Stetson that had seen some trails.

"You boys'll be lucky if you don't see rattlers. Lot of 'em this year."

"We'll share some gold with you, Charlie. That's a promise."

"Jeff, if anybody could find that damn Dutchman's poke, it'll be you. I knew him, you know. Big bullshitter, but when he came down from those hills, he'd have cholla burrs sticking all over his hide but some big sacks of gold. Now where did all that come from, you tell me. No sir, the man found something up there. Wouldn't tell nobody, nobody. And he was good with a gun. Folks learned damn quick not to follow him. Two bodies buried up there, you know. Got too close, dumb bas-tards. The Dutchman paid off their relatives, I know that for a fact, and he didn't stop at dimes and nickels."

It went on like that all afternoon, and by the time Charlie begged off, averring he had a date with a "trailer-hitch gal," we'd passed the point of rational consumption.

"No sweat, Matt," Jeff said, "Charlie says the cops are too scared to come out here."

"Not scared. Terrified," Charlie confirmed.

We had great fun getting to the foothills, as for reasons linked to terrain and heat and who knows, road grading bud-get, the dirt roads that crisscross the desert had each and every one of them a series of humps. Riding fast over them in a Beetle was like a Disneyland thrill ride, and we bobbed our way at top speed to Superstition Mountain like dervishes who'd forsaken whirling for hopping. "Hang on, boy!" Jeff yelled, on about the dozenth hump. Up, down, up, down, boom boom, dust flying behind us, but who cared—you could look a long way behind and not see a car.

We camped in the desert. I had learned from my past experience that no matter how hot during the day, nights brought a real chill, and I'd packed an air mattress for the ground and more than one blanket. After some perfunctory bullshit, mostly centered around Charlie and the past lovers not worthy of us, we slept well under a wonderful sky bursting with stars, the moon not having been invited.

In the morning I knocked off a layer of frost from my blanket, but I'd slept soundly, sans one single shiver. "The desert air," I told Jeff. "Or the desert beer."

We headed up the mountainside on foot.

Very quickly I learned one of the perils of Phoenix desert hiking. And I should have known. We trekked past numerous cholla—called the "jumping cactus" as lore claims the burrs detach from the plant and stick to your person without having been touched.

I did not have a chance to determine if the cactus did indeed jump, as I simply walked right into one. Crunch! Three burrs stuck right into my thigh. Jeff came over to help.

"Does it hurt?"

"Mother fucker suckers!"

"I understand your pain. Don't feel it though, sorry."

"It hurts like a bitch."

"Now you're talking Beth. I did feel that. Hang on."

He reached and very delicately tried to pull out one of the burrs.

"Can't. They'll rip up my hands."

"Gangrene is setting in!"

"Naw, you've got another hour. We'll have to do it one by one."

He took one of the spines, tugged—and we learned to our mutual chagrin that (1) cholla spines are barbed, meaning when firmly embedded, they had to be pulled out with some force, and (2) it hurt, took time and the burrs were thick. Very thick.

"They're beautiful if they're not stuck in your thigh. Like snowflakes or snow cones."

"Just what pray tell do you intend to do with that stick?"

Fortuitously it turned out, Jeff had found a branch, it looked like from a saguaro. Long, desiccated and sturdy.

He draped the towel he'd been using to wipe sweat from his face over the three burrs—"Going to ruin this," he said, meaning the towel, "but it's worth it if you walk again"— wielded the branch like a stick and beat them off. Once the mass were knocked off, we could pull the remainder out individually.

The procedure is far easier to write about than to experience. I nursed a thick, wide green spot on my thigh as we moved on and upward. I still worried about gangrene, but Jeff was delicately picking his way through another patch of cholla, onward and upward toward them thar hills where, history had it, gold waited.

I followed—and got another few spines in my other leg. All the way up I had little luck with the cactus, as I kept bumping into them and getting one spine after another for all my pains —and that is an apt word. "This could be a fool's errand," I said. "I mean, how could the Dutchman forget where his mine was?"

"He was one dumb Dutchman. But we're not. Dutch, I mean."

We switchbacked higher and higher, up into the rock cliffs when the cactus and verdure gave way. We were determined and into it, going higher and higher and steeper and disdaining caution. We had gold on our minds, and nothing was about to stop us but what finally did, high up on the mountainside, where Jeff found himself rimrocked—no way to make it down without help.

I'd been picking yet another cholla burr out of my thigh, spine by spine, skin pooching out each time the barbs reluctantly exited. They were not so deep as to draw blood, but deep enough to embed and make extraction a miserable chore.

Far below us lay the not yet smog-shrouded city of Phoenix, and above us the crags that we now saw stretched upward to wherever the peak was, or peaks—they looked like giant stalactites, and unfortunately we'd not bought along ropes and pitons and of course, any sort of technical climbing skills. Which hadn't prevented fearless Jeff from scrambling up on one, seeking the top as always—or heaven perhaps.

I looked up after the last spine was plucked and saw him eying the way down and off his perch. Only he wasn't moving.

"I'm fucked," he said. "I really don't see how to make it back down."

"Same way you got up."

"Doesn't work that way. Trust me."

I did. And I wasn't about to leave him up there as lizard bait. Here I was able to return the favor he'd done me with the cholla. Being more agile, I was able both to help him scramble down off the ledge and then make it down unaided myself.

It took time and wasn't guaranteed in the least, I realize now looking back—but Jeff was never going to end a casualty of the Lost Dutchman. Just our hopes of finding his mine.

"Call it a day?" he asked, though it wasn't a question.

"Anything to get away from the infamous cholla," I said.

Breathless, we took a pause to admire the desert and Phoenix, far below. We hadn't found the mine or any nuggets either, but gold of another sort, the adventure that comes from being young and foolish and willing to venture almost anywhere, cholla or no cholla.

That next spring I made a circle tour of the great Western canyons, Zion and Bryce, Capitol Reef and the Grand Canyon, one of the superb trips one can make from a base in Los Angeles, and it happened to coincide as well with a blooming romance. Phoenix made for a welcome stop, and another tubing day on the Verde in perfect sunshine enhanced my lover Lynn's esteem, as did the evidence that I had acceptable, nay congenial friends.

I had noticed that once I settled in Los Angeles, my friends suddenly found excuses to visit, or in the case of Marco from the East Coast, pass the summer hanging out. We rendezvoused in Mississippi, then drove out together with his friend Linda who "made for wonderfully pleasant company."

That at least was Jeff's immediate reaction when we stopped over for a couple of days en route. He enjoyed her company so much he invited her to Phoenix and after several weeks in LA, she accepted.

Marriage followed in relatively short order, as well as a move to San Francisco when Jeff found a job with the government. He earned a fine salary, had security and got a free apartment as he became manager of the building. He and Linda lived well.

My wife Lynn and I—now unluckily married—would visit, more often than not at Thanksgiving, and when not enjoying the Bay Area, went north to the Mendocino coast. We all learned the vocabulary of wine tasting, pretentious and otherwise, and did our best to support the local growers.

Partners in crime get together less after marriage, of course, as crime quite normally doesn't sit well with concerned wives. We did however get away one week, Jeff and Marco and I, for a raft trip on the Stanislas and Tuolumne rivers in Gold Rush country. My friends briefly thought about drowning me in one of the rivers when I began a discussion of literature with our trip leader.

"He's not just a mountain man," I said, "or river man. He's got some interesting ideas about Thomas Pynchon."

"Not while he's driving a bus down a frigging road like that!" Marco exclaimed.

Jeff just laughed. "I measured by eyeball. We had a half inch to spare."

"Yeah. We made it," I said. But Marco had a point. Getting down to the river on a death trail only made the next few days more pleasurable, with rapids and clear crystalline water and smooth silken currents below the gold-tinted hillsides.

"Gold knows where to live," Jeff said aptly.

Our guide, the literate outdoorsman, carried melancholy throughout the trip, even though he always remained professional and focused on wilderness delights. Which he hardly needed to do. "It's God's country," I said.

"Well, the Devil let in some dam builders. Another one's gone up downstream. Every year it fills up more and who knows when the next one comes. Some day maybe nobody will be able to float this river and see it like it's meant to be seen."

We considered ourselves lucky.

Marco flew back to the East Coast and I went back to LA, where I was struggling to get directing gigs. We made one last couples trip together to Mazatlan, taking the long train down and back, enjoying the country and discovering the pleasure of Mexico and dozens of genuine banana daiquiris.

Maybe the stress of work or a collapsing marriage got to me one afternoon, and a rip tide started to carry me away. Exhausted, I couldn't fight my way back. But as always Jeff was there, and with the help of a surf dude rescued me "from a hellish fate," he said afterward, watching me gasp back to breath. "Floating off to Tahiti."

"Glad I got you off that rock in the Superstitions," I managed to say.

"Let's treat each other to a daiquiri. Mutual heroes and all that."

Not long after my wife and I separated, and stayed so for years until I made the decision, after so long a time, to cut the cord.

Jeff and Linda decided it was time to have children, but not in San Francisco. They preferred Portland, a "cleaner safer non-decadent town to raise kids," Jeff said, and pulling the strings he was always able to, managed to get a transfer.

I flew up expressly to bid them goodbye, on one of their last weekends before the move. This time I was melancholy, even though I hid it well. Portland is not a shuttle flight like LA/SF, and I knew we would see each other much less. Plus they would found a family and that was 24hr+.

"To health, happiness and good wine," I toasted them.

Alas, a year later they had separated, heartstrings unraveled and they divorced. I never knew exactly why. By then I was writing TV movies, selling some and directing a few others, and nothing so complicated as this kind of real life made it to the small screen.

That strange phenomenon began where one loses track of someone who has been very close and important in your life. They are around, somewhere, but time and distance and who knows, entropy set in. When my wife and I finally got divorced, we would see each other occasionally, but eventually the get-togethers stopped, and we lived far away in distance and mind and heart, way way out of sight and mind.

I only saw Jeff twice in the years after. Once he came down to LA on business and we went out to eat. It was a small restaurant not far from my apartment, neither chic nor a trendy hangout. We kicked over old times and friends and how we were doing, and at one point I asked him if he had news of Jim and his wife Fran, the friends with whom I'd stayed when I first came to Los Angeles.

"Nothing, just lost touch completely," he said. "Don't know why that happens."

"You've got to put in the work."

"Yeah. And who does nowadays." And in just that moment of reflection: "Except, that guy over there, I could swear it's Jim." I looked over to see a man poring over the menu.

"Jim! Jim!" Jeff yelled.

And Jim came over. Both were almost trembling at the surprise and emotion of the reunion. Not to mention the incredible coincidence.

We all attributed it to the stars or destiny or "a good restaurant," I said to laughs. We observed that we'd all gotten divorced.

But we were still dating and hoping. Jim went back to his table where his curious date was waiting, and Jeff went back to Portland. The only other time I saw him in person, he'd come to LA with his new wife, to show her the city and the beach, where I met them for a fun afternoon of chat and rays. Marilyn was a darling, and I thought they would be happy.

And I noted that if this is the last time I saw Jeff, the end will be like the beginning—as once again, I'd been dumped by a girl friend. I railed far too much about her perfidy. Jeff summed up: "You've been hurt. Real bad."

Then he added: "But I know you. The bell's going to ring for you again."

"Bell?" Marilyn asked.

"We'll need tools," Jeff said, a self-evident comment only after one had decided to take on a job, which he had done in theory moments before we entered the abandoned church and picked our way through the debris, trying to avoid the multitudinous nails that stuck out from all the planks and 2-by-4s littering it seemed, every inch of the warped wooden floor.

"You couldn't make a mess like this if you tried. It's disorganized destruction on an artistic scale."

"Maybe the devil took a hand," Jeff said. "But he stopped on the way to the belfry. Too high and too close to God."

"Like we can do outdo the devil?"

"We're sinners but not to that degree. It's beautiful, don't you think?"

It had the rounded contours and burnished bronze alloy of a well cast, one could said lovingly cast, bell meant to peal tidings of peace and joy and also, alas, mourning. The variations could sound in astonishing variety, depending on how its clapper was wielded and who knows, the atmosphere and whatever waves of emotion and faith went up from the hearts assembled below.

Except the assemblies had long ago dispersed to the winds, and now the bell hung up all alone in the heat and dust and silence. The rope cord of course had long gone as well. We could see a remaining strand high up, looking like it had been cut.

"Whoever did that didn't have his eyes on the prize," Jeff said. "What's going to happen to it?"

"Well, it's not going to degrade anytime soon. Erosion's not a factor."

"One day some punk will take a match to this place and the flames will bring it down, and it'll get barbecued. It'll survive the fall but who's going to want to restore it?" He looked up. "I want to save it."

The logical question should have followed: "Saved for what?"

But I've searched the ruins of my memory, now resembling somewhat the devastation we saw in the old church, and found no relics of any such existential discussion. Nor a sensible practical one, such as, how much would such a bell weigh and could we even lift it into his Beetle? What I do remember crystal clearly is we assessed the framework holding the bell in place, a lattice of 2-by-4s that would have been easily found in these thick Mississippi woods, the poor man's construction materials. And Jeff's succinct analysis: "A good saw and some moxie and we'll bring it down."

"At least it's not a tractor," I said.

So now the aimless summer day had turned into a day with a mission, and we hauled ass back to the home he shared with his family. A big Dallas Cowboys football game was under way on the TV, and his parents rooted more or less fanatically for the team—which meant that almost literally, they were rooted to the screen.

They had no eye or concern when Jeff took saw and hammer etc., and then outside, lifted out with my help the back seat of his VW.

"You've made the calculation?" I asked.

"I've made the calculation. The only unknown is whether we can fit you into the front seat."

"Great. I'll be stranded in a ruined church with no way to ring for help."

"Some car will come along."

"Did you see any cars come along this afternoon?"

"Let's go."

We managed to get back to the church just before tea time. It wasn't like we had to maneuver through a traffic jam.

"Good," Jeff said. "We can work without noise pollution."

We fell to it. It was possible to clamber up, strut by strut, edge by the bell and arrive above it to the top of the belfry.

"It's beautiful," Jeff said, "still in great shape."

His plan—such as he had a plan—was to saw through the principal supports and once the bell was almost freed, lower it down with a rope Jeff had found in his parents' garage. The lower wood beams would allow for a step by step descent.

He mounted upward with the saw. As he was en route I said, "The only flaw—which it occurs to me we haven't considered—is what if the bell weighs a jillion tons?"

"Adrenaline will take over."

In the excitement of the moment, I did not make a critical analysis of his analysis. Assuming I could do so at that stage of my life.

Jeff fell to his work, sawing through the strut foundations to which the bell had been attached. He found pronto that the workmanship of the time had been of high quality.

"These suckers are thick," he said.

Plus intricately designed to hold the bell in place come hell or high water.

"Did they use architects in those days?" he wondered aloud.

"Remember, Joseph was a carpenter. Oral traditions and expertise get passed down from generation to generation. Even way far to Mississippi.""

I don't think he heard. He was working away. Sawdust cascaded down in a thick stream, wood from 50 to 100 years ago. I told myself what Jeff and I believed, we were saving their work from the oblivion into which time and perhaps those of little faith had made it fall. No cars came along while we worked, or if they did, no one inquired as to what we were doing in the old church. It was a Sunday, after all.

After about an hour Jeff said, "I'm cooked."

"That bad?"

"Maybe it's the altitude."

"Come on down? I'll take over."

Once he'd made it down and I'd gone up and started sawing, I understood his exhaustion. It was very hard to cut through the thick beams. "Mississippi oak, not pine," I gasped.

"The finest."

I worked to the point where I too was feeling the altitude. I took a moment to look out from the belfry at the surrounding woods. My father had grown up on a small farm in the middle of woods just like those. I dreamed of glory in Hollywood, but destiny might have fashioned a different film for me, and maybe, just maybe, these woods might be the last I'll ever see.

"I've got good news and bad news," I said.

"Lay it on." Jeff had been browsing around, maybe to avoid all the sweat that was pouring down from me to the bottom of the belfry, but now he looked up from below.

"I think I've cut through the last beam. If I kick it hard, I think the bell will fall."

We'd long ago realized that lowering it by rope was not an option.

"It might destroy it."

"Got no choice. It's the bell or me. Or both."

In all of our calculations and despite the brilliance we were convinced we possessed, we hadn't noticed the obvious fact that once the bell hung tenuously above, I couldn't descend without risking it falling and crushing me in mid-descent.

On the other hand, if the bell fell, the belfry might collapse and me with it.

"Well shit," Jeff said.

I waited for his solution. He was after all, the practical wizard I looked up to in that regard.

"Let's cross our fingers."

"Right. Good thinking."

"Brace yourself to the belfry walls. You can spider your way down."

"Stand back. Here goes something."

I waited till he'd stepped away, then kicked the last beam and down the bell went. We knew it was pretty heavy because it shattered every single strut before landing with a tremendous crash and rolling a pace or two. The clapper pealed once before breaking off.

"Holy Jesus," Jeff said.

Amazingly, the belfry had held and I hadn't tumbled down in the cascade of woodbeams. "I'm coming down," I said.

Jeff was right, and I managed to use my arms and some toeholds on the woodbeam shards and belfry walls to make it down.

We eyed the bell. It was as beautiful down to earth as above in the sky.

"We can fix the clapper. If we can get it home."

It was getting late, and maybe the adrenaline did kick in. We managed to roll it on its side and off the church porch. Jeff brought the Beetle over as close as possible, and with as much elbow grease as we could muster, managed to winch it up and into the back seat. It just fit. And the chassis held without collapsing.

"I could make compliments about German engineering," I panted.

"Not till we see if it can hold your weight."

"I lost a couple pounds in that belfry, I know that."

I just managed to wedge myself into the front seat, push forward as far as I could push, and ride all the way back to Jeff's home angled like an L. My neck still hasn't recovered.

Jeff's mother was gardening the flowers of her front lawn when we rolled up, got out and promptly went to work unloading our prize.

"Oh my God!"

"He was with us today," her son said. We all looked at the bell, shining in the last golden light of sunset, there on a green grass, perfectly manicured lawn.

"Give it an honored place," I said.

When Jeff made contact in the sundown of our lives, my lovely second wife and I had moved to the high desert near Joshua Tree National Park after our son finished university at UCLA. Robin devoted herself to fabricating artisan jewelry, most of it with desert and Native American motifs. Exquisite work, in my unbiased opinion, and for a time she ran a little boutique near the park entrance. I helped with stock and negotiation and all the hundreds of other details that came with the territory, but it was terrain far less stressful than Hollywood and TV networks. We were able to get by fairly comfortably on my residuals, part-time teaching and her sales, and in the cool of desert evenings, watched the world go by from our back porch. I'd made sure to buy a place flush up against the park, so no dirt bikers or uncongenial neighbors could disturb our retirement and recovery.

Jeff had led the expected charmed life. Stable career for the US government, then active retirement operating a one-man tourist agency. He greased wheels all over the world, and found plenty of time to check out the destinations he was promoting up front and personally. "Goes with the territory," he wrote, and I smiled because the world made for lots. "Life has been good," he concluded with his typical terse and accurate precision. He'd found time for humanitarian work here, there and everywhere.

We exchanged several emails and agreed on solutions for various world problems. He was headed off to Thailand for another wonderful trip, and we chuckled about the havoc we might cause to ourselves and the country if perchance we went together—even at our ages. "It's never too late for creative adventures," he wrote.

It was then I remembered and asked about the bell. I knew he'd reattached the clapper just before we'd left to head West. "It's just too bad you never heard it ring," he wrote. Apparently it had a deep, rich, resonant tone, and when his parents rang it after a blessed family event like birth or marriage or even birthday, the whole neighborhood celebrated. When they passed away and Jeff and his brothers were settling their estate, he said they'd discussed at some length what to do with the bell.

They decided to donate it to a state charity organization that runs telethons. Each year when the tally mounts up or someone opens a wallet with generosity, the bell tolls with grateful joy. The group was thrilled to receive it and their president said, it's like the sound track of a good film, that extra touch that elevates each and every scene.

In my emails I slid over details about Robin and her health battles and my own failures along the long road of the last 50 or so years. No need to bring clouds to a sunshiny friendship.

But he still knew me even after so long a time, and wrote back: "The bell's going to ring again for you, my friend."

Let the bell ring too for Jeff, and all those generous lucky souls who spread joy of life like the scent of orange blossoms in spring.

4. FIRST LOVE. PART 2.

When Rachel arrived back in Manhattan and opened her door and entered her apartment, she saw all the familiar surroundings, furniture and wall paintings and even her briefcase which she'd carefully prepared before leaving, as the next day she had an internship interview.

But as sweet as home seemed, it seemed to lose virtually all importance compared to the days and nights of happiness she'd just lived. She called Karen and arranged to share an "emergency coffee."

She recounted as much of what had happened as she could, hoping that Karen would help her make sense of it.

Karen had been married for several years and she thought hard before saying simply, tearfully, "I am so happy for you."

Rachel emptied her backpack but instead of scrunching it up and stashing it in her closet where it had been before the trip, she kept it propped in a corner near her bed--a sort of symbolic presence to remind her of Matt.

Then when she began unpacking her suitcase, she held close her nightgown and clothes she'd worn in Las Vegas. They still had his scent, mingled with hers, and it wrenched her so much she sat down and wrote him a letter, pouring out her desire and the strangeness of how her former life had been changed and concluding with how she desperately needed to hear from him.

The days of instant Internet communication had not yet come, though she could have called him. Fear held her back. She might after all had been dreaming and he was just out for a vacation romp that he'd managed to disguise very well as something deeper.

But she couldn't deny what she felt.

"Maybe it will wear off," she'd speculated to Karen. "A fling always does, doesn't it? I mean, if it doesn't, something's wrong."

"Or right," her friend corrected.

She set the letter on her nightstand. Come what may, she was going to post it first thing tomorrow.

Then, finally, she went to bed, wearing the white cotton nightgown from Las Vegas.

\#

Rachel knew she had to wait several days for Matt to receive her letter, and then his reply, if he replied, so she went back to her business as best she could.

Sooner than she expected, a package came to her mailbox. When she unwrapped it and found the wonderfully ornamented and crafted music box with Debussy's moon inside for her to open and play whenever she needed a mood for love, she "literally jumped up and down," she wrote to Matt.

"Screaming, crying--my neighbors were getting out a strait jacket. What a wonderful incredible extravagance." She wondered to Karen, "Does this mean he really loves me? Tell me honestly. Maybe it's just a parting gift."

"At this price, honey? Listen, I tell myself every Valentine's Day, this year Bill gave me flowers and chocolate, how sweet and different. Last year it was chocolate and flowers. Listen, what counts isn't the price even though he may have maxed out his credit card. Even if he's a guy who's going to make films about slashers and talking dogs, he had the sensitivity to know who you are and what you're all about and find the special thing that would make you happy."

Rachel said, "Whether he loves me or not, I love him."

#

Matt's letter in response to hers arrived and he confirmed his feelings for her were more than a passing adventure. He reaffirmed what they had only tentatively broached during their time together, his marriage. He had dismissed it as a stage toward divorce, rather like the trek down from Yabut Pass. They were separated and all that remained was to go through the process of a court filing and judgement. He did not give a date for same, and Rachel dismissed as best she could her concerns. She was full flush in the excitement and fever of her first love. She worked and saw friends but her real emotional life lay elsewhere, in the dreams of a future she had already started to visualize.

The practical problems of where to live together and how had not yet intervened, but she knew she had to see Matt again as soon as possible and on his home grounds.

They made plans, and on the 4th of July holiday she flew out to LA for four days.

Matt lived in a smallish apartment in West LA, not so very far from the beach. It had a rooftop terrace and distant view of the Pacific, though Matt confessed there were only a few days per year when the smog and haze cleared up enough to see it, and mid-summer wasn't one of those times.

"Welcome to the City of Angels, where the angels need to fly by instruments."

They walked on the beach and Rachel got to view up close the freak show that Venice sometimes was--"Believe me, she assured Matt, "we've got plenty of freaks in the Big Apple." Matt had been very nervous that Rachel might turn and head back to New York on the first plane once she witnessed laidback Angelenos up close, but she was amused by anything and everything.

They escaped the crowds at the swimming pool at his apartment complex, lolling in the midsummer sun and adjourning to Matt's bedroom when the sun set, though Rachel accused Matt of advancing the hour. "My watch says 4 o'clock."

"New York time"

"Aren't we ahead three hours?"

"Chronologically speaking. Here we go by pleasure time, and it's a-wasting."

And so to bed, Matt said, citing a phrase from Samuel Pepys' diaries, and she found it wonderful that out here in LA, which to all evidence was the milk, honey and indolence paradise all her Manhattan friends sneered that it was--her friend Sarah warned her not to mention Proust, "'cause the New Agers will think it's a new virus"--she was with a man who had read Pepys, aware that it was not a virus.

They went to Disneyland and joined tourists of all ages and small fry "only slightly more excited than me," Rachel laughed. She was accosted by a large costumed bear who seemed to be Winnie the Pooh, and Matt insisted on taking their picture, "so your friends will have their worst fears confirmed about strange LA types."

He cooked a barbecue for her on the terrace and she met some of his friends, including Richard, the writer with whom he was collaborating on a project they hoped would become a feature film and elevate them to long career status.

"Long career," he explained, "is when you have a hit film. You can make flop after flop for the rest of your life but will probably always find work, because producers figure you'll strike gold again."

Rachel said, "It's capitalistic but practical and clear. What if you don't have a hit?"

"Back to scrabbling."

He hoped very much to succeed, and she saw that he was trying very hard not to show how much he was counting on it happening in the very near future.

For him and her, she was sure now.

She had enjoyed very much listening to him and Richard discussing their film story. Hollywood or not, she had always admired artistic creativity and saw herself being married to someone who lived for it.

On her last evening they watched the warm evening sunset fall over the scrim beyond which the ocean lay and planned on seeing each other again in six weeks, when Rachel would have a week's vacation.

Matt would come to her home town in New York for a week, then they'd spend a week roaming through New England, which neither of them had ever done.

"No backpacks this time," Matt said. "I'd like to treat you to cosy inns and B&Bs."

"Cosy and romantic, please."

"I am bringing a suitcase though. It'll be chock full of romance."

Once again Matt saw her off at an airport, but this time he felt no need to write a reunion scene. That would be happening very soon.

Matt felt sure Rachel would never want to live in LA, dismissing Walt's down-to-earth objection that "we've got plenty of diseases out here." Walt had been off in northern California wooing his "lady of the moment" during Rachel's visit, and on his return wanted to hear about how everything had gone down.

Matt appreciated his moral support, but countered sure, a doctor could practice in LA as much as anywhere, but would Rachel be happy, being the kind of woman she was, an elegant and extremely bright opera lover who "probably never had a superficial day in her life."

"Holy shit," Walt said, "lucky for her I was out of town."

LA had no lack of Walts, Matt thought, even if he was a great guy and had a kind of screwy but insightful logic.

\#

So it happened that one hot August day Rachel opened her apartment door to a polite but firm knock to find Matt standing with his suitcase and a daypack, "to remind you who I am in case you forgot."

"Come in and see what I remember." They ate a quiet supper as the city lights waned and planned out the next two weeks.

She was excited to have him on her home turf and as nervous as he'd been in LA. Naturally, a cockroach chose this evening to make an appearance in her bathtub, but Matt gallantly came to the rescue.

"I'll singlehandedly handle this miscreant," he vowed, and did so after a high speed chase throughout the bathroom.

"I was here for backup," Rachel offered.

"Maybe, but I can see already, in this kind of dangerous territory, you need a man."

"But not just any man."

And that ended the serious discussion for the evening as they turned to other matters that lasted far into the night.

#

Rachel had taken the following week off for their planned tour of New England, but this week she worked and Matt arranged to meet his friends from college. They reunited for the first time in ten years and continued their late night college bull sessions, focusing less than in the past on the meaning of life, as they'd done little in the decade to solve this burning question.

Ben kept looking for Miss Right, whereas Charley had married right after his undergraduate studies, which had stabilized his romantic life while he finished his combined M.D. and Ph.D. Ben was a lawyer. They both found him as genially quixotic in his desire to make it in Hollywood as Cervantes' windmill swashbuckler.

"Except a windmill's got more substance than a cell of celluloid," said Ben.

"Says someone who makes cinema buffs look like amateurs."

The real Quixote, Matt thought, was Charley, who'd embarked in his spare time--such as it was--on a comprehensive catalogue of all the world's species. "Believe it or not, it's never been done."

"Because it might take a few lifetimes," Rachel said when she met the two friends at the Plaza Hotel's Oak Room for dinner. It was class and tradition and Rachel reveled in the good fellowship and ambiance and most of all, the soul satisfaction of being with her lover who felt as home here amid elegance and New York tradition as he'd been in the canyons, scaling sandstone domes and lugging a heavy pack.

"And battling cockroaches," he added.

They lunched together near the Met and he explored the museum while she worked. Mostly he enjoyed walking in the city and tolerated well the noise and bustle.

"Energy. That's New York. It's like there's a 24-hour generator underground Manhattan."

"That's called the subway. And by the way, if there's so much energy, why did you sleep till 11 your first day here?"

"Strenuous night."

Matt met Karen and liked her, and vice versa. The three had coffee together. "I've heard a lot about you," he told her, "and the kaffeeklatsch."

Rachel had grown more and more concerned that Matt hadn't followed through on his divorce, and Karen had been the most sympathetic of all her friends to Matt's emotional struggle to break bonds.

"If you're married, you can understand better the ties that bind, even when you're dissatisfied."

#

On the Sabbath Rachel invited her orthodox friends over, to present Matt and give him an idea of her religion and devotion.

Isaac and Sarah, with whom she usually celebrated the high holy days, came and also Elizabeth who arrived breathless after climbing the stairs.

In his innocence, Matt asked why she hadn't taken the elevator. She smiled--still breathless--and Rachel explained that on this day one should avoid work, or machines that did. She had shown him her cupboard, with settings separate for meat and dairy.

"I have a lot to learn," Matt confessed, and Rachel seized the moment to pass along a book that presented a concise, clear history of her religion and practices. He thanked her and promised to read it.

Matt had been raised an extremely devout and practicing Catholic, but at 21 had begun to have doubts about his faith.

"One Easter morning I was in DC and went to the Cathedral and heard the best sermon ever. The priest cited a Gerard Manley Hopkins poem that I'd studied. 'In a flash, at a trumpet crash, immortal diamond, is immortal diamond.' Meaning if you believed in the resurrection, you believed. It was your choice, but in a way could not be programed. That's what happened to me, except in reverse. One day it was lost and I haven't been able to get it back. Faith I mean."

They had this conversation after the dinner and the guests had gone.

Joshua had said the Sabbath prayer and Rachel said this was what gave her life community and meaning and structure. Her religion was like a sonnet--"or a poem by Hopkins"--freedom within form, in a certain sense shaping time. She needed that.

Matt said that was what he'd lost, but he'd grown up with a devout Catholic mother and a father who saw the inside of a church once every ten years or so, at midnight mass. As a child this had hurt him sometimes, but he'd accepted it and fiercely resented when the nuns at school affirmed that non-believers could not get into the kingdom of heaven. He could not believe that heaven would not welcome a man as upright and honorable as his father.

Rachel respected Matt's honesty and said, "If you changed your identity for me I'd think you were unstable." But the question persisted. Matt changed the subject by gently mocking Elizabeth, a born and bred New Yorker who'd only traveled to the south once, to Georgia where it happened her destination lay not far from a waste dump. "Is all the South like that?" she'd wondered.

"I said no, and she looked serious, but she was joking. Wasn't she?"

"Afraid not, " Rachel laughed.

#

They drove to Massachusetts and took in a concert at Tanglewood, spread out on the lawn grass on a warm summer night.

"Are you getting nostalgic for your camp mattress?" Matt asked after Ives and before Brahms.

Rachel had the reply ready: "This blanket will do just fine, and nostalgia's for absence, no? And you're here, darling."

She'd called a truce on her worries about their future together. "Not easy to do for me," she confessed to Matt--"inertia's not my style."

"I know that."

She took pleasure in the moment. That night after a wonderful dinner at Stockbridge's historic inn, they made love and she "became a woman at last," she said later to Karen, and shyly, days later, to Matt--"if orgasms can define a woman."

"Not even close," Karen snapped.

Rachel countered, "But now they've arrived at the party, they're very welcome."

They went north through Vermont and stayed at a rustic country inn where the main pastime seemed to be the children's swing out back. But they found ways to amuse themselves.

At a resort near the frontier with Canada they spent 2 nights at a magnificent, historic building and found an 8-walled octagon room that captured sunlight from every direction.

"People always say I've got so many sides to me," Rachel joked.

"So depending on which side you're using today, park yourself in front of one of the eight so I'll have a clue."

They climbed a small mountain, one of the several that ringed the resort, and watched the sunset.

Heading back south, they rode the cog railway up Mt. Washington, shivering even on an August afternoon. "Nice place to visit but..." they said in unison.

They spent the last night on the road at a hotel fronting the Atlantic, and Matt insisted after dinner that they carry the wine glasses out to the dock.

"I've always wanted to do this," he said, draining the last of the wine, "make a wish and..." He turned, back to the Atlantic, and flung the glass over his shoulder into the water.

Rachel followed suit, delighted.

"And your wish?"

"Can't tell you or it won't come true. You might say it involved you."

Later, Matt remembered melancholy from the evening. New Hampshire and Vermont had been supernally beautiful, but leaves were already turning as he sensed autumn coming and an end to the warm, romantic days they'd had since spring and the canyons.

He wondered if destiny were not like the seasons, regular though changeable but above all, beyond a man's control.

Rachel read his thoughts, as he learned she could do so remarkably well.

"Time to head back and make our destiny, wish or no wish," she said.

"We can do that?"

"I can. If you'll come along."

They arrived back in New York just in time for a concert at Lincoln Center.

Rachel remembered how they'd hastily dressed and walked to the concert hall arm in arm, arrived early and watched the crowd trail in.

Matt noticed 2 men who'd come dressed in overalls, and not the vintage fashion kind. With a strong country accent he said, "This mornin' we was sloppin' hogs, now here we are listenin' to Mowzart."

Rachel just managed to stop laughing before Mowzart's violin concerto began.

On Matt's last day they lounged, making a Plan for their destiny in between lovemaking.

This time it was Rachel who watched him go. She took the elevator down with him and his suitcase and daypack and they spent as many minutes as plane schedule would allow on the sidewalk, hugging and kissing very much as they'd done at the Rainbow Bridge and the Las Vegas airport. When he could wait no longer-- he had to return the rental car, then hurry to check-in--he rolled his suitcase down the sidewalk toward the river beside which he'd parked.

At the corner he turned back and cast a last look, wave and kiss to Rachel, who hadn't budged. Then he turned the corner out of her sight.

She would not see him again for three years.

#

"I love you. I do so love you." In passionate letters Rachel poured out her feelings, sure of hers but constantly needing reassurance from Matt.

He responded with as much sincerity as he could express, and swore to put the Plan into action.

The Plan's central clause required him to divorce. But weeks went by without confirmation that he'd filed or made any kind of move.

Matt reaffirmed his lack of religious faith and hope that she would understand, without explicitly promising to seriously consider converting. He did read the book she'd lent him, and thanked her for enlightening him to a new respect for her faith's "humanist traditions and beliefs."

His project with Richard was moving slowly but he met with his agent and emphasized how he needed to get a deal, any deal, as soon as possible. "Fingers crossed," he wrote, "and toes too."

Rachel recognized the obstacles keeping them apart on two sides of the continent but convinced herself that the tide of their love and passion would sweep any and all away and they would enjoy for the rest of their lives together an upper middle class life of children raised in comfort, discussions around the dinner table of life and events and religion, mental and cultural exploration of every kind. "Our life will never be boring," she wrote.

Rachel's friends cautioned her that she was chasing a transient dream. Matt would never convert, and the marriage would never work if only for that. Plus it was clear he still loved his first wife and could not break the ties that bound him to her. The proof was not in the courts, where it had to be.

Elizabeth weighed in that Matt needed to stay in LA for his career, and Rachel could never live there. "I went there once on a trip and believe me, it's no place for an I.Q. I'd sooner live in the south than LA."

Rachel had laughed. "I'm indulging you, my provincial friend," but she couldn't get past the thought that provincial or not, Elizabeth might have spoken truth. It hit her that she'd never considered living in LA for one moment. Only Karen kept holding out for patience.

One cold November day when Rachel had the blues--"and for me to have the blues," she said to Karen, "would be major depression for anybody else"--she sat down and wrote a long letter voicing her doubts that maybe she'd underestimated the obstacles keeping them apart and as for him, he'd underestimated how bonded he was to his wife, separated or not. When she posted the letter, she felt she'd only been realistic.

Matt wrote back angrily, reiterating what he'd always said, that his divorce was only a matter of time and she should not pressure him so much, as she was doing.

Rachel read the letter and recognized how upset he was. She took the bull by the horns and gave him a call. They both settled down. She suggested on the spur of the moment that he come visit her in New York for the holidays. The Big Apple was beautiful that time of year and she would organize a lovely romantic excursion to a nearby island. Matt said he'd like that very much.

Rachel made all the plans and arrangements and looked forward with excitement bordering on ecstasy to their escapade.

Then a few days before Christmas, Matt called to cancel. Something about his deal with Richard falling through at the last minute and how he'd been overstretched financially etc.--Rachel hardly listened, she was so angry and hurt. He had done nothing about the divorce and now she knew why, whatever she knew--bottom line to her, he did not love her as much as she loved him, if at all.

She got off the phone and stubbornly decided to go on the trip to the island solo. She had friends there and she'd make do. But it was a lonely end to a year that she'd marked already as a turning point in her life. She blamed Matt for not being by her side, and so much else besides, and could not forgive him.

She'd had the impression from his phone call that he blamed HER, for not understanding the pressures he was under. Maybe so, but when the year ended and a new one began, which she celebrated among friends but all alone, she put Matt and her love for him along with it in the past tense.

#

Matt received what Walt considered a "very sweet" Dear John letter, extolling "what we had" and being so grateful for his sincere, passionate love, for which she would always love him.

"So," Walt concluded to his morose friend, "now you've become history. Think, wax museum."

Rachel had also suggested that Matt canceled the Christmas trip for ulterior motives. He wrote back briskly that those motives had to do with finances, as he'd declared.

Rachel did not write back, and Matt seized the occasion of her birthday to send a card he thought was one of the nicest he'd ever seen, a rendering of an Art Deco music box. Walt thought this "laying it on with a trowel," and Matt thanked him for the nth time of ridiculing what was for him heartfelt gestures. He just hoped that Walt's wavelength was not Rachel's.

This time she did reply, thanking him very much, and updating him on what was happening in her life. "The operative syllable was not 'us'," Matt grimaced. She qualified though that no one in the wide field she was playing measured up to him.

"That was the coldest of comforts," Matt said, and Walt replied very concretely, "Two can play at that game."

For a while Matt had played at the game. In the summer in mid-romance with Rachel he had continued to see his wife from time to time and also his sometime girl friend--the student having become history very quickly to both Matt and Walt, she having found a lover as young as she was.

Matt considered these forays a kind of insurance policy in case Rachel "came to her senses and decided she could do better," in Walt's helpful assessment, and also normal--he had affection for both and they for him, and neither pressed him for fidelity or commitment, including his wife who nonetheless let it be known very clearly that she did not plan to divorce him any time soon. "I still love you," she said, while giving no sign whatsoever that she wanted to live with him again.

Walt had been studying French at UCLA Extension in order to somehow add to his allure for the opposite sex, who he was convinced desired all things français, and he summed up, "Love sans cohabitation, sounds like a trend to me. You and her both must have French roots--they don't care who loves who, as long as they're one of them."

Matt found this a much more effective strategy on his wife's part--if it was a strategy--than jealousy or possessiveness, and he had hesitated and hesitated despite Rachel's mounting pain and growing bitterness.

After their New York-New England trip however where their future came more into view, he'd left off his side adventures and concentrated on making his career happen, as Angelenos in the film industry liked to say.

"Happen" was the right word, with its connotations of an event not under one's controL.

Matt knew the film business and LA by now, how precarious one was and brutal the other, and vice versa, on life, nerves and psychology.

Deals had to be pursued 24/24.

A small deal was better than no deal, which meant nonentity, non-person, but small deals gave worth only for the short period before the cash ran out and Square One beckoned.

Big deals gave a few months or perhaps a year of validation and psychic harmony, but if the film or telefilm was not made, it hardly counted for an entry on the resume, for it would have to be explained to producers and financiers who would blame you for the project being dropped.

If the film was made, a grace period would ensue of real "heat" where deals could be had in the fervor of the moment and expectation of success, but if the film tanked, one had to climb back just to get to Square One, and many never did--they could stay out of the game for a lifetime.

If a film succeeded big time, one could live high on a very big hog until Time took over and a moment came when the phone stopped ringing and one had to remind the young who got younger every year the name of the film and what it was about. As if they cared.

"You want laurels, but you can never rest on them," Matt had written once to Rachel.

Walt kept speaking of LA as if it were a breeding ground for every form of past and future pestilence afflicting mankind, hence in need of Rachel's presence to help and heal.

But Matt saw his future wife enjoying a suntan, a cactus garden with eucalyptus trees, year-round dinner parties on the patio with other exiles, and him--but not much else. She would have to travel a long way for the opera.

Then there was the matter of religion. Matt sought faith, less for his own sake than Rachel's. She had protested that this was "my problem," but if they had a future together they would have to solve it together.

When his deal with Richard fell through just before Christmas, Matt had panicked. The trip would empty his bank account which he'd overextended. His pride refused to ask Rachel to contribute, or to explain in any clear fashion, as to do so would reveal how precarious her life with him might be, for all the guaranteed career she would have.

His motto for the film industry had always been the title of an old B-movie, "I Died a Thousand Times," because deals fell through at any moment despite looking so promising. Rejection and humiliation stalked LA's streets like the living dead in a B-movie.

When Rachel erupted and banished him, he died more than a few times.

#

Matt moved from sadness and self-pity to anger. He decided to "move on." He met Kacey at a party and wooed her and they had many hot and heavy nights, which Matt interspersed with less heated nights with Clarice, whom he'd met through a friend of Walt's.

He got in touch with Randi who said she'd love to see him, but when he traveled to the low mountains on the California/Mexico border, he found her living with her girl friend. Matt could tell she liked him very much--and said so--but for the moment she was "*hors de combat*," he said to Walt, delighted that he understood the phrase from his French class.

At the 6-month mark of his affairs with Kacey and Clarice, Matt came to the realization that his passion for them, and theirs for him, was dimming to darkness.

And he knew why. He'd been operating on the energy and excitement stored up from his love for Rachel, but reserves could only go so far, like rebounds and ricochet romances.

He felt more and more foolish explaining how he was still married but that meant nothing as they were separated and it was over etc. etc. etc.

He called his wife and announced he'd be filing for divorce.

"Well, you're right," she said, a bit sadly, before declaring firmly that he'd have to sign an agreement renouncing any claim to any of her property or assets. He could have custody of their cat, however. "She always preferred you."

He wrote to Rachel with the news when the divorce became final. She congratulated him for taking the long-bruited step but gave no sign whatsoever of welcoming him back from purgatory.

Matt let some time pass, doubling his efforts to get a deal and a film that would elevate him from the ranks of wannabes.

He'd lost his enthusiasm for casual affairs. He missed Rachel.

He sat down and wrote her a letter telling her so, and proposed a rendezvous and trip somewhere--anywhere. He realized he was coming out of the blue and she might have a range of reactions, from desire and delight to disgust. So he concluded that if her answer was no, she need not reply.

She did not.

Matt plunged pell-mell into his work, and after myriad meetings and prospects that ended in zip and nada, a friend of Richard's helped them find a home for their project at a studio.

And just like that, after years of futility, Matt and Richard had one month to rewrite their script, then six weeks before going into production.

It was madness, but that was Hollywood, and for four months Matt went into purdah, writing and directing a low budget film that he knew "had a lot of heart" and humor besides. He counted on it to launch his career. Finally. He figured the story's merits would shine through the rushed production and hasty casting choices he'd had to make.

He'd pitched the film thus: "A reckless hipster throws his life away and misses out on love and a family. Heaven sends him back one last time to make amends with his ex-girl friend."

Walt had thought a long moment when he heard this before asking, "Does he succeed?"

"Yes. There's a happy end."

"But not for him. He's still dead and gone."

"But headed for heaven."

"Let's hope he makes it." Walt had been very vocal in blaming Rachel for their breakup. "That's not official," Matt reminded him, to which Walt--"Yeah, but when a woman consigns you to history, you're history."

Walt had met Meg at his French class and they'd spent many a date trying to communicate in French, and somehow or other she'd understood when he proposed in fractured phrases.

Matt drove up to a small town near Sacramento for the wedding ceremony, so small he was drafted to make a toast to the newlyweds and find some flattery to say about the groom. He managed to do it and Walt thanked him for his creativity. "You're going to make it," he assured Matt, "with imagination like that..."

Matt had found himself very popular with women with the aura he had now of hot up-and-comer, and he indulged in flings--he knew very well by now how to recognize them and differentiate from the real thing.

Walt had said, in one of the insights he occasionally albeit rarely had that rang true, that "everybody's alone in LA." Hence his welcoming the move to northern California. Matt remained in LA, but while his editor assembled a rough cut of his film and the composer worked on the score, he bought a plane ticket to New York.

He was going to present Rachel with a fait accompli, i.e., himself. Now he had a film and a future. Three years had passed, but he still refused to become history.

#

When Rachel received Matt's phone call out of the deep blue, she instinctively reacted protectively, suggesting a rendezvous two weeks later, toward the end of his stay. He protested, and she reduced the wait time to a week.

When she confided the news to Karen--"Oh my God!" was her response--over an emergency coffee, she admitted she'd been surprised by her defensive reaction. "After all, it's been three years."

"It proves you're not over him, like I've been saying for three years."

"But I am. I got closure a long time ago. It's just old wounds, you know. You don't want them reopened."

She'd been dating continuously but a good man was hard to find. She'd had a couple of more serious flings, and recently had met Max, who had a prosperous textile business and let her know very quickly that he'd like much more than a casual relationship. They had both just crossed the threshold of 30. As the day of her meeting with Matt approached Rachel found herself increasingly panicked.

"What do I do if he says he wants to get back together?"

"I doubt he'll do that," Karen replied.

"Why not? He came to New York to see me."

"You don't think he's been seeing other people while he's here?"

"He has to. I made him wait. "

"Look honey, you blew him off. If he expects wedding bells overnight, he's not as smart as I remember. The question is, what do you expect?"

Rachel reflected for a moment, which was about 59 seconds longer than she usually needed to express a view.

"I don't know. You know what? We were only together about 4 weeks total. And just about every day was heaven. The hell came after. "

Karen said, "Look, have a quick drink, kick over old times and get him up to speed about what you've been doing, wish him a good time in the Big Apple and beat the proverbial retreat."

"You know me. I never retreat."

"In that case, do the sensible Big Apple thing and take Valium."

#

When Rachel heard the elevator at their appointed time, she understood so very deeply the meaning of déja vu. She opened her door and there he was, just as if that day years ago when he'd left he'd just gone to the local cafe for a drink and come back with the Times and tales of the colorful types he'd overheard at a nearby table.

He said he'd passed the afternoon attending his first opera, Wagner's Lohengrin, and had to admit he'd fought off sleep more than once.

Rachel said, "Not surprising. I detest Wagner. Long, boring, Teutonic ponderous."

He said her apartment seemed to him as cosy as when he'd left it, and he noticed the music box on her piano.

"It hasn't budged," she said.

"And Debussy hasn't changed his tune?" She laughed, and he delighted in its melody more than Clair de Lune.

#

Matt found her strange. Outwardly she reacted to what he said and made conversation, but at the restaurant particularly she seemed only half-awake, not at all the dynamo she usually was. He wondered if she'd taken Valium. But she assured him she was normal and no more "out of it" than she usually was. They discussed present plans and life and she invited him to see her office, where she'd begun to accept patients after finally finishing her schooling.

When he took her home she invited him to stay, but afterward they did not get very far. He found the encounter too strange, as if she'd decided to dip her feet in brimstone so she could better deal with the devil, or in her medical jargon, take the vaccine so her immune system could thwart the virus she'd been infected with.

He invited her to a play a few days later.

#

He'd chosen a revival of Cats and he'd been allotted good seats very near the stage, so the musical numbers hit them front and center.

Rachel seemed to Matt to have reverted to the self he remembered, lively and confident and ready to laugh whenever he succeeded in making her do so, which he happily found was as often as he remembered and not half narcotized.

They chatted together and enjoyed the play as much as the music concert at Lincoln Center, long ago, as Matt realized toward the end when Grizelda took the stage and mourned her past in the melancholy song "Memory." At the lyrics where memory is lamented "all alone in the moonlight," Rachel broke out in tears and found it difficult to stop them.

Matt understood why she was crying and found no words to console her. Nor did she elaborate. They left the theater and took the subway home without much conversation.

At her door she did not invite him in, but said she wanted to see him again before he left and they planned an afternoon aperitif the day before he took the plane.

#

Matt saw other women in between his dates with Rachel, women he'd met in LA and stayed in touch with, and found it particularly ironic that Lynne, whom he took to an Italian restaurant, aspired to sing opera and had done so at local productions in Manhattan. Having studied Italian, she delighted in hearing the waiters rave about her beauty, assuming of course that she didn't understand a word of the language.

Matt found his thoughts drifting away from Rachel to a lover he'd met just before he left LA, and wondered if Rachel was doing the same. Like her, he'd posed no questions about her love life the past three years, and he did not when they went out. He'd bought tickets to another play and intended to go solo after their drink, but he found she wanted to hang out together and suggested dinner at one of her favorite restaurants. She wanted to show him her office on the Upper West Side.

"What do you think of the interior? I did it all myself."

He looked around at the mix of modern and some Western style, and said without an ounce of false sincerity, just the truth of his exact opinion, "It's perfect."

"What do you mean?"

"Just what I said. To my taste, everything is perfect. Just beautiful. It's like I designed and chose everything myself, except I wouldn't have done it so well. It makes me want to get sick so I can enjoy the decor."

She loved that, and laughed heartily. In the back of his mind he despaired. Where would he ever find someone who shared his taste so well, and could go him one better, if not multiples?

#

At the restaurant they talked like old friends. She said she had gone on another backpack trip, to New Mexico, but "I don't know why, it didn't have the same ambiance as ours."

"I'm sure my not being there had nothing to do with it."

"And you?"

That same spring he had taken a long trip, his first since theirs together, in the Grand Canyon. "Really hard and I had to train, but the sights were extraordinary. Not sacred, though."

"Did you stay at the El Tovar?"

"No, I couldn"t."

She knew that the word had different senses but did not follow up.`

#

They walked back from the restaurant in the cool of an autumn evening.

Matt hadn't wanted to come to New York in October and be reminded of winter and lost leaves and the end of warm golden days. But here he was, and he did not know if he'd ever be back on her street.

"You know," she said, "I never could understand why Lassiter hesitated before he rolled the rock. The bad guys were charging after them with guns blazing and even if they dodged all those bullets they'd have taken Jane away from him."

"He did roll it though. All he needed was for her to say 'I love you.'"

He flashed on something he'd heard from one of the spring backpackers about the Rainbow Bridge. Waters from Lake Powell had continued to rise and though they hadn't yet touched the buttresses of the Rainbow Bridge, which would hasten its erosion, they'd filled the stream which had created it so much it now flowed more like a spring freshet. Neither he nor Rachel now would be able to cross the streambed to the rock ledge where they'd begun their love affair.

She continued, "What if the rock had rolled down and squashed all the bad guys but left the entrance to Surprise Valley free. What would Jane and Lassiter have done?"

"Gone back to her ranch, I suppose. It was a beautiful ranch. Horses, pastureland, everything."

"Would they have been happy?"

"Lassiter was a gunfighter, used to roaming and happy trails. Who knows if he was really ready to hang up his holster."

"She might have reconnected with her religion, now that the villainous elders had been squashed."

"Probably. I don't think Lassiter could have lived with that so easily, after what they'd done to his sister. I spare you the details."

"And if Lassiter wandered off and came back years later. Would she take him back? "

"Maybe. If she hadn't found somebody else. She was a very attractive woman, you know. A rare jewel."

They arrived at her building entrance and she said, "You told me once in one of your letters, 'You're like a stream one could spend a lifetime knowing.' I never told you but that made me cry. It was the most beautiful thing anyone's ever said about me."

"And true."

He thought for a second she might tear up, but it was dark and he couldn't be sure.

He'd come to New York to see if there was still time to roll the rock, but she'd given him the answer at the theater, when she'd cried over the song about memory and lost love.

He was no good at voicing sentiment but figured now if ever was the time, and said, "In one of your letters you said I'd loved you so much that you could always love me just for that. True?"

"As anything anyone ever said. It's in the music box, all tucked away nice and snug with Clair de Lune." She smiled warmly, lovingly he thought, but made no move to invite him up.

After a moment he said, "Thank you for the evening. And the company."

She kissed him and said, "Happy trails, pardner." It was good to end with a laugh.

After a few paces he turned around for a last look and wave, but she had already gone into the building.

Life would go on, but he knew that a part of him would regret her till the end of his days.

Less than a year later Rachel married Max, in a ceremony reported in the New York Times.

5. TOO DEEP FOR TEARS

featuring Private Detective John Marriner.

The   corpse of a former nun turned actress/model has been found in the desert near Joshua Tree National Park and her onetime Mother Superior asks Banning private detective John Marriner--a decorated war veteran with stress and other disorders--to search for her killer on the mean streets of LA, where he was last seen bitchslapping the city Police Chief.

...the meanest flower that blows can give
Thoughts that do often lie too deep for tears.

—Wordsworth

1. ANNABELLE

Late summer nights in Palm Springs can be wonderfully fresh and even a bit cool, like this night, when the daytime temps had reached 115° Farenheit. Most of the party guests had stayed and now at midnight, many still circulated around the grand S-shaped pool, sculpted like the house from the side of one of the desert mountains ringing the Springs.

To the west Mr. St. Jacinto could be seen in profile under a half-moon, and for urban scenery, the city sprawled below, thousands of lights keeping restaurants, bars and other sorts of nightlife thrumming in a basin that a hundred years ago seemed too hot and barren for lizards. Water lay abundantly below the desert dust and sand, and when over the course of time and technology it could be extracted on a large scale, a city boomed, first as a resort, then a famous playground and getaway for the rich who wanted to escape LA and urban stress.

This house flanked the mountainside like Ali Baba's castle. Guests came and went from an interior all glass and marble, to the poolside fringed with palms, cactus and exotic blooms.

The grounds were a blaze of light and glitter, including the human kind.

Three massive, exquisitely wrought crystal punch bowls, full to orange slice-ringed rims with newly poured and well-spiked punch, were set up on long tables festooned with hors d'oeuvres.

Beautiful people milled around it, conversing, laughing, enjoying the music from a small orchestra. Most all of them rivaled the decor and some eclipsed it.

A stunning blonde woman in a lowcut dress dipped a ladle into one of the punch bowls, ruffling the smooth surface. She spooned a quantity into her glass, and took her time, because she knew she was being noticed and even though habitual, it pleased her anytime and everytime and she knew she would collect names and numbers tonight from which she could pick and choose, or not.

But a hand disturbed her moment. It dipped into one of the punch bowls, swirled the punch back and forth, around and around.

Pulled out. The blonde followed the hand up to Annabelle as she put her hand in her mouth and sucked the punch from her fingers like a popsicle. She sighed with pleasure at the taste. A dowager grimaced in disgust at what she had just witnessed, but the blonde had another reason for disgust. She had been eclipsed.

Annabelle wore a white one-piece linen dress and had the kind of figure that needed no other support. Many men who saw her that night dreamed of holding her and making love, with or without affection.

Pure physical pleasure would be more than enough to make the night memorable, if not unforgettable. But no one held her attention for long.

One cowboy type in a $5,000 outfit with Stetson and boots tried, and when he went to fetch her another drink, came back to find her surrounded by a half-dozen admirers.

She let them admire, giving nothing away, when the orchestra began to play a song that struck her soul.

Annabelle danced away from the flock, inviting no one to join her, but was momentarily blocked by Barry, a good-looking young guy who had no chance with her but didn't know it.

"Have we met?"

Annabelle pushed past him.

Dancers moved onto the lawn, merging into a swirl of motion. Annabelle watched the dancers. Her face was bright, happy with the music which increased tempo.

The dancers gyrated faster, in keeping with the new beat. Annabelle joined them and began to dance with joyful fervor.

"What's your name?" Barry asked, rocking up beside her, not giving up.

"Annabelle Angel."

"You're kidding, right?" She began to dance faster. Barry kept up, happy in her presence. But Annabelle began to dance to her own music. Her pace increased till she was almost writhing…a spinning, whirling dervish.

She yelled with delight…again. Annabelle lifted her arms to the moon, a bright oval in the sky overhead. Some of the other dancers gradually eased up, their attention drawn to this oddity in their midst.

Barry stopped dancing altogether…but Annabelle didn't notice or stop. She spun, whirled in odd but graceful pirouettes of motion. Soon she was in a circle of space all her own, the other dancers clearing her way. The band slowed, then resumed, gradually--as the other dancers desisted--making music for Annabelle alone.

Barry asked one of the dancers beside him, "What's she on?" The partygoer answered with a gesture, tapping his temple with his forefinger.

As Annabelle continued her solitary dance...spinning, whirling under the light of the moon, her face radiant with exhilaration, another man in the crowd watched her, and had been since she passed by the pool, in the glow reflected by the submerged pool lights resembling Neptune.

His eyes fixed on her like a treasure of infinite price. He was ready to pay it. He would do anything to have her, and would.

2. MARRINER

Master and pet were having a fabulous time on this sunny afternoon in the park, even though the clock had ticked past 4 and the brown haze cloud of Los Angeles pollution had begun to arrive and choke throats of "sensitive people," as local TV weatherpersons liked to characterize such atmospheric sufferers.

John Marriner was not one of those people, not being sensitive in any way, shape or form except when it came to tracking miscreants. He had one on his radar now, the master, a middle-aged man named Harold who was playing with the dog, a mixed breed named Gershwin--though Harold called him Sunny, "like the sun" he said more than once to his buddies at the Sphinx, one of Hemet's less than hip bars.

Hemet lay on the other side of the San Jacinto Mountains from Palm Springs, geographically speaking, but many worlds away from the elite posh of the Springs. Marriner knew the city well, as he lived down the freeway in Banning and did most of his clothes shopping at Hemet's Goodwill store.

For some reason--maybe because the store had a pipeline to the Springs denizens who trashed shirt and pants after one engagement or shopping expedition, which would require a traverse in the blazing hot sun from one air-conditioned interior to another, hence sweat and body odor--Hemet's branch customarily had fine designer offerings at rock-bottom prices, though Marriner once vociferously complained to management when an Armani reached 10 bucks. He couldn't go past $6 at that point in time, between jobs.

Now though he was about to break a case, and on this case he left Armani at home and opted for jeans and sleeveless leather shirt, the kind of garb that could get him mistaken for a Hell's Angel just recently released from the eponymous Hades. He had tied his hair back and slung a Bowie knife in a belt scabbard. One could mock him as a caricature, except he sometimes had to angle his way into a room if the doorway had been constructed in another, narrower epoch, and looking up at one big ass dude like him made mocking more problematic to all but the occasional world championship wrestler or NFL lineman.

Harold and Sunny were gamboling about, playing tag, the dog barking, Harold laughing. When the master had had enough, probably thinking about the beer he deserved to cool off with after this daily exertion, he and Sunny walked in tandem toward his car.

The dog suddenly bolted forward. Harold's look of surprise suggested this was an unusual occurrence. He hurried after him, shouting Sunny's name. But as he reached the parking lot, Harold stopped abruptly. The dog was happily barking, jumping and pawing over Frances, a middleaged blonde. There were tears in Frances' eyes. "Oh Gersh, God how I've missed you!"

The dog barked a happy assent. Harold's surprise gave way to concern. He turned and saw...

"Dognapper," Marriner spit out disgustedly.

"You horrible criminal," Frances seconded. Harold collapsed to his knees, all too aware the jig was up. Groaned, "I couldn't help myself. When I saw him on the street that day--" He could barely go on, but recovered and aimed a cri de coeur at Frances. "I've been so lonely since my wife died."

Frances came over to Marriner. "Poor man. I almost feel sorry for him. What should I do?"

"Forgive and forget. But not before we take Gershwin home." Frances nodded. As if on cue, the dog moved over to Harold and began licking his face.

"You've taken wonderful care of him," Frances said. She moved over and consoled Harold with a pat on the shoulder. Marriner eyed this tender scene and suddenly worried about the Stockholm Syndrome.

"My jeep is waiting, Mrs. Randolph. We can't risk Gershwin developing canine schizophrenia. Serving two masters, well since time immemorial it's been a clinical condition without cure."

"You're so right, Mr. Marriner." She turned and headed toward Marriner's SUV in the parking lot. She was thrilled when Gershwin followed. Harold looked stricken.

Marriner said consolingly, if firmly, "Be thankful for the time you had together. "

"No other dog can ever replace Sunny."

"That's exactly what I said about my ex-wife, and once she got through taking my last penny I had to start chasing low lifes like you. Don't make me do this again. Let sleeping dogs lie." He turned and headed back to join Mrs. Randolph, who stared back at the chastened Harold and repeated, "The poor man."

Marriner knew that Mrs. Randolph was not poor, and that brought joy to his heart even as he went through the motions of sympathizing with his client's humane sympathy. "He'll be a better man after this," he said.

#

Marriner shorthopped Interstate 40 and took the Banning exit that led to his office. He'd rented a space formerly used by a tax consultant who'd had to flee the IRS and many financial forms still remained, which Marriner used to form elaborate paper airplanes that he sailed around the office and sometimes the parking lot when he was waiting for his next client.

Ana Louisa spent much of her time gathering them up and sailing them around herself. She'd gotten quite good at it, and Marriner told her so.

"Practice makes perfect," she replied. "It's not like we're going to hit anybody in the face."

The office sat between a Chinese restaurant and coin laundromat that had the distinction of retaining one of the very few public telephones in the region, if not whole state of California.

"Does it even work?" Ana Louisa had asked when she began on what she soon laughingly referred to as "your payroll," but she learned it did, as Marriner frequently gave out the phone as contact number to his numerous bill collectors. Laundromat habitués had gotten used to its frequent ringing and some even engaged in conversations with the angry interlocutors, who could have cared less about clean laundry.

Marriner ran a tab at Mei Ling's restaurant, where he greatly enjoyed the frog legs. Once he had gotten up enough curiosity to ask Mei Ling's husband Jun Yi, the chief waiter and bottle washer to his wife's cooking, where such delicious, plump and nourishing frogs came from.

"Water," he answered.

"Yeah, but what water. You know, like lake or pond or river."

"Deep water. You want more? On house."

Marriner dropped the subject, figuring that what he didn't know wouldn't hurt him, and thus far the frogs of unknown origin hadn't. California had many such mysteries, and that's why he'd gone into business--to solve them.

Ana Louisa was on the phone when he walked in. "He like shoved his nose right in my face. I could not believe it! Have you like seen his nose? Puke. He said he wanted to have a relationship

127

and stuff. Guess again, pukenose. Hey, got to go to work. Call me in five, ok?"

Ana Louisa went to college in Palm Desert and, it seemed to Marriner, spent most of her class time avoiding leers from horny fellow students and teachers. He had gotten used to the slow cruisers who passed in front of the office hoping for a sighting, but he'd drawn the line at guys pretending to mistake the office for the laundromat, popping in with some clothes sack half-full--"like the morons don't have GPS or can't read," Marriner groused.

"Come to our college," Ana Louisa said, "you'll see."

"See what?"

"That you're right. They can't read." But Marriner remained skeptical and knew they were just bopping in hoping against hope that she might deign to notice them, and they'd gotten so numerous that now he didn't even want to waste breath on them. He'd placed his .45 Magnum on his desk and when they entered, he just waved it to the right, laundromat direction. They got the picture.

Ana Louisa didn't even bother to say hello when he walked in, but got to the bottom line. "Did she pay you?"

"The check is in, uh, is going to be in the mail."

"Crapola."

"She was so into renewing her relationship with her dog, I had to respect that. There's a time for everything, you know."

"Yeah, like the end of the month and paycheck time. Here's some good news for you and me." She'd opened a letter from a Delaware Bank and paper clipped its contents to the envelope--a new Visa card.

"Haven't these rubes heard of credit checks?" Marriner marveled. "Cash advance your salary."

"Already have. Your new code is 0007."

"Good choice, thanks."

"Take some time before you max this one out, okay? Rick Smith got your new number and he's been calling every day."

"The guy's a true professional. I give the other debt collectors 3 months minimum before they track me down."

"He sounded really down."

"His shit job doesn't help. All day calling insolvent deadbeats like me and getting insulted."

"His wife kicked him out."

"Don't tell me she moved in with that dickhead from Thrifty she was boffing, uh, having sexual relations with."

"Next time he calls you should like, raise his morale, you know. Talk about how you scraped bottom and crawled your way back up. Even if up means Banning."

"Right."

"So I aired out your mattress and threw out the beer cans and whiskey bottle. Now you've got some financing maybe you can think about getting a new one. The mattress I mean. They've got a sale on at Target."

"God I'm glad I hired you."

Before he'd cadged enough credit to find a rental Marriner had sacked out in what he laughingly called his back office. As Ana Louisa surmised, the mattress had seen better days and nights.

As if on cue, a very wet behind the ears and clearly very amorous young student type--his gaping stare focused on only one person in the office and it wasn't Marriner--entered. Like so many others, he'd taken the trouble to simulate mistaking the office for the laundromat and had a cloth bag from which a dirty white sock protruded. Marriner liked that touch. "The kid's got a future as a production designer in movies," he said later.

"The laundromat's next door," Ana Louisa helpfully enlightened.

"Oh yeah, I guess I like didn't notice. Hey, haven't I seen you around at school?"

"Yeah, I'm majoring in nuclear physics."

"Really. I didn't know they offered that."

"You?"

"Uh, sports management."

Marriner interjected, "You need her to show the way?" The admirer was so transfixed he'd had a lapse of short term memory, so Marriner added, "To the laundromat."

"Hah, no, I think I can find it now. It's like right next door. Well, maybe I'll see you around campus."

Marriner thought he was going to bump his head on the door on the way out, because it was still jerked around toward the interior, or more precisely, Ana Louisa.

"Listen," he said to his secretary, "maybe you should start dressing down when you come to work. Or what I call work."

"I am dressed down. You haven't seen me dressed up."

"Save it. My heart's weakening these days. Unemployment does that."

"Presto bingo." She handed him a note written on one of the accounting sheets. "She wants to talk about a case." Marriner eyed the name and address.

"Is she kidding?"

"You want my honest opinion? She didn't sound like she knows what kidding is. You better like, behave yourself. And hit the Goodwill store in Hemet." Marriner looked reflective, and Ana Louisa added, "You want me to GPS the address?"

"No. I know LA."

3. CONVENT

Marriner dressed for the meeting, which for him meant a white shirt with jeans instead of the usual plaid. He had found several nice ties at the Goodwill store but finally decided they would not do for a private investigator who meant to display an image of firmness and if necessary, controlled aggression--though he had acquired a reputation for the uncontrolled variety.

Ana Louisa had polished his boots, and when she saw his eyes moisten up, thinking she'd done it for him, she corrected, "That counts for overtime pay." All things considered, she and Marriner felt he was as presentable as a basic savage like himself could be.

He'd come back after serving in several of the USA's campaigns to "stabilize the Middle East," plus Afghanistan, and done various deeds that would have surprised his mother but pleased very much the brass. In the process of stabilizing, he himself had been destabilized. He did not have clinical PTSD, but some members of the LAPD, chiefly the Chief, swore he'd acquired this and other disorders and assimilated them. "He's a high functioning psychotic crazy," the Chief said after the incident that'd made Marriner persona non grata in the City of Angels and sent him drifting to Banning, where he'd run out of cash and gasoline.

But he was capable of acting like a civilized, non-violent human being "if I put what's left of my mind to it," admitting that it took a huge chunk of effort.

Today he was trying, even respecting the speed limit as he rolled into the LA megalopolis and then turned north toward the San Gabriel foothills. Our Lady of Hope Convent lay a good ways past the entrance, at the end of a long circular drive. It was an impressive 1920s red brick building, somewhat incongruous for the Southland style that flourished when the LA Basin first flourished, boomed really, after Mullholland brought water to a desert basin and a garden grew.

No one waited at the wide open entrance door. It reminded Marriner of some churches that never closed or locked, as sin and sinners could happen by any hour of day or night and need penance and, depending, forgiveness and absolution.

Marriner hadn't known many churches or faiths, but he'd definitely sinned from time to time and once or twice had found it necessary to enter a church, kneel and reveal what he'd done to "the Higher Ups," regretfully.

Penance had come down, and he'd felt a bit better afterward and gone back out into the world, knowing he was liable to sin again but hoping to do it less.

Marriner crossed the long corridor that led to the grounds in back, which he could see like the light at the end of a tunnel. His boots clattered, but no one came to greet him and it occurred to him that everyone might be at prayer.

As he exited he heard noises and shouts, and saw the source: under a wide, tall and majestic palm tree which surely dated back decades, in a space that served as an exercise ground, with footpaths leading toward the hills and mats for exercise, yoga, prayer or meditation--as he thought--a woman had placed various wood planks on two saw horses and was karate chopping them in half.

She did it with fierce cries and tremendous energy, showing the wood no mercy. Marriner approached and waited for her to pause. Breathing heavily, she hadn't noticed his presence. "I can take lessons," he said. She turned then. She was dressed in sweat pants and top.

"Mr. Marriner. I am Sister Mary." She extended her hand and they shook.

"Mother Superior?"

"Yes, not a martial arts wizard. We have to exercise our bodies from time to time, not just our souls. Thank you for responding to my request. It's very unusual, you know that."

She had prepared tea and they sat around a hand-carved wood table under the palm tree. At intervals Marriner saw nuns in traditional habit exiting the convent to stroll. It was a peaceful place, with the mountains in the background and flowers and verdure gracing the grounds everywhere.

Sister Mary asked, "Did you hear the sad news about Annabelle Angel?"

"It's a name hard to forget. It was big news in Banning. It's just down the road from Joshua Tree, where the body was found."

"Annabelle lived here with us for a year. A very sensitive, fragile soul. She tried so hard to worship and serve God, but in the end...she had many compulsions, you see. We missed her when she left. Now we'll always miss her."

"That was about six months ago as I remember. An eternity for the homicide cops in Riverside."

"They've put the case on a shelf, one might say."

"And LAPD? She lived in Los Angeles."

"They came for an interview. Since then...well, if you're wondering how and why I chose you, it's because I know you will not take no for an answer from that particular police department."

Marriner knew what she wanted him to do, but he wanted to be sure she did.

"Sister...she's gone to God. Her heavenly reward, isn't that what it's called? I mean, if you're asking me to find her killer... LA's a big place. Home to a lot of rats and some people on leave from hell. If Annabelle ran into one of them, the wrong person...the desert's a dumping round and most victims are never found. The killers go back to their lives like normal people and seem normal to everybody who comes into contact with them. I have to be honest. This could go on for a very long time and I can't guarantee anything."

"The Lord said, 'Render unto Caesar the things that are Caesar.' Earthly justice is one of them. I know the person who did this to Annabelle will be punished in hell. But if we let him stay free, he may do it again.

"In my previous life I had some resources and in exceptional circumstances like this, I can draw on them. Let's just say you have an indefinite retainer." She handed him a check.

"Will this suffice for the moment?"

Marriner looked at the amount, blinked, looked again. "It will suffice."

4. LONG CANYON

Marriner spent the night back home in his Banning rental house. He'd still not taken the time to do much furniture shopping even though he'd lived there for awhile. His rationale was, as each month's rent that came due added to his debt to the owner, a Mr. Tubbs, at some point in time that came nearer and nearer he'd be obliged to vacate the facilities. And why burden himself with cumbersome possessions like a sofa and dining room set?

So he spent most evenings grilling on the veranda, then watching the sunset with whatever beer he hadn't emptied yet, watching the play of light on the cholla cactus and a distant Joshua tree and the arid hills to the east that led to the national park. A coyote had taken to descending most nights to within howling distance. Marriner looked forward to his nightly serenade.

He'd prop up his chair after a meal of barbecue hamburgers or takeout from the local KFC--Marriner enjoyed the 5-piece dinner meal, and employees knew not to even ask what he wanted to order. Saved precious time--Marriner calculated an extra beer's worth.

Once he'd spotted a puma who'd wandered down from the mountains, insouciantly traversing the low terrain that sloped down to his neighborhood of inexpensive '50s homes.

Marriner had been very impressed at sight of the big cat, and so had all the neighborhood dogs, who raised a ruckus from a discreet, guarded distance.

Marriner could have taken down the puma easily as he had the Army surplus hardware to do it, but first, he never killed animals for sport or almost any other reason except self-preservation, and second, he preferred to save ammo for miscreants. Human variety. He had a feeling he'd encounter some of those on this case.

He savored the beer and the silence and the desert night.

#

Long Canyon deserved its name, as it extended not far from Joshua Tree National Park's westernmost entrance at Black Canyon, down to its southwest boundary at Desert Hot Springs.

A branch of the LA Aqueduct passed there, and various signs threatened humongous fines for anyone caught parking there. Marriner parked his SUV in front of the signs and walked past them into the canyon. Whenever he needed desert silence to refresh and calm current demons, he resorted to the desert. He loved the back-country. Some trails cut through the splendid and splendidly wild acres of the park, but much of it in and near the Eagle Mountains remained virtually unexplored.

He'd wandered into the unknown more than once, and more than once come close to exhaustion, water deprivation and death, as any side wash or canyon could look similar to the one his map said led to a road or trail that would in turn lead to an escape route, but in fact led to a cul de sac or yet another way to nowhere.

And even if you did choose the right route, you would have a very long trek to get to water and/or vehicle where you'd stashed it. If you miscalculated the distance, some day someone would find what was left of your sunfried corpse and add it to the list of heedless desert explorers. But that day might not come for decades.

Annabelle's killer had counted on that fact.

He, or whoever had employed him, knew that one could simply drive up the canyon as far as a 4-wheeler could go. Dune buggies and ATVs did, and no ranger ever patrolled to stop them. It was a big park, bigger than its NPS budget.

Marriner started very early, before the heat of the desert day fried body and mind, and walked briskly upcanyon. The sand was hard and made for easy hiking. The tracks made by rescue and support and police vehicles had thoroughly blended with the killer's car tires, but Marriner still studied the imprints and felt sure he discerned them from time to time. About 4 miles from the entrance Marriner turned into a side canyon on the left. A rusted remnant of corrugated tin lay on the desert floor, and had lain there for decades--nearing a hundred years.

Another few minutes of steady hiking gradually uphill and Marriner came upon the ruins of a stone cabin. The canyon abruptly deadended here at a small waterfall trickling down from upstream. The cabin's roof had long ago fallen, and stone building blocks lay all around the interior, but the intact fireplace still bore the name of one of its tenants, Chuckawalla Bill, and a date: 1933..

In his heyday in the '30s, taking refuge from the Great Depression--or so Marriner imagined--Chuckawalla Bill would have lived quite comfortably here, when the water no doubt fell down at several times its current rate, creating a small oasis.

If Bill had persuaded a woman to share his rustic lifestyle, he'd have had many moments when life seemed wonderful. When he needed provisions from the civilization he no doubt distrusted and disliked, with the exception of certain well-stocked bars, he could just hop into his Model T and head into town. Maybe even Banning.

The killer had driven up canyon as far as he could, then packed his victim up over the cascade and into desert he undoubtedly thought wouldn't see footprints for an age--at which time the gravesite would be effectively covered by winds, sand and time.

He hadn't counted on Juan De La Costa. Desert prospectors still lived and wandered here, and Juan knew the desert enough to recognize upturned earth, carelessly--one could say, contemptuously--smoothed over with a boot.

Someone else would have passed on and let sleeping secrets lie, but Juan was about the most upright person Marriner had ever met. While his burro sipped precious water, Juan pulled his shovel from a side sling and turned up just enough sand and gravel to see what lay down there.

"Didn't have to dig deep," he confided to Marriner. "She looked like the angel she was named for, even in that hellhole. That's what old Juan calls grace, John. Like these flowers we're seeing now. They'll be gone next week. Just got to be grateful they graced us for a little while."

Marriner clambered up on the right side of the little stream and began to crisscross, looking for the gravesite. He didn't have far to go.

A stick had been stobbed into the ground by forensics people or the investigating officers. They hadn't bothered to fill in the hole which wasn't very deep. It lay in a wash to the side of the stream--eons ago when more rain fell, it would have been filled by running water. Now the sand lay loose and abundant and made for easy digging. Marriner figured the killer wouldn't have wanted to exert himself and picked the first soft spot of ground he could find, up here where no buffalo or much of anything else roamed.

Marriner scrutinized it for a moment, squatted down, took a handful of dirt from the hole and held it up in his palm. The dry dust eddied away in the desert wind--part soil, part perhaps the mortal remains of Annabelle Angel. He thought he saw a red tinge of dried blood on the grains.

Marriner let his gaze swing round.

In every direction down below was desert, plenty of ocotillo and cholla and scrub tamarisk, but no humans. Very few of them came here to live, people like Chuckawalla Bill who didn't stay and certainly didn't choose to die here.

Neither had Annabelle. Someone had made that decision for her. He'd come and done the deed in broad daylight. Not so very far away lay a megalopolis of 20 million people. But none of them lurked around here, with a cell cam to record Annabelle's last moments of life.

Marriner would have to find the killer among those millions.

The desert wind had begun to pick up and it whistled around him.

#

Juan de la Costa lived in an oasis just outside Joshua Tree National Park. Marriner had stumbled upon it once when he'd hiked long past Cottonwood Springs. Decades ago Juan had blazed a kind of road to his handbuilt cabin amid palms and tamarisk. It wasn't the kind of road anyone would take who feared loneliness and rugged individualism and saying fuck you to the beaten path, because this one wasn't.

Juan liked it that way. "My cats and dogs and Bucky get after me sometimes, but they don't crowd my space, if you know what I mean, John."

Bucky was Juan's trusty burro, who packed his provisions when they went prospecting. Juan rarely found anything, but he wasn't looking for gold or silver so much as open spaces.

Marriner knew his visit risked crowding on Juan's space, but on the contrary, he'd never seen Juan so happy as when he told him why he was there.

"Those so-called authorities did what they're paid to do, no less and I can damn sure tell you no more.'

"They ask the right questions, Juan?" They were sitting around a stone table Juan had crafted himself out of a stone block--"hell of a job," Marriner complimented.

"Well, I'm getting toward 90 now--got a lot of time slipping away and I got to leave my mark, you know." Even though he had no electricity at the cabin, Juan had found a way to keep beer cool. Marriner had brought a few in--"in case you have any hot days."

"Cool or hot, me and beer don't give a damn." Juan reflected a moment, then answered Marriner's question. "Yes, but it didn't seem to me like they'd remember the answers. It was hot out there, and I could see 'em thinking, this senile old man's talking about

137

something he don't know nothin' about. Plus, the ranger didn't like one bit that I couldn't show him my Lifetime pass to the park."

"My guess is, because you don't have one."

"Hell yes I do. It's called life. That's what it means, no? You pass during your lifetime."

Marriner held out his beer and they toasted to wisdom and right thinking.

"Size 12 boots. He's a big bastard. Watch yourself. He didn't care about lung cancer, neither."

Juan finished off a beer and opened another.

"God, I'm happy you're on the case. See, me and Bucky'd been out for a while and we were heading home. You know these parts. Out there where we were, you don't usually hear a jeep come and you don't hear a jeep go. I figure, well it's the rangers and we don't get along too good. They don't like it when I tell 'em stories about how this used to be free land and then the government started calling it a monument and then a national park and suddenly I ain't welcome anymore unless I give 'em my hardearned money--and hell, I don't earn any money. Against my principles.

"So we don't get curious, Bucky and me. I don't rush down that little streambed and see what's going on till the next day. And I should have, John. I should have."

"Yeah, and he'd have put two bodies in that hole. Hell, maybe Bucky too. This kind of bastard would have had a real big gun and know how to use it."

Marriner had never seen Juan so anguished, or at all. He'd lived long and gone to war after lying about his age and seen a lot of action and developed a resistance to all kinds of evils that men do.

"I saw his tracks and wanted to see what he'd buried, even though I knew I didn't want to see. I took my shovel and started to dig and then when I saw her, that little angel...find him for me, will you John? Before I leave this desert for good."

#

As Marriner got out of his car and approached his office he saw a familiar face: a dog's. Gershwin's. He was tied up to a bike rack that never had any bikes, so it made for a perfect hitching post. The dog wagged its tail happily at sight of Marriner.

"Hey boy, how you doin'. Getting back in the Springs lifestyle? "

Marriner noticed Gershwin now wore a miniature ankle bracelet, custom made for a canine and quite obviously effective in tracking.

It no doubt cost a pretty penny, and Marriner looked forward to receiving many pretty pennies from Gershwin's mistress who no doubt waited inside, grateful for his services.

But when he entered, he found Harold and Frances sitting together. His gaze moved downward. They were holding hands.

"Gershwin brought us together," Harold said.

"Harold reached out to me," Frances said, "just wanting the right to a visitation every now and then. I said to myself, this man has so much love in his heart for Sunny Gershwin, he's got room for me. And he does."

She squeezed his hand and Marriner thought her eyes had developed a tear or two.

"I'm glad," he said. "Everybody's happy. As soon as we conclude the business side of this passage in your lives, you can move on to the next one. I'll have some real satisfaction knowing I helped bring the three of you together."

"Satisfaction. Yes," Harold said. "Well, under the circumstances we..." He stopped and looked to Frances for support. She urged him on with the prod of an elbow. Marriner saw it coming, as he wasn't born yesterday and hadn't become a private detective without some slight understanding of human nature and how homo sapiens could spin around on a dime.

"Keep talking," Marriner said, "I have to get my equipment together. Big case, you know. Some really bad people. Hey, where's my secretary?"

Frances answered: "Oh, she had a history class or something like that. A young man came and picked her up. They both seemed so sweet and she trusted us to look out for the place." Harold mustered firmness: "Frances--well, both of us really----we don't feel your fee is entirely reasonable. There, I said it."

Marriner looked directly at Harold, who stared back with stiff upper lip. "We'd like to renegotiate." Frances squeezed Harold's hand proudly.

Marriner dropped on the desk what he'd pulled out of his desk drawer: a handgun. He dropped it on the desk with a CLUMP. Harold looked impressed by the .45 Magnum as Marriner moved over to a closet. Rummaged.

"I've seen a gun like that. In the movies."

"They're real," Marriner said.

Frances confessed, "I feel so guilty, persecuting Harold like we did."

Marriner laid a shotgun on the desk beside the revolver. "That's a hugely honest statement. I said to myself when you hired me, Mrs. Randolph is the soul of honesty, and if I succeed in my mission, I'm going to find a dog that's been raised well and the kidnapper's going to be one lucky man, misguided as he may be. And I was right. My problem is, I'm stopping off at the bank on my way to LA--big case you know, might get violent--and I'm afraid they're expecting a check. This is one time when honesty can't pay."

Harold said, "It's not that you don't deserve payment."

Marriner laid down on the desk another shotgun and three hand grenades. "Souvenirs of my time in the military," he said.

Frances assured. "We respect our military." Marriner laid down a rocket launcher on the desk. It landed with a THUMP. Then several rockets.

Harold and Frances watched for a long moment. "Ex-military, huh?" Harold reflected.

"We feel honor bound to pay a portion of your fee. Maybe even all of it," Frances said, looking to Harold for approval. He reflected further and nodded yes.

5. LA

Marriner hit the freeway, taking the 60 instead of the 10. He would hit the 10 later, but the 60 led over mountains and he liked the scenery. At Riverside he would start to hit the big traffic and soon enough merge again with the 10.

This morning remained fairly clear, as the prevailing west winds didn't really push the noxious cloud of LA pollution into the Inland Empire, and afterward desert, until late afternoon.

But the closer he came to the megalopolis, the more the haze intensified and soon the sky had been blotted out and he couldn't tell how blue it was, if it was, or whether any clouds had managed to form this day.

When he topped out about 20 miles east of downtown he'd had to slow for congestion but still rolled, and he made fairly good time. He took the first exit and went surface roads to the coroner's office.

He'd notified Red Ralston he was coming and why, and Red looked happy to see him again.

"Hiya Johnny. Where you been holed up?"

"Just down the road in Banning."

"Banning. Kind of a cow town ain't it?"

"It would be, if we had any grass."

"Hey, don't drip any sand on my floor. How are your kidneys holding up?"

"I flush them out every night with beer."

"Water's better, but you know that."

Red handled many body parts in his job and knew the importance of healthy ones, and Marriner had always counted on him to keep tabs on his--even though Red knew Marriner's prostate, kidneys, lungs and cardiovascular system--not to mention everything else--were liable to suffer a great deal of abuse, in one form or another.

He used to repeat, "One day I'm gonna be workin' on you," and Marriner would ritually reply, "Nobody else but you, okay? And let me know if you find a heart."

"Yeah, I'm gonna scribble some graffiti on it."

This time Red asked, "So what illegal and against-the-rules shit you want me to do this time?"

"Annabelle Angel."

A few minutes later Marriner was poring over photos and an autopsy report. Red said, "They brought her back here and somebody paid for burial at Forest Lawn. You could say she lived poor and died rich."

"My friends at LAPD run a DNA?"

"Yeah. Couldn't find a match. And they had plenty to work out. He had some fun with her."

Marriner paused a moment before continuing. He found it necessary to tamp down the anger he felt rising in him.

"I owe you another one, Red."

"Hell, that makes a dozen now, give or take 6. Come back to town, go back to work--I need favors too, you know." Marriner looked startled at what he read and looked up at Red.

"Yeah. She had some shit in her blood I couldn't identify. I'm getting old and behind the times, you know. This was some real sophisticated shit. But it didn't kill her. They buried her alive, John. I've seen a lot in my time, but to do something like that to someone who looked like her...why didn't they put a bullet in her, show a little mercy."

"Either they hated her, or something worse."

"What's worse than that?" Marriner shuffled the docs and put them back in their manila envelope. Took a moment. Handed them back to Red.

"They didn't think she was worth a bullet."

6. PRECINCT

Ed Gorton was a good cop who'd spent years on the force and was moving up in the ranks and esteem of Chief Bentley, the only opinion that ultimately counted, but he had a huge black mark on his resume--he'd remained friends with Marriner.

The Chief had been a good cop once--once. When Marriner worked on the force for a brief, eventful year, he'd even complimented him on his results, if not dubious methods. But then came the "imbroglio," as Marriner referred to it. The Chief used other words, less literary.

Marriner had pursued an investigation into the death of a prominent citizen's daughter, and as it led closer and closer to the son of an even more prominent citizen, huge donor to the city's welfare and not incidentally, law enforcement organizations--the Chief and his minions, mostly a lackey named Frank Harbison, had done everything they could to block it.

The shit hit the fan on an annual Law and Order Day when Chief Bentley gave his ritual self-serving speech, standing at the podium in front of a carefully selected crowd of dignitaries. In the front rows of the audience sat a number of the precinct's officers, among them Gorton and Frank Harbison. The Chief proclaimed, "People come to me and say, 'Captain, you came to this division with a mandate: clean up the crime and corruption that has plagued this city. Tell me. How are we doing?' Well ladies and gentlemen, I'm here today to tell you, we're doing fine!"

Applause followed that sounded to an informed ear like the canned response of a TV episode.

Except a lone voice in the audience dissented loudly: "Bullshit!" A few feathers ruffled on the podium's dignitaries, but the chief continued.

"Sure we need more officers. Sure we can do better. But we're not doing bad."

Scattered applause and murmurs of approval, with the same lone dissent: "Bullshit!"

The Chief's jaw tightened. "This city can take--"

"How much do you take?"

This rankled. Chief Bentley leaned forward. "From jerks like you, too much."

The crowd laughed at this comeback. The Chief resumed.

"This city can take pride in the job we're doing. But we're not satisfied."

Suddenly a hand grabbed the microphone, and along with the astonished crowd, the Chief came face to face with his heckler.

Marriner mic'ed to the crowd, "I'm not satisfied either." The Chief recoiled. Dignitaries stirred. The crowd reacted.

"This department stinks," Marriner continued. "Six months ago a woman disappeared. What has this department done? Nothing."

There was much scrambling down below among the officers. Harbison asked Gorton, "Has he got a gun?"

"He's a private detective. Probably."

Marriner continued, "They're too busy lining their pockets."

Harbison said to Gorton, "Goddammit, do something."

"What?"

Harbison looked flustered at having to make a decision. The Chief was paid to make decisions and take action, and he'd had enough. He grabbed Marriner by the shirt. "You're finished in this town, Mister."

Marriner chose his words carefully: "Bullshit." The Chief took a swing at him. Marriner parried the punch, then slapped the chief, once, twice, again, resounding blows that echoed like hammershots in the microphone. The stunned Chief stumbled back, then fell out of sight behind the podium.

It happened so fast the reaction was stunned, silent: dignitaries, crowd in front, gaggle of newsmen and action cams, even the assembled officers. Harbison and Gorton stood motionless, watching.

Marriner eyed his handiwork--the prone police chief--then turned to the crowd. "Have a nice day," he said cheerfully, before calmly marching off the stage where he was finally surrounded by a gaggle of LA's finest.

In a just world the Chief would have been sacked and assigned crossing guard duty, for assault and worst of all, as vicious comments summed up on the Internet, "getting the crap slapped out of him," but Department PR branded Marriner a veteran deranged by military duty, a decorated veteran who'd gone over the edge and needed more psychiatric help than the Chief needed balls.

In fact, PR went, the Chief had behaved heroically in recognizing very quickly a psychologically challenged individual who needed careful handling. Thus he had turned the other cheek, in recognition of the poor man's wartime service and what it had cost him.

It cost Marriner further when he saw his license revoked, 24-hour tails placed on him, and more than once a beat cop--always with backup--trying to provoke him into drawing his weapon. Eventually he had to go with the prevailing winds and drift to Banning, where his credit cards maxed out--not for the first or last time--and he rented a dirt cheap house with plenty of cheap dirt in front and back.

Common sense would have told Marriner to avoid the minefield that was the interior of the Department, with so many of his enemies prowling around looking for an ass to kick, but Marriner had renounced common sense the day he took on the Chief in public view.

He strolled in past security based on his appointment with Gorton, and the young guard condemned to repeat past history for not remembering it let him stroll. He immediately encountered Officer Pinckney--young, wise-ass--hustling an elderly black wino through the station. He was enjoying his work. When the wino slowed, he shoved him forward.

"Hey, man. What's the charge! What's the charge?" the man asked plaintively.

Pinckney leaned in close. "The charge is you're a piece of shit." Pinckney gave the wino another contemptuous shove to punctuate his point. A hand grabbed his shoulder.

"Easy there, Officer...Pinkie." Marriner had squinted at his badge. "Scuzzballs have rights, too."

Pinckney turned his full attention to Marriner. "Pinckney. Perry Pinckney. And you want your ass handed to you, call me PP." He looked him up and down, noted with disgust Marriner's hand on his shoulder. He shoved his nose into Marriner's face.

"This looks like assault. I'm going to book you, asshole."

"Hell son, this is an assault." Marriner had suddenly flashed on the morgue photos of Annabelle Angel and without taking the time to analyze why, or why the anger was rising again inside, cold-cocked Pinckney with a punch to his right jaw. The officer fell back and as luck would have it, slumped into a sitting position on one of the weathered, wood and iron chairs set against the wall.

The wino gaped. "Oh yeah! Man, he didn't see that coming. I mean, he did not see that coming. How you swing fast like that, man? "

Marriner said to him, "Nice meeting you."

"Yeah, yeah. Right." He shook hands with Marriner and hustled out. "I got me a new lease on life."

On his way he brushed past Ed Gorton, who rolled his eyes at the sight of his friend Marriner. He said, "The Department's Most Unwanted Man and what does he do--walk into the building."

"And hello to you too. We've got a date."

"At the coffee shop, for God's sake."

"I get confused--you know, I'm screwed up in the head."

"Don't I know it."

Gorton shook his head in wonderment, with reason as Chief Bentley chose this moment to pass by. He was accompanied by another old friend of Marriner's, Lieutenant Frank Harbison.

The Chief said, "Well. I thought you were dead, Marriner."

"Wishing won't make it happen, Chief." The Chief turned to Gorton, "Whatever we're booking him for, make it stick."

"Let me," Harbison said. "I'll enjoy it."

Marriner retorted, "First you'll have to learn to read, Harbison. I'm here on a case, Chief, want to see how much progress you've made on the Annabelle Angel murder." Gorton explained to the chief's puzzled look: "Cold case."

Marriner continued, "Officer Pinckney here was updating me but can you believe it, fell asleep on me. In mid-sentence! Guess he's been working overtime plus."

Chief Bentley nodded at Harbison and he moved over, shook and slapped Pinckney--who came to, groggily.

"Hey there, Perry," Marriner greeted.

Pinckney was stunned a second time at the sight of the bigwigs. Harbison growled, "What the hell happened?" Pinckney shook his head trying to clear it and held his hand to his sore jaw. "Fuck! This man assaulted me!" He had trouble pronouncing, and his words came out as if they'd been mixed in a rusty blender. "I find a witness Mister, you're in deep shit."

The Chief responded, "Mr. Marriner doesn't care about witnesses. He'll slug people in broad daylight and damn the consequences. One, he figures you'll be too embarrassed to pursue charges. Second, he banks on his war record. But the war's over."

"Hey, is this the same guy who bitchslapped you, Chief?"

Pinckney was right, but the Chief's look told him what anybody else would have--it doesn't do to be right sometimes. The Chief said to Gorton, not taking his glare off Pinckney:

"Take this trash out to the nearest dumpster, Gorton. Before he hurts someone else." And for Marriner's benefit: "If you step in here again, you won't be stepping out real soon."

Marriner had a parting shot for Pinckney as he headed out with Gorton. "You were so right, Officer. Lot of deep shit around here."

At the door and out of earshot Gorton just shook his head again. "One word: why?"

"Two words: Annabelle Angel. Case isn't cold any more, and now they know it."

7. GWEN

"Nice place," Marriner said to Gorton.

They had seated themselves in a coffee shop just off Hollywood Boulevard, the antithesis of a "nice place": vinyl and fake wood, scuzzballs and low-lifes galore, a hum and buzz of noise, activity and anger.

"Any action out there in Banning?"

"Yeah, I cracked a big case just the other day." A young waitress, very attractive in a punked-out way--e.g., her hair frighteningly frizzed but tied down with a giant girl-next-door bow--brought them menus.

"Hello to you and good afternoon. My name is Gwen and I am to be your waitress today."

She was sniffling. "Cold?" Marriner asked. He liked her accent very much, and that wasn't all. She nodded. "I was up late last night walking my snake."

"He sick too? "

"He's not sniffling."

"What's good here?"

"The atmosphere."

"Anything else?"

"The atmosphere."

Gorton said, "I'll have a BLT."

"I am sorry, what is that?"

"You don't know what a BLT is?"

"I am so sorry. I come from France. I am here since 2 months and you know...I am just learning LGBT. "

Marriner said to Gorton, "And you thought her accent came from Brooklyn." To the waitress: "Make that 2. The cook will know what it is. Being Spanish."

"How did you know? Yes, his name is Miguel. I call him Miguelito, because he is cute little guy. "

"I'm Johnny." Marriner was curious if she considered him a cute big guy, but he remained all business.

"How is the coffee?"

"How you say, it's your funeral." Marriner got the hint.

"Ice water."

"Make that two," Gorton said.

"So nice to meet you. I will bring your food very soon." Marriner watched her as she moved away to fill their order, a slight smile creasing his face. Gorton said, "Bring me your tired, your poor, huddled masses."

"Yeah," Marriner said, "and most of them ended up in this coffee shop."

"Look, on the Force we get an hour lunch time now, and anyway, if I took you to a respectable place and respectable people see me with you, my career's over. If it isn't already after all that oil you just poured on the flames."

A customer at the adjoining table suddenly raised his voice.

"What the hell is this?"

Marriner and Gorton turned and saw he'd just opened a styrofoam doggie bag to find--bones. The waitress Gwen said, "It is what you asked for, the bag for your dog."

"Jesus Christ, where's my chicken! I want my chicken, not a bunch of goddamn bones."

"But a dog, he likes the bones."

"Jesus Christ!" The manager came hurrying up to calm the storm. "She's new here, sir, please accept our apologies." She handed the Styrofoam doggie bag to Gwen. "Take this back right away and fill it with a full course.."

"Damn foreigners," the customer said, glaring at her. "You some kind of dumb frog or what?" He said to the owner, "Since when you been hiring dumb frogs?"

"We'll add a dessert too, on the house."

Gwen looked upset and teary at the insults and the owner led her away quickly.

Marriner got up and moved over to the table. Gorton just shook his head--here it comes.

Marriner stood over the customer. He glared down at him. It was the kind of look that could have resembled a maniac's except it seemed more controlled--the look of a psycho in perfect command of his destructive capabilities. Or as Gorton once described his friend, "one bad SOB."

"You were pretty nasty to the pretty lady."

"Excuse me?" The customer said it brusquely. "Mind your own business, pardner."

"When she comes back, you're going to say thank you real real politely and then get the hell out. If you don't, I'm going to bitch-slap the brains out of your head, if you have any. Then I'm going to start on your teeth. You understand me, pardner?"

The customer looked up, ready to object in very clear terms, but Marriner's psycho look made him pause. Not to mention he was, by any angle of vision, a very big dude. He looked over at Gorton for succor.

"You going to let him threaten me like that, Officer?" Gorton answered, "Until he assaults you, I can't intervene. He could just be BSing you. If he does knock out some teeth, be sure to keep them for evidence."

The customer thought this over. Marriner spat out, "What's it going to be, you weasly fuck?"

Gwen came back with two huge Styrofoam doggie bags. "We are so sorry, Mister. This is all for you." The customer said, softly, "Thank you." Marriner added, "He's sorry he overreacted. Isn't that right, sir?"

Marriner was glaring. The customer swallowed hard and nodded. Then stood, turned and walked out.

Gwen said, "Have a nice today, sir. And come back so soon." She watched him a moment, then said to Marriner: "How you say this funny expression, the tail between the legs. What happened?"

"He forgave and forgot. Let's give him credit. Sorry for his dog, though. That was a good dinner."

Marriner went back to their table.

"You make loose cannons sound like firecrackers," Gorton said.

"What can you tell me about Annabelle Angel."

"Nothing. Officially. Harbison had the case and didn't do shit. As far as I could tell from his reports, he didn't get very far, less from his own incompetence than there was nowhere to go. Come on John, you know the type. Girl comes to Hollywood with dreams and ends up in a nightmare. Last trace was a kind of halfway house run by Jesus freaks. Apparently she went off with a guy no one ever could ID and a few months later, some desert rat kicks up some dirt and there she is. Terrible thing but we've seen worse, right? Whatever family she had back in Iowa wanted no part of her or her story, just couldn't be bothered."

"More likely, Harbison couldn't be bothered. How much you going to share, like the good buds we are? "

"You know I can't do that."

"Yeah," Marriner said, "I know you can't."

Gorton shoved a few Xeroxes across the table. "Hell, the Chief probably likes it that I'm the point man, so I can blow the whistle when you go off unlocked and unloaded and we'll have to arrest you. My question is, who in hell hired you?"

"You wouldn't believe me if I told you, so I won't."

"Couldn't have much cash, or you wouldn't have asked me to pick up this bill."

"No, that was for old times sake when I used to treat you."

"And when would that be? Somehow I can't remember. Look, let's face facts. One, your license is revoked. Reason obvious. Two, after today every cop in this town is going to have your picture taped to his sun visor. Three, this case is textbook 'persons unknown.' So what are you gonna do besides spend your retainer, which you're so damn good at?"

"Well to begin, I'm going to save your life." Marriner had seen the derelict shuffle into the coffee shop, but not his gun until the barrel was shoved point blank against the back of Gorton's head.

"Freeze!" he screamed. Gorton did.

Movement and activity in the restaurant ceased. All eyes focused on the derelict. His own were wild, stoned. Gwen had arrived with condiments for their table. Marriner reached out to touch her leg and push her behind him. The derelict shouted, "You people are going to die! Him first."

Marriner raised his hands in a calming gesture, stood very slowly, shielding Gwen.

Gorton said, "Take it easy, man."

"I hate cops. Cops harass my space. My freedom to live. I'm going to blow out your brains."

This was said to Gorton. A middle-aged woman in the restaurant broke out in sobs. "It's no loss, lady," the derelict said.

"The food ain't that bad, pal." The derelict whirled toward Marriner. "What did you say? "

"I said kiss my ass." The derelict glowered. Marriner pushed the waitress further behind him.

"No, you're first." He came over, placed the gun at Marriner's neck. Smiled. Squeezed the trigger slowly. Gorton reached for his gun. The derelict whirled, getting the drop on Gorton. "Don't fuck with me!"

The waitress suddenly reached in her uniform pocket, tossed an object on the table in front of the derelict. He looked down.

It was a baby boa constrictor, its ghastly eyes staring upward. The derelict gasped at the horrific sight.

Marriner slugged the derelict. He fell to the floor, out cold.

Gorton leaned down to cuff the unconscious derelict and said to Marriner. "You could have skipped the fucking conversation."

The patrons hummed and buzzed, returned to their food and drink. Another LA moment. "Poor Wally," Gwen said.

"You know this clown?" Marriner asked.

"When his teeth of wisdom hurt he goes crazy. "

Gwen petted the snake maternally. To Marriner and most any objective observer the boa was a revolting sight.

"My eagle eyes see what might freak an eagle's. Boa constrictor."

"They make great pets," Gwen said.

"Every kid should have one."

Gorton pulled the derelict to his feet, led him out past Marriner.

"Remember what I said."

"What was that?"

Gorton moved past with the groggy derelict. To Gwen: "On my bill, with a big tip for you."

Marriner looked upward as if making an effort to recall. He counted with his fingers. One, two…"Can't remember the third," he confided to Gwen.

She asked; "How much for this tip?"

"Just add 100%. If he complains next time he's in, tell him he might not be in if it wasn't for you. See you later."

"I hope this so much."

8. APARTMENT

Marriner got lucky and found an apartment in Santa Monica near the 10 Freeway, a small bungalow amid one of the rare properties that rented by the week. The manager Joe, who to all empirical evidence wore a sleeveless T-shirt morning, noon and night, had some slumlord in his blood. He explained to Marriner that he'd have to pay in cash each week and that if he expected repairs, he'd better be prepared to wait.

"Good handymen are hard to find, you know."

"Is that why the front door won't lock and just barely closes?"

"Naw, that's because of Tony, the last tenant. He had so many chicks and they got so jealous they'd just bang the shit out of that door till he opened up. Then they'd cat fight inside. One day he took up with a bodybuilder and there went the lock, know what I mean? That's what happens when you reach a critical mass. Explosion. So one day Tony just up and skipped town, or wherever. Didn't leave an address or phone number. Some underwear, though, still under plastic, designer shit. Some sex tools, too. Hey, apartments in this property don't come vacant too often. You ought to thank Tony and that busted door."

"I get the picture even if I didn't hear 50%. God bless the city fathers for sinking the freeway below street level. Otherwise I'd have semis crossing through my ears."

"Hey, after a while it turns into Muzak. You'll sleep like a baby with a rattle."

Marriner paid him a week's rent. Joe asked, "Hey, what business you in?"

"The kind where you don't answer personal questions."

"Oh. Right. Well, enjoy the apartment."

"I'll try to do without the sex tools."

#

Marriner dined at the local KFC on Wilshire Boulevard and though he knew the Colonel's menu recipes were standardized, thought the quality fell short of his favorite High Desert franchise.

He had hoped the traffic barreling down the 10, then turning onto the PCH for Malibu, might diminish some in the evening, but if so, his ears couldn't parse the difference. Anyway as Joe said, after a while eardrums became so battered they mushed the noise into a constant decibel range that could be tolerated--at least for a certain period of time. Marriner hoped that would be short.

Joe had been taking the air and a beer from the comfort of a canvas lawn chair in front of his apartment office, and it didn't take a crack private eye to understand he'd welcome any kind of chatter to pass away the evening, and any tenant who got caught in his web, willingly or not, could expect to pass some time and at least a six-pack.

But Marriner let it go at "Have a nice evening" and zipped into his bungalow. He had work to do.

Annabelle Angel had not been very active on social media, but she had a couple of accounts and they'd stayed up. Marriner followed her from the beginning. She'd posted a short bio, her roots in Iowa--"just like John Wayne!" With the exclamation mark--then rhapsodized about her trip West to Hollywood as if it were taking her to the Promised Land. In many ways she was a cliché, like so many others who had come West to LA and crashed and burned, for one reason or another, and there were thousands of them.

On her sites she said nothing about an absent alcoholic father, depressed and suicidal mother who harbored what used to be called wayward passions, a series of lovers who brought nothing but more heartbreak.

Marriner had gotten this background from the Mother Superior. "She prayed with a fervor that not all who come here had, but like a blazing fire, one day it just burned out. Along with her faith. I prayed for her. And I still pray."

The movies showed a right shining happy life could be had, and even though Annabelle knew she was chasing a fantasy, she lived for fantasy. What else did she have to live for? In Hollywood, if nothing else the eternal sunshine might cure unhappiness.

On the Web Annabelle put up a front worthy of the cinematic sunland she aspired to.

She reveled in a beautiful day as if it were her last, lyrically describing a clear day when she could see the mountains "like they were there all along, just waiting for me to look up and see them in their glory."

Various people "liked" what she posted, and she had a few people who counted as her Internet friends, but none seemed to be close to her heart.

She reminded Marriner of a butterfly, beautiful, fragile, fluttering and prey to stray winds. From her first post to her last, he saw a progression, or more accurately, repression.

Thoughts would not be finished, phrases became so cryptic they were incomprehensible. Something was driving her to a kind of desperation, if he read correctly between and below the lines.

In the last photos she grew even more beautiful--softer and more tender, he thought. She looked wistful, as if she knew very soon she'd have to let her dreams die. In her last post she'd taken several photos of desert flowers. It had been a rare southern California winter, exceptionally rainy, and it had created a wealth of wildflowers scarcely seen in a generation.

One video had shown her dancing around a swimming pool that Marriner thought might belong to a desert home, possibly even Palm Springs, as the mountain slope behind reminded him of the San Jacinto eastern foothills. In the last, Annabelle strolled in the desert among a magnificent splurge of flowers.

She wore a white dress and seemed to dance even when standing still. For once, she seemed happy, smiling and acting for the camera, which caressed her with its lens, moving closer and closer through the flowers until her angelic face filled its frame, lovely and wistful and, Marriner thought, in love.

He wondered who was behind that camera. Whoever it was, he thought, had fallen in love with her like others had, but she was there with him and his camera and nobody else. That meant something.

9. TURKEY

Farmer's Market on Fairfax bustled throughout the day, but early mornings before 9 the cafes brought retirees and the rich and famous and anybody else who wanted to begin the day with coffee and bagels and any other form of breakfast starter. When the sun rose enough to heat up pavement and smog, most of them left for other pastures.

Marriner had gotten up early and gone surface roads. He wasn't looking for avocados at Farmer's Market, but a person who resembled one minus the green, and he found him. One of many things that set Turkey apart was that he didn't hide his presence. He'd worked enough in past lives for intelligence-gathering agencies-- that was his own euphemism for enterprises both above and below board--to know that if they wanted to find someone, they would, especially if he was the one doing the finding, so no need to go through the motions of incognito. Nowadays, he knew well and often said, "everyone is cognito--God bless our connected world." It had made him prosperous enough to while away daybreaks at Farmer's Market, shooting the bull with whatever circle of cronies he could ingratiate himself with. The flipside of his open source policy of course was that Marriner had no trouble spotting him.

"The answer's no," Turkey said as Marriner took a seat across from him. "I don't work in an operations capacity no more." He pointed to the medical alarm strung around his neck. "Nurses and docs can hear everything we say if I beep the button. Understand what I'm saying?"

"Yeah, and I bet it's been juiced up enough ET could call home with it. And hey, good morning, I missed you too. I drop by for a bagel and who do I see but my old friend Turkey, enjoying the good life he deserves for jobs well done."

"Yeah, real small world we're living in. LAPD's inhouse Net went berserk yesterday after you just 'dropped in.'"

"So you're still listening in. That's naughty, you know."

"It's fun. I can tell you some stories."

"Want to hear what I got for you? Besides some extra cash?"

"No." Marriner opened his computer. Turkey grimaced.

"Some day real soon they'll put that model in a museum. Or junk yard."

They drank more coffee and Marriner ate a bagel, even two. He showed Turkey what he'd seen last night. It was surprisingly hard for him to see the images again. "Her name--"

"I know her name."

"Lot of names here too. Could be fans from nowhere, could be her killer."

"Do you realize how many systems I got to hack to trace these addresses? No, I don't think you do."

"Stupid me. And here I thought you had an in at the NSA."

"Even if I did, I might not be able to do the job. Which I won't anyway because as usual you ain't got a dime's worth of pennies to pay me."

"Man, you really are retired, thinking I'd come here and ask you to work for free. You can shake off the rust, here's two days of unofficial employment." He wrote a figure on a napkin. Turkey said, "Not even half of half what this costs." But he added, after tapping on the keyboard and replaying the video of Annabelle dancing, "I'll do it for her."

10. BOARD AND CARE

Marriner brought his SUV to a stop outside what looked like a converted farmhouse. A sign on the patchy lawn read: RIDGELEY BOARD AND CARE.

There were two men in the ragged, ill-kempt yard as Marriner approached. One was sitting at a cheap metal patio table, staring ahead blankly, never changing expression, oblivious to Charley, the man behind him who was trying to shatter karate-style a plank of plywood set on two sawhorses.

Charley gave a fierce cry, brought his hand down BANG on the plywood. It rattled but remained intact. Charley looked pained.

Marriner knew someone who could give Charley lessons, but she was not available so he approached the blank-faced man, who obligingly wore a name badge like Charley, in the shape of a cross: Horace.

"I'm looking for Jillian Layne," he asked.

Horace stared ahead, impassive, imperturbable. Marriner knew the look. In the very old days it was called shellshock, but modern times had given it many more dimensions and causes.

"Been nice talking to you," he said, and moved toward the home's entrance as Charley again banged the plywood vainly. "Better this way," he said to Charley, and held up his hand in rigid, slashing, proper karate fashion.

Charley had been banging his flat palm on the plywood. Marriner's insight hit him like a magnificent revelation and changed his day, if not his life. As Marriner nodded his approval, then headed inside, Charley turned back to the plywood, raised his hand high, shrieked, brought his new weapon slashing down. The sound of shattering wood and Charley's exultant cry of echoed behind him as Marriner stepped inside the home where a group of the residents were gathered around a television set watching Rev. Jubal Joy preach his distinctive word.

The home was furnished in the simplest, most basic vinyl and metal cafeteria style. The residents were motley--all ethnicities, elderly, younger men and women. They were all staring, without conversation or animation or hint of emotion, at the television. It was a prerecorded evangelistic meeting whose fervor needed no boosting. When the Rev. Joy exclaimed, "Friends, despair's just a word. Strike it from your vocabulary!" the television congregation heartily cheered this sentiment. Marriner eyed the group. Only one bearded man had seemed to notice his arrival. He was staring at him. This man's badge read: Richard.

On the TV Rev. Joy raised his voice even higher: "No matter what your lot, no matter what your pain, lift up your hearts in joy, right now. Let me hear you!" A roar from the crowd was followed by a copycat roar elicited by Richard.

"Let me hear you!" he echoed, and all the denizens who'd seemed comatose or indifferent raised their voices all together.

"Louder!"

And it was.

"All right. You're doing fine." He flipped the channel of the television and an old B-western starring John Wayne appeared. The spectators settled in.

Marriner noticed Richard staring at him--a long, suspicious stare. He moved on.

The back lawn had a paved basketball court and a game was in progress where every play was an adventure. Most of the players showed various degrees of skewed coordination. They were shooting at a weathered backboard and ragged-net hoop. Refereeing this endeavor was counselor Jillian Layne, an attractive woman in jeans and sweatshirt.

Marriner entered the yard. One of the onlookers, badged as Larry, noted his arrival. "That Jillian?" Marriner asked him. Larry nodded. Studied him for a moment.

"You going to have sex with her?"

"I hadn't planned to."

"I have sex. With women. It feels good."

"More power to you."

"Yeah. Power." Larry turned to watch the game and Marriner did likewise.

One of the players, Joey, had the ball but was prevented from driving or feinting by a very tall gangly man who had a tight grip on the back of his trousers. Joey was spinning and twisting futilely. The other players desisted and objected loudly. Joey raised a loud wail.

Jillian blew her whistle. "All right, game's over."

From one of the women players, Joanna: "Who won?" Jillian responded, "It was a tie."

This puzzled the players but after a few moments of hard thought they nodded--sounded right. Jillian motioned to Joey for the ball. The gangly man had let go of Joey and was lumbering away.

"A tie?" Joey asked Jillian, who nodded yes.

"I had the shot! "

"You never shoot."

"Doesn't matter!" He slammed the basketball on the ground. It bounced high and rolled away on the grass toward Marriner. Joey stalked away teary-eyed with anger and frustration. Jillian stared after him, finally turned and noticed Marriner, who'd picked up the ball. He said, "Guess the ball's in my court."

"Mr. Marriner? " He nodded.

"I have some information for you."

Moments later Marriner was eying a photograph of Annabelle Angel smiling happily with the other residents of the board and care home, some of whom he now recognized.

"How long was she here?" he asked Jillian Layne.

"Two months." She showed him another picture. Annabelle was solo, smiling for the camera. "That's how she looked when she left. One day she just packed up and departed. She had changed. You've seen the kind of residents we take in. All of them are damaged in some way. Annabelle was open, honest, full of life, even if her hold on what was real and what delusion became more and more delicate. She became secretive, troubled. She wouldn't say why."

"Where did she go?"

"Address unknown." She paused. "I should tell you, all the while she stayed with us, a man would come by sometimes and pick her up; then she'd return very late. I had to make a special arrangement with the night guards. You could almost believe he'd parked her here for two months to keep her out of mind, out of sight until he needed her. "

She anticipated his next question. "I never caught a glimpse of him. Like I said, very secretive. When I read the news about her death--murder--I felt very guilty."

"So did everybody who ever knew her, apparently--except the killer. She lived in a mean world."

"We did all we could to help her but you know, we only provide some necessities. The population changes every week and it hardly makes for stability."

"Who runs the place?"

"That I can't tell you, very sorry. I probably shouldn't even be talking to you. The organization prizes confidentiality. Please do understand."

"If I do, it'll be one of the first times. But I do thank you for your time and cooperation."

She handed him a piece of paper. "I do have this." Marriner took it, eyed it quizzically.

"The place she worked before arriving. We had to have some work history, otherwise...well anyway. Do you know it? "

"From the outside. The people who go inside need other kinds of necessities."

11. HOUSE OF ECSTASY

It was a garish purple building with a bright yellow neon sign blazoning HOUSE OF ECSTASY. Lighted signs on the walls and front advertised the offerings: MASSAGE, SAUNA, WRESTLING, OTHER TACTILE DELIGHTS. Marriner could almost see it from the bar at the Formosa Cafe, where he had been wont-- "I like that word," he had said many times about cocktails, before one of the Formosa bartenders who had studied English literature before deciding to become an actor informed him of the true definition--to relax after a hard day chasing the guilty or the next client.

Or to wash down the bitterness of a case gone foul, like his last one in LA.

He'd come to the fabled Formosa after navigating past the "strumpets"--a word the literature major barman had taught him- strolling the streets not far away. One of the strumpets had implored Marriner, "Come on honey, let me suck it for you."

"I declined," Marriner told the current actor/bartender, who opined philosophically, "When duty calls, sucking distracts, you know." The Formosa had been known for generations as a place where one could digest failure and bitter philosophy as well as cocktails in the pitiless world of show business. Hearing this, Marriner felt right back at home.

At nightfall the neon lights of the House of Ecstasy were flashing garishly when Marriner entered.

Inside behind the counter was a man dressed in a grotesque imitation of a cowboy: boots and rhinestone-studded pants and huge unwieldy Stetson tilted rakishly on his head. His name on the manager's plaque on the counter matched the getup: Percy Laredo.

Percy was fiddling with one of the sex novelties in which the House of Ecstasy abounded. A customer entered. Percy looked up, watched him for a moment, then returned to his task.

Percy tilted the object up--a porcelain replica of a woman's breasts. Percy flipped a switch. Red lights in the two nipples started blinking.

"Hot damn," he exclaimed.

Satisfied it worked, Percy got up and moved over to greet the customer: Marriner, dressed to resemble a rube and displaying a rube's open-mouthed wonder at what he saw in the sex parlor.

Marriner was inspecting an object that resembled an electric cattle prod. A logo on it recommended that you "give your baby a charge."

"Some place, eh?" Percy ventured.

"Sheeitt..."

"Massage, motion pictures, full participation activities. Whatever your little wee-wee wants, we got."

"Sheeitt..." Marriner whistled.

"Just don't ask for the burro. We shipped it out." He cackled, enjoying his own joke.

Marriner chuckled: "Don't want no goddamn burro, I'll tell you that. I want Annabelle."

The cowboy's laughter faded right quick.

"She was real real nice to me last time. And so pretty. She's about the most beautiful woman I ever seen. And I seen some. Don't you think I haven't, Mister whatever your name is."

"Percy Laredo."

"That means...you're from Texas!"

"There you go, I just knew you'd figure that out, you're quick on the draw there, hoss. Listen, Annabelle don't work here no more."

"Where'd she go?"

"Can't tell you. Private life means private, man. That's our philosophy here. Whatever you do within these walls stays, and that includes certain organic byproducts."

"I really liked Annabelle. Really really."

"Hell I did too. We played house all the time." He laughed again. Marriner zapped him with the cattle prod device. Percy yelped and hopped like a jumping bean.

"Hey, it works," Marriner said. Percy was angry but had to stifle it for the customer's sake. He rubbed the sore spot in his ribcage.

"Hey, we got some new girls here'll give you all the action you want. Try 'em, you'll like 'em."

"Well..."

"Hoss, the nooky train's rollin' out of the station. You climbing aboard or not?"

Marriner thought a moment...then answered by goosing Percy again. The electric shock made Percy jump in the air like a frightened cat.

A short time later Marriner was flying through the air, hurled over the shoulder of a very large, very muscular woman clad in a skimpy bikini named Tawny. Marriner landed with a thud on the canvas-matted floor. He had stripped down to his socks and a pair of ridiculously long and baggy boxer shorts.

Tawny rushed over, pinioned him and looked toward a huge man, the referee Magog. He held up his fingers, counting. One, two, three. The round went to Tawny.

She got up, moved over to her corner and sipped a glass of water. Marriner lurched to his feet, rubbing his throat. "Sheeitt, you're something."

Magog rang a bell, signaling the start of another round.

Tawny yelled "Aieeee!" and rushed over. With amazing gymnastics she used Marriner's own leg to leap onto his back and grab his neck in an armlock...trying to wrench him to the floor.

He managed to squeak out, "What happened to Annabelle? She treated me real nice."

For answer Tawny sent him tumbling across the floor and into a wall. Marriner got up slowly, rubbing his neck. Tawny strutted and flexed a moment, reveling in her prowess. "You just one big all-talk sucker."

"Last round," Magog yelled.

Marriner said, "I'm not getting through here."

Tawny came running over toward him, leaped high in the air, attempting a karate kick. Instead Marriner ducked and knocked her legs to the side, causing her to land hard on her back and head. She yelped, feeling real pain.

"The name was Annabelle."

Tawny got up quickly, angered by her fall. "Aieeeee..." She leaped into the air, attempting to kick him with her feet, but Marriner ducked and knocked her legs out from under her again. Marriner pinned her arms.

"Annabelle."

Tawny struggled to break his hold. "Never heard of her. Honest."

Tawny looked nervous. She looked over frantically at Magog, who quickly gonged the bell, signaling the end of the round.

"Match over, man."

"Already?"

"You did a job."

Marriner kept Tawny pinned and applied some pressure.

She said, "I just started here, man. Talk to Percy."

"You swear you don't know where she is?"

"Hey, I swear." She looked scared now. Marriner got up slowly. Tawny rose to her feet, rubbing her back.

Marriner looked downcast. He started to go, then turned back to Tawny. "Cross your heart?"

Tawny nodded, quickly crossed her heart. Marriner walked out slowly, looking like a man bereft. "Gonna be so lonely on the ranch. I had plans."

"Fuck," Tawny said to Magog, "any more like him, I'm outta here."

Magog opined, "Love's a hurtin' thing, baby."

12. PSYCHO

While Marriner waited for Turkey's info, he dined--if that was the word--at the Hollywood coffee shop. Gwen seemed happy to see him and neglected a couple of customers while she advised him on what to order. After some discussion, she basically concluded that nothing on the dinner menu was worth eating. "I'll have a steak and fries," Marriner said.

"First Miguel must kill the cow," she countered. When Mariner didn't respond, she explained, "That was a joke."

"Sorry. Too hungry to laugh."

"Ok, I get this picture."

"How is er..."

"Bobby. Last night he was so happy. I let him run around--well, like the snakes run you know--"

"Slither."

"Slither?"

"Yeah. English, she is a crazy language. I don't know boas. Rattlesnakes, yes. I can even imitate one. You ever met a rattlesnake?"

"Oh shit no." She pronounced it "sheet," of course.

"Tell Miguel I'd like it medium well done."

"Ok, I get this picture."

As she moved away to fill his order, he made a mental note to himself to not let her get away any further than the kitchen. He had fallen under her charm, and just hoped that his would make an impression.

The boa constrictor would probably come with the territory, but perhaps with age and full growth, Gwen could be persuaded to give Bobby a better home in a nice zoo or better, the Amazon. Marriner had always wanted to see Rio and Sao Paulo and the jungle from a discreet distance, just enough to release Bobby into a land where he'd belong better than Hollywood.

The call from Turkey came while Marriner was ordering dessert. He scribbled Turkey's info on a napkin.

"Pie," Marriner said.

"What kind?" Gwen asked.

"Pie."

"We have lemon, chocolate and blueberry."

"Does it make a difference? "

"Not really." Gwen wrote the order.

Marriner said to Turkey, "John Smith? What's his middle name? John. John John Smith. No wonder he changed to Percy Laredo. And what about his employer? Hell yes it's a shell company. You're being paid to look into the shell. Pretend you can live up to your reputation. I know a great place, the steaks are fabulous, dinner's on me."

He signed off. Gwen brought him the pie. "I have to go see a guy on business. You working tomorrow night?"

"If it is the night, I am working. It's very late for you to do business, no?"

"This guy is a real rat. Night vermin. Except Bobby would spit him out."

#

The rat, Percy Laredo, came down the hall of a rather ratty-looking building, stopped at his apartment door. Fished around for his keys. Maybe he'd had a few before leaving his place of employ. The apartment was small but well furnished. Percy dropped his hat on the coffee table, puttered around, yawning.

Suddenly a hand reached out, wrenching him around. He choked with alarm when he recognized the intruder: Marriner.

"Annabelle's dead," he said with a look of as much anguish and despair he could muster. He was still playing the rube.

"How did you get in here?"

Marriner snarled his words. In his eyes was the glare of a psychopath. "You killed her!"

"You better get the hell out of here, man."

Marriner took out a length of nylon cord from his pocket and deliberately whipped it taut between his hands. Percy's eyes widened as Marriner started advancing slowly toward him.

Percy retreated, but managed some bravado. "I don't want to have to hurt you, hoss," Percy said, "get your sorry ass outta here."

Marriner stretched the cord tight, whap. "I didn't kill her," Percy protested. "I swear. Cross my heart, see?"

As Marriner advanced, his face registered uncontrolled emotions. "Who killed my Annabelle? Who?"

"How the hell would I know?" Percy took a swing, figuring he'd suckered his intruder and would catch him off guard. But Marriner, quicker almost than the eye, raised the cord in defense and caught Percy's hand in a loop.

He wrenched the cord tight and thoroughly trapped Percy by the arm, then dragged him over to a kitchen chair. Marriner deftly pulled the cord around and tied Percy to the chair.

He moved around to face him. "I loved her. You're going to die like she did, and not quick." While speaking he'd ripped off one of Percy's shoes and pulled off a sock.

He stuffed it in Percy's mouth. Percy let out muffled yells.

"Yeah, it stinks," Marriner said. "Like you." He went over to Percy's small studio kitchen, opened up a drawer and pulled out a butcher knife. It was lean, large and mean and he looked satisfied.- Marriner came back, held up the knife in front of Percy's eyes.

"One by one, body part after body part. You're gonna feel the pain." He grabbed hold of Percy's ear and stuck the edge into the cartilage. Percy struggled and Marriner had to hold him down.

But suddenly he left off, as if realizing what he was about to do. He bent over as if overcome by pain and emotion. He clenched his fists, closed his eyes, suppressed a sob. Percy relaxed a bit.

Marriner straightened up. His lips were now foaming. He gurgled--the saliva came sputtering out. Again he leaned in close.

"We'll start with the tongue. So you'll never bullshit a helpless young girl again."

He wrenched the sock out of Percy's mouth and with his left hand grabbed him by the hair, jerked back his head. Brought the knife down slowly--

"Wait, wait! Wrong man, I swear! I swear, I'll talk." Marriner hesitated.

"You don't got no tongue, you can't talk. That's a fact." As if this was just dawning on him.

"Yeah, that's right! Lemme keep my tongue!" Marriner lowered the knife, then quickly stuck the edge in Percy's crotch. And not gently.

Percy yelped. Marriner leaned in, frothing at the mouth. Some of the foam splattered him. Percy cracked.

"She slept with the wrong guy. Understand? Somebody big." Marriner spat more foam onto him. He slowly raised the knife.

"Who?"

"I don't know."

"Liar." Marriner put the knife to Percy's throat. Tears came to his eyes.

"I loved her so much. And you don't need a tongue."

Percy screeched. "My boss ought to know. Talk to him. I swear I just work for the guy, Spoke Lacey, that's his name. Spoke Lacey. He learns I'm talking to you he'll kill me, so hell, go ahead and get it done, boy. I'm one fucking burnt piece of toast."

"I believe you," Marriner said in a calm, non-psychotic voice. "Spoke's got his dirty hands in all kinds of shit." He straightened up, mopped his brow.

"Whew. Hard work being a psycho." He backed away nonchalantly. Pulled out a tube of toothpaste from his pocket, dropped it on Percy's lap.

"More dentists recommend it," he said. Percy's terror gave way to rage.

As Marriner strode jauntily out the door Percy screamed, "Asshole! Bastard! I'm comin' for you, hoss!'" Marriner closed the door and he stepped out into the hallway, ignoring Percy's screams that suddenly gave way to: "Hey, untie me!"

13. UNTRUE CONFESSIONS

In front of the Catholic church near Sunset two types who looked capable of felling redwoods without axes, Bob and Elfego, were horseplaying.

Bob said, "Come on, taco bender, lemme see what you got." Elfego held up his palm. Bob pummeled it with his fist--POW. Elfego's palm moved slightly from the force of the blow. He smiled at Bob's futility.

Bob held up his palm. Bob smiled, daring Elfego to do his worst. He did--POW. Bob's face contorted with pain. He doubled over in agony, holding his palm.

Bob was still holding his injured hand when the church priest came up to them. "I am Father Gilroy."

Elfego and Bob exchanged puzzled looks. Father Gilroy was beaming.

"I was told you want to join the church but you have some doubts. Tell me my sons. Let me show you the way, the truth and the life." Elfego and Bob were at a loss. Elfego said, "But...I'm Catholic, Padre."

"When was the last time you received Communion?"

This gave Elfego pause.

Inside the church a number of parishioners were taking places one by one in pews, waiting to make their confessions. A tall impeccably dressed man, imperious and imposing, strode in with the air of, "Get in my way at your peril"--but that was an exceedingly polite way to describe Spoke Lacey, who noted the red light above the priest's booth in the confessional came lit. Without pausing he brushed past an elderly lady who had started toward the confessional and entered the penitent's booth.

The lady looked none too pleased--perhaps she would have to confess to immoderate anger when her turn came.

Inside the confessional Lacey kneeled, made the sign of the cross and zipped into his confession--he was a busy man--indicating it had been one week since his last confession and "I took the Lord's name in vain many times. Missed mass last Sunday. And Father, I'm still afflicted by impure thoughts." He heard what sounded like a snicker from the priest's booth. Lacey blinked, but concluded. "For these and all my sins, I am heartily sorry."

Lacey waited to hear his penance, which he knew from experience with Father Gilroy usually consisted of several Hail Marys and repetitions of the Lord's Prayer. Instead from behind the latticed sliding port: "Oh cut the crap."

Lacey was stunned. "Pardon?"

"What about the pimps you put back on the street? The girls you turn into hookers? Pardon, my ass." Lacey's eyes widened. "Confess," the voice said. "You're an asshole."

The panel to the priest's booth slid open violently...revealing—

"Marriner!" Lacey blurted. Marriner reached out and grabbed Lacey's tie, jerked him forward. Lacey's head came slamming forward through the partition, effectively pillorying him.

"Happy to see me, Spoke?"

"Screw you!"

"That's no way to talk to your confessor." Marriner wrenched the tie, choking Lacey, pulling his head tighter in the narrow partition.

Outside the elderly woman looked askance as the confessional rocked with the commotion going on inside.

Marriner said, "Annabelle Angel. What happened?"

"Who the fuck is that?" Marriner slammed him forward again with a harsh jerk of the tie.

"Somebody took her swimming in the desert. Who?"

Lacey shook his head--as much as was possible, managed to gurgle out: "Somebody big."

"Who?"

"Somebody big enough, I'd sooner you kill me than tell you. So go ahead, do it. And go straight to hell while you're at it." Marriner jerked on the tie, choking him. Lacey's face started to turn blue...

"You're going to hell first." But at the last minute Marriner let go. Lacey gasped for air. Marriner concluded, "I forgot your penance."

He slugged Lacey in the jaw and he tumbled out of the confessional booth. The waiting penitents, the elderly woman among them, eyed this in astonishment.

Compounded when they saw Marriner, not a priest, exiting the confessional.

Outside the church Marriner encountered Father Gilroy, still administering the gospel to the bewildered Elfego and Bob. "Did they come around, Father?"

"Well, I'm afraid they need a great deal of instruction."

"Have them help with the collections. They're what you might call specialists."

Marriner suddenly whipped his hand up in a pistol motion, snapped his thumb like a trigger. Elfego and Bob both reflexively slapped their breast pockets where their guns were holstered.

Marriner chuckled at his ruse, moved away.

Lacey exited the church, disheveled, rubbing his jaw. At a glance he took in his men and Father Gilroy, saw Marriner getting into his car.

To the former he said--he would have many other things to say later-- "Remember that guy."

14. BOZOS

Marriner was seated at a table in his favorite coffee shop. It was late. He was the only patron.

As Gwen the waitress moved around him cleaning up, Marriner eyed his cup of coffee. Curious, he took a straw from the bunch furnished in a dispenser on the table, dropped it into the coffee.

The thick, viscous liquid soaked it up. There was even a slight hiss--as if it was immersed in toxic waste. Marriner noticed Gwen peering over his shoulder at this demonstration of the coffee's lethal potency.

"Me, I would not drink another one of this coffee."

"Me, not either."

She wiped the table.

"You're a woman," he remarked.

"And me, I am proud of this."

"Hypothetical question. You change your appearance--hair, clothes, everything. Move. Don't leave a forwarding address. Why?"

"You are running away or you are hiding something. Or yourself."

"There's one other possibility. You're not right"--he tapped his temple--"up here."

"Who is?"

"Good point." She sat down across from him.

"What kind of girl keeps a snake? "

"I'd prefer a man."

"Glad to hear it."

"But you know, these guys I've been meeting, Bobby he has more the personality. "

As if on cue the snake popped its head out of a carrying case that she sat on the table. "We're going home, little boy. It's late and you need your how you say, beauty sleep."

Marriner couldn't help but flinch at the sight of the snake's ugly head. "How big is that--he--going to get?"

"Let's just say I will need a bigger pocket."

"He ever try any hanky-panky? "

"*Comment?*"

"Mischief. Bad things."

"No. He hasn't reached the adolescence yet. Me, I think he will be a good boy."

She turned…bumped into a man's chest. A big man. Magog. She gasped at sight of his leering face. He grabbed her, held her fast. At about the same moment Percy put a gun to Marriner's head. Cocked the trigger. "Feel that? Huh? We're talking brain sandwich, boy. Frisk him, Magog."

Magog nodded and started frisking Marriner. Gwen asked him, "Who are they?"

"A pair of bad boys. Dildoes you might say."

Percy tapped Marriner's head with the gun barrel.

"Hey, you wish." Percy picked up Marriner's coffee cup. "This yours?"

"Have some. It's delicious."

"You lying fuck." Nevertheless Percy took a sip. "Good coffee. Too good for a psycho like you."

"Toxic is as toxic does," Marriner said.

Magog pulled out Marriner's gun, pocketed it. Then Marriner's wallet. Percy said, "See if he's got a gold card, Magog."

Magog held up the wallet. No cards. "Cheap fuck," Percy spat contemptuously.

The cook Miguel came out from the kitchen area, one of his larger butcher knives in hand. Percy had turned his back to conceal his weapon when he spotted Miguel, who asked: "Everything all right here?"

Magog looked to Percy for direction. "We were just leaving," Percy said. "Ain't that right, folks?"

"I'm leaving," Magog affirmed. "Got shit to do." Marriner said to Miguel, "No sweat, Miguel. Even if he did have a gun, he wouldn't know how to pull a trigger." Percy glared at him, in a rage.

"Everything is okay, Miguel," Gwen said.

"You're sure?" he asked.

"Yes. You can lock up?"

"Yeah." He still eyed the newcomers suspiciously. "You need me, give me a shout."

"Sure thing," Percy said. "We'll shout in Spanish, too."

Now it was Miguel's turn to glare, but he turned and went back into the kitchen.

"What are you going to do with us?" Gwen asked. "We don't have money. You want more coffee or a dog bag?"

"We're gonna put this boy in a dog bag," Percy answered.

"You collateral damage, baby," Magog added to Gwen. He went back to frisking Marriner.

Percy said to him, "All right, that's enough. For Christ's sake, you'll give him a hardon."

"Jealous?" Marriner said.

Percy leaned in close. " Pretty soon, yours'll be just a memory."

"Let the girl go."

"No, I need her. To replace Annabelle. Now we're gonna go outside and jump in my truck. You wanna run, go ahead. I ain't one of them cowboys who won't shoot a man--or woman--in the back. Let's go. "

He waved them toward the exit.

"She can't leave her snake," Marriner said.

"Yes, he would die," Gwen said. Without asking for permission, she hurried over, pulled the boa out of the carton cage and picked up the boa, wrapping it around her arm.

"That is one ugly sucker," Magog said. "What is it?"

"Earthworm," Marriner said.

"Aw, you're shittin' me now."

"Let's go!" Percy yelled.

#

Percy led Marriner and Gwen into a room at the House of Ecstasy occupied by a large glistening pool. A sign above it read SENSUOUS SAUNA.

"See there, Magog. This big cowboy psycho acts tough but he's a pussy. All I had to do was aim this little pistolero at his girl friend, and he turned into pansy candy."

"Drop the guns and I'll take on both of you," Marriner said. "Come on, you chicken shits. Hand to hand, let's do it."

Magog said, "You want some of me you gonna get it, man, and you ain't gonna be tellin' nobody 'bout the experience."

"Down, boy," Percy said to Magog, "first I'm gonna show him some tricks with his little lady."

Magog said, "Stiff her, Perce."

"Hell, I am. Get me some of them self-help devices."

"What for?"

"I need 'em, dammit."

Marriner said, "I was wrong. He isn't a dildo."

"You gonna be ok?" Magog asked Percy, eyeing Marriner.

"Yeah. I got the gun and he loves every hair on his lady's head."

Magog headed into the other room.

Gwen said, "You are how you say, a creepy."

Percy hovered near her lips: "Creeps make good lovers."

"Back the fuck off," Marriner said, but as he stepped forward Percy put the gun closer to Gwen, threatening to shoot. Marriner stopped.

Gwen raised her arm with the snake in Percy's face and he recoiled in horror.

"Ahhh!"

"Sic him, boy."

Percy said, "I'm gonna shoot that fuckin' reptile too." Magog returned with an armful of "devices" for Percy--apparatuses designed to assist or substitute for sexual performance. "No, man. I been wantin' me a pet." To Gwen he said, "Lemme have him."

"He doesn't like you."

"Gimme, baby. Else I'll be followin' Perce and I ain't gonna be usin' no tools."

"Go ahead, Gwen," Marriner said. "Boas like the smell of dung."

"Dung?" Magog said. "What the hell is that?" Even Percy rolled his eyes at that one. Magog took the boa.

"Wrap him around your arm, like I did."

"I know that, baby. This is how you do it."

Suddenly the snake bit into his arm.

Magog screamed in pain.

Marriner seized the chance, rushed forward and belted the distracted Percy full on the jaw.

He obligingly fell backward into the pool sauna and let go of the gun, which Marriner gratefully took. Magog was preoccupied with Bobby, who despite his best efforts to loosen the snake's grip clung fast. Magog kept yowling and hopping around in severe pain.

"He an iguana or something?" Marriner asked Gwen.

She said, "When boas do not know someone they bite and they do not let go. Unless you really pull and then the skin…" Marriner nodded. He quickly moved over and grabbed the snake, and with fuller leverage than Magog could bring to the situation, wrenched.

The snake came free, taking a huge chunk of skin with him. Magog screamed, grabbed his bloody arm. Marriner picked up one of Percy's sex apparatuses--a green cord with phalluses stenciled on it here and there--and looped it around Magog's neck before he could react.

In a moment he had pinned him back against one of the support pillars in the room. Magog could reach back and grab the cord but do nothing to loosen it.

"I'm hurtin' man! Get me to a doctor!"

Gwen said, "He is drowning I think." She meant Percy, who was floundering in the pool, still stunned and half unconscious.

"Oh yeah," Marriner said. Marriner moved over to the pool area, grabbed Percy by the hair and dragged him to the edge of the pool. He slapped him a couple of times and Percy revived somewhat.

"Talk to me, hoss." Marriner said.

"Kiss my tumbleweed."

"Your little posse. Whose idea? "

"Me and Magog put our heads together."

"Not many IQ points there."

"Figured we could impress management. Get a pension plan or something."

"You are a moron."

"Hey, that ain't no reason to shoot me."

"You're right…unfortunately." He let go of Percy and stood up.

"Next time we will shoot you," Gwen added.

Marriner was amused. "Yeah. We will."

Magog shouted, "I need help here, man, I'm bleedin' bad. Call 911 or somethin'."

Gwen wrapped the boa around her arm, cooed. "Did he hurt you, Bobby? He is a bad man."

"He's a bad snake!" Magog yelled. Marriner handed the gun to Gwen. Went over and untied Magog, who coughed as the tension on the rope around his neck slacked.

Marriner confronted him. "You wanted me. Here I am." Magog held his arm.

"I'm handicapped. Wouldn't be fair. Next time."

"Okay," Marriner said, then hauled off and punched him backwards. Magog fell into the pool beside Percy.

"Jesus," Percy said disgustedly.

Marriner took Gwen by the arm and they left. Marriner had a parting shot, shaking his head at Percy's stupidity: "Right. Pension plan."

Percy watched them go. He made no effort to help Magog, who floated in the pool like a dead whale. He leaned back against the pool wall. Grimaced, suddenly realizing how battered he was. He felt his jaw, winced.

Percy said aloud to Magog, "I been beat up, verbally abused, stomach hurts like hell--and I got gas. Fucking coffee. It ain't been a good night. What else can happen? "

Magog was in no position to respond, and Percy could have cared less anyway.

He managed to lift himself out of the sensuous sauna and slosh over to one of the mirrors set up all around the room to excite sauna denizens. He examined his jaw. "Fuck," he said aloud, "sucker's gonna swell up like a balloon." He touched it softly, winced.

Behind him he heard the front door open, and footsteps. "I told you everything, goddammit. Don't know nothin' else."

He said that without turning. When he did turn, he saw not Marriner, but Elfego and Bob.

15. UCLA

Marriner and Gwen walked down the mean streets of Hollywood toward his car. It was late and they passed the late-night life of the town: drunks, a few gawking tourists, panhandlers, cyclists, hookers, three hulking transvestites in black dresses and blond wigs, ordinary people...all merging in the faded glory of Hollywood's underside.

"What did you do to make them so mad?"

"I was trying to get a database. For some reason they didn't approve."

"Me, I think they were not nice people."

"You could tell?"

"Everybody calls you John, but I prefer Johnny. Do you mind this?"

"Me, I don't mind."

"Is your life always this dull?"

"Only in Banning. That's where I live. But I've got a chic apartment in town and I think you should spend the night there. You and Bobby. Those bad people might come back."

"Well, I appreciate your saving Bobby's life and my honor but--"

"Both had top priority."

"But--"

"Yeah, you have to get to know me better. "

"Are you keeding? That's what nights are for. I just wish I had my nightgown. It's really cute, you know. This is no problem for you?"

Marriner gave her a long look. She seemed perfectly sincere, and untroubled by the possibilities inherent when a man and woman passed a night together for the first time.

She read his thoughts, which Marriner had thought would be impossible in the current post-combat state of his mind and thoughts.

"I am French, you know. I don't have so many of what you call them, hangups."

They passed a short night, sleepwise. Gwen was amused by the unlockable front door but less so by the nearby freeway. "How you say, 'sweet nothing'?"

"Sweet nothings. They're supposed to be whispered in a woman's ear."

"Do not waste your time. My ears are occupied."

Nevertheless they enjoyed each other and the sensuous night. In the morning Marriner took a long shower, one of the apartment's amenities that manager Joe said he was very proud of, to the point where Marriner wondered if he was aware that every apartment in LA possessed the same amenity. While he was wondering, he thought he heard voices, and worried about Gwen and the return of more of Spoke Lacey's goons, he hurried out.

Two women were just leaving. From what Marriner could tell from the back, they were the kind that could stop traffic even on the nearby freeway. "Poor girls," Gwen said. "They were looking for this guy Tony. They were so sad to hear he had skipped the town. The blonde, she said she is very rich and will pay you so much money to find him. She is afraid he knocked her down."

"Up," Marriner said.

"Up where? She doesn't live in Beverly Hills. She said Pacific Palisade."

She meant Palisades, but Marriner didn't bother correcting her this time. "And the other one?"

"Tony dumped her so bad, just like a so hot potato. That's what she said. She just wants to strangle him. They made friends, these girls. So many angry girl friends, they can form a posse, you know."

"From what I could see, they won't have trouble finding new boy friends."

"They are not your type. One is too rich and the other too sexy." Marriner had to think a moment, wondering whether he should thank her for saving him from making a serious error of judgement.

"What is my type?"

"Are you blind or just silly?"

She pronounced it "seely."

Marriner drove Gwen home to her apartment in Westwood, near UCLA.

"I'm studying ecobiology in the graduate school."

"What the hell is that? "

"The study of the environment. How it sustains itself. The interactions. How it degrades."

"No wonder you work in Hollywood. An A number 1 degrading environment. "

Marriner had gotten off the 405 at Santa Monica to avoid a bottleneck, and on the surface streets he came to a stop to let a group of children pass on their way to school. When they had done so Marriner leaned out his window and said to the crossing guard:

"You're doing a great job, Officer. Our children and their parents appreciate it to the max."

Instead of grinning at the compliment, the guard glowered in a rage and came over. It was Pinckney.

He said to Marriner, "You're scum. The worst kind. "

"Hey, I was serious. You've found a niche here."

"I know it was you stole my badge."

"You lost your badge? And you told your superiors? Good move."

"I'll be back on the beat, and when I am, you're toast." Marriner was blocking traffic and the typical LA motorists behind him responded in typical LA fashion, by honking as if the Big One was coming and life or death depended on the next few seconds of speedy travel.

"You know what you should have done? 3-D printing. I know a guy could have duped your badge in five secs. And nobody would have looked twice. You'd still be on the beat and--"

The klaxoning had become deafening and Pinckney, frustrated to the max, interrupted and waved Mariner on. "Get the hell outta here."

"Keep up the good work, Officer."

As they rolled away, Gwen asked, "Did you really take his badge?"

"I'll give it back when he earns it."

Gwen lived in a student apartment in Westwood and she explained to Marriner that she had a tenuous relationship with her roommate, an exchange student named Tasha. "We have a one-bedroom and two single beds and Tasha loves capitalism. Me, I appreciate some of the capitalism but I don't feel the need to sleep with every capitalist I meet."

Consequence, Gwen frequently had to sleep on the sofa while Tasha continued her studies until the wee hours of the morning.

"She does not appreciate Bobby."

"Can't imagine why." Marriner had slept well, if briefly, but had dreamed of a grownup Bobby pissed off by something he'd said or done, and Gwen reprimanding the rascal when it was way too late to save him from compression.

At least, he said to himself and her in the dream, she would have less body mass to litter the environment when she disposed of his cadaver.

Gwen dropped Bobby off at her apartment, which was in the heart of the heart of the Westwood student district. Any thrown rock would have hit someone on his or her way to class or from same, or just as likely, the spacious lawns ideal for sunbathing.

Tasha had commandeered the bedroom again, and was spending the morning with the latest capitalist.

"She is how you say, skipping? Skipping class again."

"Politics makes bedfellows. Or so I've been told."

Gwen gathered up her books.

"I met the FBI. They came by and asked me to keep an eye on her. This is legal?"

"If the FBI says it is."

Marriner drove her to campus and blanched at the astronomical parking fee, but they passed a very agreeable moment at one of the school snack bars, drinking coffee and watching the passing parade.

"You can audit the class if you like."

Marriner knew he wouldn't like, but it was another opportunity to pass time with her, albeit passively. He sat and squirmed repeatedly while the professor lectured to 100 or so students on the virtues of sustainable development in Third World countries. Marriner couldn't help but wonder if Banning qualified as Third World. He decided he would invite Gwen for a weekend and have her make an assessment. She was a serious student, taking copious notes and at one point posing a question for which the professor complimented her.

Marriner understood neither the question nor the answer.

Afterward Gwen asked, "Did you enjoy this class?"

"I learned a lot."

"The Green Revolution is coming."

"Any green plant in Banning would be most welcome."

"Well," Gwen said, "now we can do what everyone here does. Have a lunch in the sun."

"Sounds good."

Marriner's cell buzzed and he answered. Gorton was calling, and summoning.

Marriner said to Gwen, "This afternoon you have to skip a class."

16. INTERROGATION

When Harbison and Gorton arrived at the House of Ecstasy that morning, they found the Sensuous Sauna charred and blackened from an electrical fire. Two lab technicians were lifting Percy Laredo's body from the smoking, soot-stained water. As the body was lifted up a uniformed officer retrieved a charred radio from the pool. Gorton quipped, "Must have been listening to the Firebird Suite."

Harbison wasn't amused. He was examining the array of sexual devices meant for Percy's use. Gorton moved over to where Magog's body still slumped, held to the post by the cord that had been used to strangle him. Harbison commented, "They took their time with him. Bad way to go."

"Like being barbecued isn't?"

One of the uniforms came over to Gorton. "Got some interesting video for you." He inserted the recording on his laptop. It showed Marriner punching out Percy and stringing up Magog.

Gorton stared at the footage, not believing what his eyes were seeing. From behind he heard Harbison say, "Well well well."

Harbison insisted on interrogating Marriner and Gwen together. "She's a French chick, right?" he asked Gorton, who he also insisted should be present despite his demurs. "She doesn't cooperate, we'll put her on a plane back to gay Paree."

"That hellhole," Gorton said, "yeah, she'll cooperate."

When the suspects were seated Harbison growled, "No goddamn handholding here."

"She's new to this country and LA's finest," Marriner said. "Somewhere she read how the boys fired thirty-five bullets into a woman who didn't pay her electric bill."

"I paid my bill," Gwen said. "I can show you the *facture*."

"Lady, we're talking murder here. A Mr. Percy Laredo got deep-fried and his buddy"—he turned to Gorton, who cued, "Mr. Magog Roosevelt"—got hung out to dry, permanently."

"He is dead?" Gwen said. "This is a strange metaphor."

"She's studying ecobiology at UCLA," Marriner said to Harbison, "ask me to translate if she uses words you don't understand."

"She wasn't at UCLA last night. She was with you at the House of Ecstasy when you attacked both these gentlemen. We've got the video."

Marriner said, "So you saw Mr. Laredo waving his gun. He lacked a vital male organ, you know."

"That why you killed him?"

"When we left," Gwen said, "he was wet and unhappy but how you say, kicking and alive. You saw the video, yes?"

Marriner added, "Somehow I think the video ran out at that point in time. What a misfortune."

"Yeah," Harbison said, "You shut it off to cover up your crime."

"Come on, Frank, don't compare your brain to mine." Gorton intervened before Harbison could do something the police manual forbade--"Come on, John, tell us something we can work with. I'm stupid enough to think you're not stupid enough to off these losers. So who did?"

"They worked for Spoke Lacey. If you didn't know that before, you do now. When Spoke disapproves of your work performance, you can end up out of work." He looked directly at Harbison and added for his benefit: "Permanently."

Harbison turned to Gwen: "You'll get bored with him real soon. And when you do, give us a call. I'll see you get a Green Card real quick. Life in LA's real good."

"If you pay your electric bill," Gwen said. This astonished all three of the men in the room and for a moment they were speechless.

Marriner's lawyer Sklar Jeffries arrived late, as per usual. He shuffled in, sweating heavily and disheveled and not up on the case, also per usual. But he worked on contingency and Marriner appreciated this aspect of his practice.

"Chasing ambulances wears you out, doesn't it Sklar?" Gorton said it with irony and as a joke but Marriner knew that Sklar probably had, in fact, been out chasing an ambulance.

"My client--clients"--he'd noticed Gwen. He thrust out his hand, "Sklar Jeffries, glad to meet you. Don't worry, we'll beat these charges." He turned to Marriner: "What are the charges?"

Harbison shook his head. "Talk about lowering the bar. When you passed it--if you passed it--they must have subbed a driver's test by mistake."

"Careful, Officer," Marriner said, "you're talking to my attorney here. He's won a lot of defamation cases." He turned to Jeffries--"Haven't you?"

"What I'm hearing here is what I am not hearing. You don't have doo-doo," he said to Harbison and Gorton, "and pardon my French."

"You speak French?" Gwen asked him, and for a second time this gave everyone pause.

"This meeting is over. Harassment, that's what it's called. Police brutality. My clients invoke the right to remain silent." He turned to Gwen. "In this country the law provides a powerful counterweight to abuses of authority." Harbison said, "Take your clients outta her before I puke."

Afterward Marriner complimented his lawyer: "Your usual excellent job. Very thorough." Marriner knew that Sklar drove his opponents nuts, and this often proved very useful in quickly resolving cases, as opponents preferred settling anything, everything rather than deal with him a second longer.

"You'll get the bill. You got a fixed address? If you're back in LA, I'll have plenty of business, so stick around for a while."

He handed his card to Gwen. "I handle a lot of immigration cases. Spicks, micks, frogs, you name it, I respect cultural differences. That was a joke by the way."

"You got a car?" Marriner asked.

"Hell yes I got a car. What attorney at law doesn't?"

"You, the last time we met."

"I'm doing well. It's classic, a vintage model I've fixed up."

"Keep the motor running. Like you said, I'm back in LA."

17. FARMER'S MARKET

Turkey was working where he relaxed, Farmer's Market over bagels and coffee that kept coming with free refills. From time to time his cronies would stop back to shoot the breeze, or manufacture one if, as so often happened in LA, there was none.

"They're like skeeters buzzing around," Marriner told him, "and how the hell can you get any work done?"

"First, they are oldtimers who've earned the right to be irrelevant and sit here and watch the world go by, like myself. Second, haven't you ever heard of multitasking?"

"Yeah, but in Afghanistan and other places like that you don't want to be on your cell checking messages and miss a bullet that's got your name on it."

"Here you can't get killed by a chocolate donut. Check out these names."

He handed him a list. Marriner glanced at it. "Her social media friends. I'm paying you for what I already know?"

"Check the addresses. You're lucky because I've already eliminated the casual acquaintances--which I might add I was able to do in one afternoon in between heavy conversations here with Josh Lichtman. She didn't have many deep friends, even back home.

"And you will note that it's lean in the men department. They 'like' and sometimes they comment but she never responded. Never. Like she was media deaf."

"Who's Barry? He checked in three times."

"A hound dog man. He met her at a party and she blew him off, and that got him really pissed. He's the type from what I figured from my limited knowledge of human nature, pokes and runs, and she cut it off before it leaped into action."

"Don't undersell yourself. I've always said if you'd been around in Freud's day, no one would've heard of Freud. How's the DNA analysis coming?"

"What DNA analysis?"

Marriner sipped his coffee and just stared. Turkey blanched.

"No. You are seriously asking me to track down and cross check and double cross check and basically spend hours and hours finding a family tree? Where we ain't even got a tree and the twigs are lying all across the country. You said yourself Gorton wouldn't give you the breakdown. How am I gonna get the readout?"

"They had to send it out to the Bureau and NSA. You know those places like the back of your bagel."

"We're getting serious here."

"Spoke's boys took out a couple of flunkies. He's fronting for some big bucks this time."

"Yeah. I ain't getting anywhere with my completely legal informatic intrusions."

"We have to get creative. What's your trouser size?"

"Oy oy vey and oh shit. All the ohs. You don't worry about bringing on a coronary to an elderly gentleman in retirement?"

Marriner finished his coffee and put some bills on the table. Turkey said, "Hey, I could buy lunch and dinner with all that."

Marriner didn't respond, but Turkey read his expression.

"Right. I'll get on the DNA. Search the known universe if I have to."

"It's garbage the known universe doesn't need. We're going to remove it."

18. ANNABELLE'S FRIENDS

Marriner confirmed Turkey's assessment of Annabelle Angel's social media friends, who were just that, there for the listing and occasional "Like."

But Linda Harrell was different. She had met Annabelle at a one-week rental building north of Hollywood Boulevard and they'd clicked, to the extent of having dinner and drinks together sometimes.

"She went off into these bizarro jobs and sects, you know. And I'm like your basic salesgirl. I don't do crazy shit and I don't like people who do. But she was different. You wanted to hold her and hug her and say everything is going to be all right. She was the kind of person you wanted to be happy. She deserved to. And not because she was drop dead. I mean, when we walked here it was like crash city, all these rubbernecking guys on skateboards banging into palm trees."

Marriner had met Harrell at a snack shop in Santa Monica and they strolled along the beachfront promenade. It was a picture perfect day.

"When I got my place here I said come on Annabelle, I've got some space and we get along, it'll be great. Rent's sky high but I'm working and I can carry you along for a while if you get in a crunch. It made sense but she wasn't practical, you know. She didn't care about practical shit. That's why she fell in with the Joy crowd."

"What's that?"

"You don't know the Ministry of Joy? They make Christian Science look like a Mickey Mouse pom-pom team. Last couple of times I saw her, it was like a light would come on behind her eyes when she talked about them. Like she'd found the answer to whatever she was looking for. You know, typical sect victim. But then, what's scary, I'd see the light go out and it was like, is anyone home? Are you losing your mind, Annabelle? After a while she'd be back to her sweet little self but that was like...scary, that's all I can say, real scary."

"She ever talk about a lover?"

"Yes and no. She had somebody, but she'd never say who. She'd have these trysts you know--is that the word, where you meet and screw around and it's like forbidden? Anyway that's what it seemed like from what she said, which wasn't much. I didn't push it. I respect private life, you know."

When they said goodbye Marriner thanked her and Linda said, "I don't understand why anyone would want to hurt her. Was it like some sick psycho or something?"

Marriner thought a moment and said, "That would make it easier to understand."

Barry was harder to track down. He worked two bartending jobs like most handsome young guys in LA who wanted to make it in the film business, and when he wasn't working he was dating the girls he usually met in his line of work or on auditions.

All this per Turkey, who'd done a good job of backgrounding.

Marriner found that the only way to pin Barry down was to queue up to his bar at a chic "bistro" in Beverly Hills near Rodeo Drive that specialized in champagne.

He asked Gwen what the word "bistro" meant in French.

"It means bistro. A place you can eat and drink *pas chère*, pretty cheap."

"Not this bistro. If I get back late, it's cause I'm washing dishes or looking for a way to sneak out the back door."

"No problem," Gwen said, "I'll just drink some tea with Tony's girl friends."

Another two had dropped by looking for Tony while Marriner spoke with Linda, and Gwen confirmed that she'd saved him again from making a mistake consoling beautiful girls who were almost too beautiful to be true, ergo not his type. Marriner wondered if Tony had fled to the suburbs or, conceivably, Banning, and how he would fare in a territory not so fertile with goddesses.

As for Barry, he was cut from the same mold as Tony, but not in the same league. He served from behind the bar and did his job well, insofar as it could be done in between buttering up wannabes and chatting up the ladies.

Marriner was neither, but he was able to catch 25% or so of Barry's sporadic attention. He had to nurse a couple of champagnes by the glass, both of which were far too rich for his blood or Banning's, but Barry remembered Annabelle well.

"She shot me down," he said, "or I guess you could say, didn't bother shooting me down. That was kinda worse. I was nobody with a capital 'N', and that doesn't happen too often to me if you want to know the truth. That's one reason I remember her."

"What's the other?"

"Sex. I mean, I licked ye olde wounds and picked up this girl who was a real babe, like 10 and a half on a scale of 10, and we banged like bunnies all night. And all the time I was thinking about this skinny blonde."

"Didn't seem skinny to me."

"Compared to who I was with, yes."

He moved over to serve a customer with a Rolex who wanted Crystal champagne for his lady. Marriner recognized him as a director who'd just had a hit action film. Given the scene and Barry's inevitable sucking up, it would be a while before their conversation would resume. Marriner nursed his drink and waited. At the appropriate interval he downed the champagne which was not Crystal, but would have to do considering his budget.

Fortunately, the house had the capitalistic consumption philosophy and Barry wasn't permitted to let a customer's glass go empty more than a minute. He scooted over.

"Another?"

"Hit me," Marriner said. And while Barry the barman poured: "Tell me about the party."

"I'm not religious or anything and for damn sure haven't been born again--hey, I'm still going through birthing pains. But this guy Joy gives great flings. He invites producer types and big shots and presses the flesh, know what I mean? The mayor of Palm Springs made the scene for a while and I shook his hand."

Marriner said, "God knows you might become a big star but right now you're climbing the ladder. How did you make the scene?"

"Well, if you want to know the truth--"

"I do."

"I crashed the party. Everybody knows if you arrive late the security's thinner. I caught a look at the invitations and forged one, just like that. It's easy to do, you know. And then I rushed past the gatekeepers so they wouldn't have time to look it over too close. There, you've got my secret. Anyway, at that point who the hell cared? I didn't even have a room reserved. In a crunch I'd head back to LA, but I believe in myself. A lady blows you off, you move on and get luckier the next time."

Marriner was glad that Barry's prowess was interrupted by more customers. It was a while before he made it back, and his pocketbook was going to take a big hit if he kept chugging. So he just hung.

In the past, when he wasn't on a case, this had proved a useful strategy, as proven when a very attractive, and young, dark-haired girl named Liz sidled up to him.

"Are you going to buy me a drink?" she asked.

"No. Broke. You got a tin cup I can use?" This set her groping for a comeback, which she found: "You're bullshitting me."

"This is kind of my last drink before the streets."

She was getting annoyed.

"If that's true, you're using up bar space." Then calming. "But I don't think it is."

Marriner knew that if he continued the conversation, it could very well lead to a place he didn't want to go, and his place had a fiery French mademoiselle waiting, not to mention a rapidly growing and faithful boa constrictor.

He came clean and recounted this to Liz.

"I think you're full of shit but when and if you get it all out of you, give me your phone number. Maybe I'll call you one of these days."

Marriner sacrificed a cocktail napkin. LA was a fickle, capricious, stormy place and one never knew when one might need a port.

Barry came over and said, "That's about all I can tell you, man. If I think of anything else I'll get in touch." Marriner sacrificed his other cocktail napkin.

"You don't have like a business card?" Barry wondered.

"Private dicks don't do biz cards."

Barry was distracted as the bar was really hopping now and he was losing valuable networking time, so Marriner got his attention: "Somebody killed her. You're innocent till proven guilty. We can't rule anybody out."

"Now look--"

"You see anybody else hit on her?"

"Yeah. A guy."

"How did he look?"

"Just some guy. I remember thinking, Annabelle, this guy's minor league and once you find that out, you'll come running over here to old Barry."

"But she didn't."

"I lost sight of her. Got involved, like I said."

"Thanks for your time."

"That dance around the pool. It was like a vision. I'm not easily impressed, you know. Uh, we go up to 25% here." Marriner didn't get it at first, so Barry explained: "The tip."

"No problem," Marriner said. "I just got a new credit card. And add a glass of champagne for Liz."

19. EXTERMINATORS

Marriner and Turkey exited a truck across the street from a tall office building. They were wearing green uniform shirts and pants.

Turkey said, "The day I get to pee in a bag, I'll tell all the old farts like me all the shit you made me do."

"If you'd broke into his system like usual we wouldn't be here. You sure he's gone for the day? "

"He's in Santa Barbara with a lady who wouldn't notice us if we were peeled onto her nose. Her husband's in Saudi as per often. They lunch on lobster and 500-buck French wine at their favorite restaurant and then spend the afternoon at her beach house. Spoke don't want to be disturbed at these precious moments."

"Good work. What kind of wine costs 500 bucks a pop?"

"I'd tell you but it'll just be wasting vocabulary."

"Try me. I'm going to have a French girl friend."

"Something called Corton Charlemagne." Turkey pronounced it "Charley-main," but he was right, Marriner didn't know it from a water main.

Inside the building the security guards raised more than one eyebrow at them. BASH-A-BUG EXTERMINATORS was stenciled on the front of their uniforms. They were both sporting cheap shades and Bash-a-Bug caps. Each carried a pump can of insecticide.

Marriner said, "Got a work order. Mr. Lacey's office." A brief glance at the official-looking invoice and the two were waved on.

One of the guards shook his head and said "Damn. Bugs in this building."

Spoke Lacey's offices took up a whole floor and it wasn't on the ground. It took a while for the elevator to arrive. Marriner took a moment to admire the view.

"Nothing like this in Banning," he said. "Our idea of a high rise is two floors. You could say it keeps us grounded."

To which Turkey: "Hey, we got work to do." They entered the principal office. The Secretary working the reception desk looked up, as surprised as Security.

"Got a work order," Marriner said to her. He shoved the order form in her face. She looked at it. Surprised.

"We don't have bugs," she protested.

Marriner said conspiratorially, "That's what they'd like you to believe." He pointed at the signature on the work order.

"Mr. Lacey's never kept something like this from me."

"Lady, he was trying to shield you, and I respect him for that. But lady, while you're talkin' them bugs is breedin'."

"Worse than bunnies. Some of 'em," Turkey added.

"No time to lose," Marriner added.

"Roger."

They headed toward Lacey's office.

"Wait…" the secretary said, but they were already inside. She thought a minute, then got on the horn. "Get me Mr. Calvin."

Marriner and Turkey entered, shutting the door behind them. It had a bolt. "Convenient," Marriner said. "For discreet 5 to 7's." He looked at Turkey. "Well? Mr. Hacker Supreme. Since when do we need to bust in? "

"Since Lacey decided to download sensitive material to drives and sticks. He ain't as stupid as you think, you know."

"Almost."

Turkey got to work on Lacey's computer while Marriner looked around for storage. He fell upon a file cabinet immediately.

"He hasn't turned off paper."

Turkey said, "If you can read, do it." Marriner quickly rifled through the files.

A short time later, too short for the exterminators' efficiency, a well-dressed officious man, Calvin, strode briskly into reception and confronted the secretary.

"What in the hell is going on?"

"They say we have bugs."

"We will now, but not the insect kind. What the hell were you thinking?"

"They had an order from Mr. Lacey."

"Haven't you heard of something called a mobile phone?"

"He's incommunicado, if you know what I mean."

"Fuck that. Make him communicado."

Calvin marched over to the office door and turned the knob. Locked. He started banging on it.

"Open up!" He yelled.

In Lacey's offices Marriner was stuffing appropriate files in his equipment bag. Turkey said, "Got what I need to got." He looked over at Marriner. "What are you doing?"

"My job."

Marriner was spraying insecticide all around the office, in the least likely (for bug prevention) places: Lacey's desk drawers, spare cells, sofa for business associates . . . Marriner noticed a wet bar. He moved over, uncorked an expensive whiskey bottle and sprayed a dose of chemical for added flavor.

Calvin banged on the door again, then heard the bolt released. He angrily shoved the door open-- only to get a spray of insecticide on his pants, knee-high.

"What the hell!--"

Marriner said, "Sorry man, but you got any lice, that'll take care of em. "

"Who called you people?"

Turkey had hefted his own can of insecticide and was dutifully spraying in the background.

"What was that gentleman's name?" Marriner asked him.

"Lucy."

"Yeah, Lucy.Strange name for a guy, unless he's not really a guy, know what I mean?" He sprayed the floor, almost splattering Calvin's expensive shoes. Calvin jumped back.

Marriner said with satisfaction, "We had a job to do, mister. Now you're bug-free, 6-month guarantee. Give it 24 hours for the odors. Let's go man," he said to Turkey, "big job in Bel Air."

"I'm hungry," Turkey said.

"So are them goddamn cucarachas." They brushed past Calvin and the Secretary, headed out, moving at a professional pace, un-hurried.

Calvin pondered whether to call Security...settled on: "Hey, you guys show me your badge." Marriner and Turkey exchanged looks.

"Badge," Marriner said, shaking his head, and Turkey chortled.

"Check out our Website, sir," Turkey assured him as the elevator door closed.

Calvin scoped out Lacey's office. All seemed in order, undis-turbed. Two uniformed security guards entered.

"It's about time," Calvin reprimanded them.

The guards noticed Calvin's wet pants, smelled the smells.

Smirked while Calvin stewed.

As Marriner and Turkey exited the building, Marriner asked: "We really got a Website?"

"Hell yes, took me five minutes. That's bonus money, by the way."

"Desertlands Realty," Marriner said. "Is that a front or what?"

"It's a front," Turkey agreed. "Correct me if I'm wrong, which I never am, but you're going to be wanting to know for who."

"Whom. Like, now or five minutes ago."

#

Spoke Lacey had felt sufficiently worried by his Secretary's call that he'd left lobster and lady and choppered back to LA. When he stalked into the office he knew right away from the looks on the faces of his Secretary and a nervous Calvin that something bad had gone down. Lacey said, "Which enterprises are concerned?" The Secretary handed him a list and Lacey quickly scanned it.

"Should we call him?" Calvin asked. Lacey gave his underling a withering stare.

"Not we. You."

He stormed out.

Calvin was on the verge of shitting bricks. He glanced toward the wet bar, moved over to it and grabbed a cocktail glass.

Got a couple of ice cubes from the fridge. Chose his poison-- which would be, alas for Calvin, closer to reality in his case, because he chose the whiskey Marriner had fortified.

He glowered at the secretary. "For my coming to Jesus moment."

He took a big gulp. "Jesus!!!!"

20. CANYON DUSTUP

Coincidence or not, and Marriner thought not, an emotional Jillian Layne called him and proposed a meeting.

"I didn't tell you the honest truth when we met," she said. "I have a good idea who the man was Annabelle went out with. I don't know his name but I know enough about him for you to track down."

Marriner asked why she didn't tell him this "honest truth" before now.

"I was scared. I'm still scared. But I keep seeing her in my dreams, in that desert grave. I haven't slept well for days."

She said the Care Home owners--she swore she would tell him now who they were in person--held retreats from time to time at a ranch home in one of the Malibu canyons. She was spending the weekend there "for mental recuperation time" and it was secluded and private and suggested Sunday night for a rendezvous.

Marriner easily found the home from one of the oldtime mailboxes stobbed next to one of the myriad eucalyptus trees shading the extensive grounds, turned off and passed through the entrance onto a dirt lane leading to the house. He parked his 4x4 to the side.

A Honda was stationed there, also to the side. It might be Jillian Layne's car. Or it might not. Marriner reached the front door and found it was unlocked and open. Lights were on inside but when he knocked, no one came to the door.

Marriner pulled out his cell and called Jillian Layne. He got a message saying to leave a message, but he did not.

He went inside, closing the door behind him. "Jillian Layne!" he called out, to no response. Marriner began to move through the expensive salon, with a chimney for winter chill and your basic ranch style furniture and decorations--first taking care to draw down the shades on the two windows.

A faux Remington sculpture rested in an honored place on a flat marble stand near the fireplace. As Remington was one of the only 2 or 3 artists Marriner could cite, he moved over to take a look. It was magnificent, and Marriner realized it was not a faux.

He was in no hurry. He saw a wine rack with some well-aged bottles near the wet bar, which was formed in Western style from petrified wood and boasted an imitation Remington--check, Marriner thought, it looks like the real thing, too.

Gwen had promised to teach him a thing or two about good wine--"You keedding?" she had said. "With you we don't stop at 2." But even Marriner could tell that a vintage that had a label that seemed Bordeaux from 1926 would cost more than a typical month's salary.

He opened it, but left it there in the air to develop without tasting. Then another. And another. Soon they would become vinegar.

He found in a tall cupboard the kind of vacuum cleaner he was looking for.

Marriner called out again: "Jillian! Jillian Layne." He went upstairs and there too found what he was looking for: a closet full of shirts and pants.

He chose what looked to be the most expensive, a belt with a gold buckle and some exceedingly shiny black leather shoes. The furnishings in this bedroom were expensive and in the same ranch style as all in the house, as if it were a museum piece or model for a Home and Garden article. Nothing distinctive or individual. Even the Remington in the salon downstairs Marriner felt had been bought because the owner could buy it without worrying about money, and it fit a certain image of gentleman farmer.

Marriner suspected the owner was no gentleman. He went downstairs and began to clothe the vacuum cleaner, strapping trousers with the belt. In daylight it would have looked like a half-ass imitation of a scarecrow man, but in the dark and from a distance, and if someone didn't have time to look closely, it might seem humanlike.

Marriner decided to kill off another ten minutes before leaving. He went over to the wine rack, chose one and filled one of the crystal glasses arrayed neatly behind the bar. He gave a silent toast to Remington and sipped the wine.

"Fuck!" He said in admiration. He vowed to becoming a willing pupil for Gwen's wine course, and regretted he couldn't share with her some of these obviously extraordinary vintages.

On second thought, he picked out several of the oldest vintages, white and red, and stuffed them into his backpack, first lifting out his night vision infrared goggles. Marriner moved over to the front door and placed his vacuum man just in front of it. He turned out the lights and stood to the side of the door.

He reached over, turned the handle and jerked the door open.

Instantly a barrage of gunfire blasted his imitation man, blowing it to kingdom come. Some shots missed and blasted wall and lamps and whatever else lay in the line of fire behind the decoy target. Marriner thought that the owner might not appreciate this much collateral damage, but by then he had exited the house by the back and was sneaking to a perch he'd picked out behind a eucalyptus earlier that day when he'd come to reconnoiter.

His rifle was there, and while the would-be assassins were discussing between themselves whether they should move forward and body bag their victim, he put on the goggles and made out the two. They were not as well equipped as he, relying on their naked eyes. They would regret that, as well as falling down on their job. For sure, they would fall down.

Marriner aimed at the first killer's foot and fired off a shot. The scream echoed in the night air, maybe all the way to the beach, it was that loud.

The second assassin reacted like a frightened rabbit, whirled and looked around for the marksman, then panicked and took off running, leaving his associate to his pain and fate.

Marriner shot his foot off at the heel.

Now there were two men caterwauling through the night. Marriner got up and moved toward them. He took care to train rifle on them, though he knew that most men in their positions, badly wounded and in excruciating pain, would not have the guts and gumption to search around for the guns they'd dropped when wounded. That was the movies, and this was real. Nevertheless he took care to kick the first man's gun away. Through the howls he recognized Elfego, and not far away, Bob lay writhing.

"Fuck!!" Elfego screamed.

"Don't kill me!" Bob wailed.

"Call 911 boys, before you bleed to death," Marriner said.

"You'll make it if you don't take off on a marathon. Now you're probably thinking about calling Spoke Lacey, but Spoke doesn't like failure and it's likely to be your last discussion with the boss. You could tell 911 you were horsing around and shot each other in the foot. That might get you off, but then Spoke's B team would be waiting for you when you left the hospital. My advice is to blame everything on Spoke. You were just two dumb assholes following orders. LAPD won't have any trouble believing that."

While speaking Marriner had lifted off the fake "Canyon Security" badges they'd clipped to their shirt pockets. The boys nodded as best they could, but they had pain on their minds, and to an extent, how they were going to cope with a cane and other prosthetic paraphernalia.

"Well I see you have other priorities. Have a good evening."

Marriner headed toward his car, with some last bit of advice.

"Think about a tourniquet."

21. BANNING

Gwen looked in the back of the 4x4. Bobby was lying in a flat carton she'd fashioned for the trip. He shared the space with Marriner's entire armamentarium, covered only partially by a blanket.

"Do they all work?"

"The US Army doesn't screw up when it comes to weapons and ammo. There's something for every eventuality. Sometimes they invent an eventuality.,"

"Give me one good reason I'm doing this. Just one."

"It's more fun than graduate school." This, the truth, squelched her.

They had driven past the typical jams and slowdowns and along about Riverside, hit the hills before descending into the Morongo Valley.

Marriner told her, "When we arrive in Beaumont, we're almost home."

Gwen asked, quite logically: "Does your front door lock?"

That evening Marriner cooked swordfish steaks on his trusty barbecue grill, which Gwen insisted he scrub for the occasion, as it reflected many evenings of carbonized meat.

She had insisted he stop at a vineyard along the way, which he'd been astonished to know existed--"I have the eye of the eagle," she said--and ask for some trimmed vines that were just lying around baking in the sun and waiting to go up in flames, but she convinced Mariner that they contained juice still and lent excellent flavor to any grilled meat or fish.

"Plus they are not toxic like this carbon stuff, these bricks you use."

"Briquet. It's a French word."

"We gave it to you and this made us happy, to say bye bye."

Gwen made her own vinaigrette salad dressing, a mix of olive oil--which had never before graced Marriner's cupboard--mustard and a touch of spices Marriner knew existed but had never thought could enliven a dressing. He thought they grew in the wild and mostly stayed there.

In fact, he scarcely knew that one could prepare a salad dressing in your basic kitchen. "It comes in bottles at the market," he said. "Ranch, Thousand Island, French, Italian--why go to all this trouble?"

"You are so seely."

Finally Gwen threw him out of the kitchen with the firm request to prepare the vineyard wood for the grill, and chill one or more of the wines he told her a good friend had given him.

Turkey called and Marriner took it on the patio where he'd been exiled, watching Bobby curl around the ground below and wondering what the coyote would make of this undocumented immigrant.

"I got him, Mr. Big who needs fronts to hide his dirty linen," Turkey said, "and like we say in the information business, the easier knowledge to obtain, the less important it is. The bigger the info, the bigger the big shot."

"Stop before you drown me in metaphors," Marriner said, "and anyway I know what you're going to say and I'm going to be grilling fish steaks, drinking French wine and making out with a French damsel. You know the lady and you know when she says we eat at 8, she does NOT want me discoursing to you.

"Jeez, three-syllable words. All right wise ass tell me who I was gonna tell you who who is. And don't say 'whom'.

"His name starts with 'J,'" Marriner said "and if you listen to him, he's got a stairway to heaven waiting for him if he ever shuffles off this sinful earth."

"I'm betting he sins with the best of them. Or worst. How the hell you figure this out?"

"Call it divine intuition. He's going to welcome me into his flock on Sunday."

"You need any details from here?"

"All you got. We have broadband in Banning."

"And you got a broad who's way too high class for you, but she'll learn. So make hay while the sun shines. I'm gonna have sole and some appropriate veggies, not that you know what they are. She cooking the sides?"

"Call me when you've got the DNA on the killer."

"Yeah, well it won't arrive before dessert, so enjoy."

A lovely dinner was shared on the back porch--"Terrace, I prefer to call it." Marriner knew how to tell a white wine from red, and that was the extent of his oenological knowledge, as well as the general rule to drink white with fish. He chose one of his contraband bottles at random and found it extraordinary, but hesitated to say so in the event she detested it and his lack of taste would be displayed.

"Hey, it's drinkable," he finally ventured. She fired back, "You keeding? Search this wine on Internet." He did and found this particular vintage was selling--if you could find it--for a price that would pay his rent for quite a few fortnights.

"Your friend, he is very generous with you."

"He blows hot and cold. We'll see on Sunday."

They watched the sunset and listened to the coyote serenade. "This is like the Westerns," Gwen marveled.

On Saturday Marriner took her for a tour of the city.

"Well, what do you think?" he asked after she'd seen the sights.

"The oak tree on Elm Street is very beautiful."

"I think so too."

They stopped by the office.

Marriner hadn't heard much from Ana Louisa, and when he entered he discovered why. The mooning admirer had made such progress that he was sitting in Marriner's chair with his feet up on the desk. "You remember Toby," Ana Louisa said, making the best of an awkward situation.

"Yeah, but I forgot his feet." Toby got the picture and got up, offered Marriner the chair. "I've uh, been helping Ana with the paperwork."

"What paperwork?"

Neither one had an answer for that. Toby said, "Holy shit, what's that?" He meant Bobby, curled around Gwen's arm.

"My rat catcher," Marriner said. "He's going to clean up this place right quick."

Ana Louisa said, "You must be Gwen. I've heard so much about you. And the snake, too."

"So pleased to meet you. And Toby."

Toby said, "Sorry but I've like I've got to run. Big test, you know. Real braincruncher."

Marriner said, " You looked like you were studying hard."

"Yeah, well uh, have a great day everyone." Ana Louisa gave him a big kiss on his way out. "Ace it, okay?"

Toby got out as quick as his feet that Marriner had come to know would take him. "That kiss will really get his mind on his studies," Marriner said.

"You got a message from a Mr. Lacey. You know him?"

"To my regret."

"It's like, just one word. 'Truce.' What does that mean?"

"It means truce. You taking any English classes this semester?"

"No way. You have to read books and stuff." Marriner turned to Gwen. "Let's have lunch before I despair for the future of our country's youth. I know a great place." To Ana Louisa: "Want to join us?"

"Thanks but I'm lunching with Toby."

"Right. These one-hour separations can be tough."

Marriner's "nice place" turned out to be the restaurant next door.

"The frog legs are great," he told Gwen, "but you've probably eaten a million in your time."

"Never. That is such a seely cliché. Like every American eats nothing but hamburgers."

"That's mostly true. Try the frog legs."

"Where are they from?" Gwen asked Jun Yi.

"From water. Lots water."

"So they are very authentic," Gwen averred.

"Very authentic," Jun Yi agreed, and gave her an extra helping.

"A French girl comes to Banning to eat frog legs. This world, she is crazy," Gwen summed up.

They drove up into the mountains and passed the afternoon hiking on a trail above the picturesque village of Idyllwild.

After an excellent dinner at one of the town's haute cuisine restaurants--"No frogs tonight," Gwen vowed--they headed home for a nightcap on Marriner's "terrace."

He chose a red Bordeaux and they found each glass a wondrous experience.

As had been, Marriner thought, their day together. It was not Paris but Gwen said, she did not know Paris well and for all she knew, Banning might contain more delights than the City of Light.

"Are you keeding?" Marriner joked.

He was growing very attached to her. She was from a small village in the south of France and had come to LA with her boyfriend, who quickly grew homesick and fled back to familiar shores. Gwen, who had been reluctant to leave the shores she'd grown up on, found Hollywood and environs an adventure, and her studies stimulating and exciting.

"I do not give up," she affirmed. "I will get this degree."

There was adventure, and there was danger, and on this case Marriner was encountering both. And it wasn't finished. Tomorrow he would enter a lion's den in Palm Springs.

"Let's don't get too close," he said. "Like you said, these are bad people."

"*Au contraire*. That's why we must get close."

22. REVEREND JOY

The Rev. Jubal Joy, perspiring heavily and alone on a stage before his congregation's adulation, dialogued with them in the throes of evangelistic fervor.

"Lift up your hearts to the Lord! Tell him, Lord, I'm not worthy of you. I'm not fit to clean your boots. I'm a sinner. I've got hellfire and damnation in my soul."

"Amen!" the huge crowd seconded the reverend. A lineup of the afflicted and supplicant stretched at the foot of the stage on which Rev. Joy moved back and forth, playing the masses like a cathedral organ. In background were security guards, a gospel chorus and signs proclaiming the "Ministry of Joy."

"But Lord I love you," the reverend proclaimed.

"Amen."

"I fear you."

"Amen."

"And I'm a blessed member of the Ministry of Joy." He walked along the line of suppliants, bestowing hands, looks, blessings. The wrought-up reverend's ministrations brought their eyes alight, their swollen and aching limbs back to life, their spirits revived to wild fervor.

"I give my heart, my soul and my hard-earned dollars to the Ministry. Look kindly on me, Lord!"

"Amen."

"Let me hear you!" The congregation began chanting as in a Negro spiritual: "Amen, amen, amen."

Various factotums moved through the crowd with collection baskets. Donations piled in as the fervid excitement mounted.

Joy said to a supplicant: "Heal, brother." To another: "Give me a smile! A smile. The Lord said I am the way and the truth. Listen to my minister."

Joy had not always served "my Redeemer." He'd worked as a scientist at a top pharmaceutical and pioneered various innovative drugs whose commissions brought him a healthy fortune, so that when he was born again--"like Saul on the road to Damascus," except he'd been attending a conference in Palm Springs and found enlightenment on Bob Hope Drive—he left science behind and formed a ministry that had become countrywide, with a television show that pulled big ratings and even bigger contributions.

He had an estate in Palm Springs and this immense arena that seemed as much theater as church, and maybe both were intended. The Rev. Joy claimed though that he'd never lose contact with "each and every one of the faithful" and would press their flesh at every revival meeting--even if closely watched by a horde of security.

Suddenly the reverend was grabbed by the collar and jerked down to his knees. Marriner had him in grasp.

"I need answers, Reverend."

"You came to the right place, brother."

"The devil took your follower Annabelle Angel, killed her, reverend. Help me find the reasons."

"Leave that to the Lord, brother. His ways are mysterious."

The Reverend struggled to get loose. Marriner held him fast. Various members of the congregation glanced askance at this variance of the rite.

"No can do, Reverend," Marriner said. "Help me." The reverend looked more and more uncomfortable, unsure what to make of this devotee, motioned behind his back for his security guards. They came forward, led by a huge hulking man dressed impeccably, and incongruously, in a 3-piece suit.

As the security guards reached the edge of the stage Marriner held up his reconstituted badge. Recognizing the LAPD insignia, they came to an abrupt halt. Marriner held the badge in front of the reverend's eyes.

"Perry Pinckney, Reverend. Please, give me a sign. Take me under your wing. Enlighten me. Speak in tongues if you like. I'll find a translator."

Marriner let go of him. His eyes were aflame, a mix of fervor and fury.

The Reverend straightened, regained full composure. "The Ministry welcomes you. When duty calls, faith can follow." He turned to the crowd. "This man looks for salvation!" Marriner screamed, "I seek the way and the truth! Hallelujah!"

And the congregation followed: "Hallelujah!" Marriner repeated, "Hallelujah!" The Rev. Joy watched and listened with some discomfort as the crowd yelled to his prompt: "Hallelujah!"

Marriner had recognized Charley among the supplicants, and now in the crowd he picked out the bearded Richard and Horace, chanting to the Lord or maybe him and his Hallelujahs--would they care about the difference?

After the spectacle the well-dressed hulk--Marriner assumed he was head of security for the Rev. Joy--accosted him.

"Follow us. You got a car, don't you? Officer."

"Respect the speed limits," Marriner countered. The rally had been held at the huge open-air space constructed to the north of the 40 interstate. Cars barreling to and fro from Palm Springs had provided a constant thrum of auto Muzak in background to the Reverend's exhortations.

To the west, the desert wind turbines spun unceasingly, and Marriner had thought they marked the passage of time better than any watch or clock, and desert dwellers needed only to lift up their eyes to be reminded of man's earthly journey. But of course the Rev. Joy would have disagreed profoundly. Marriner followed behind the string of cars in Joy's entourage. The guru himself traveled in a limo. Marriner rang Gwen.

"I can't come too?" she asked.

"You don't need salvation."

"I don't feel this. All this bull sheet screaming and yelling and taking money, it is bull sheet, you know?"

"If I don't call you, it means these bad people did something bad. Wait till Bobby grows up and turn him loose."

"This is not funny. I am scare." She pronounced it that way, which amused Marriner even as he worried for her.

"Relax in the sun. It will fry your cares away."

"I don't think this." The Rev. Joy's compound loomed ahead, a vast expanse ringed by palm trees, sitting like a green island in the midst of the desert.

Marriner followed through the entrance gate but a surly ursine guard, his ID tag reading Mario, stopped him at the guard booth. "Detective Pinckney," he confirmed to the guard, who eyed his badge for some time.

"Want me to read for you what it says?" Marriner asked.

The guard gave no sign he understood. Marriner eyed the wall of elaborately constructed stone--not the usual brick and mortar affair--at least ten feet high that extended completely around the huge estate, fronting a ring of palm trees.

Marriner said to the guard, "Some wall of Jericho."

"I don't follow," the guard growled.

"Yeah, don't." Mario didn't understand this either, but grasped that he was being mocked. He gave the badge back and waved Marriner through.

He drove up to the house, on a long, straight paved driveway that gave the impression of leading to a castle or, more probably, the Lord's heavenly house. But Marriner noted that the entrance gate hadn't been pearly.

When Marriner got out, he moved past a well-manicured lawn and luxuriant flower garden and a row of garages in front of which several expensive cars were parked. Beyond the house, a long low rambling structure of expensive glass and wood which had been built against the side of a desert mountain in the San Jacinto foothills, a small private golf course had been built for the owner's pleasure.

As Marriner approached he came within sight of a luxurious swimming pool at the back of the house. He moved that way rather than the front entrance.

Marriner spotted three young women reclining on lounge chairs and sipping energy drinks. They were all strikingly attractive. Marriner watched one of them, a voluptuous redhead, dive in.

It seemed to him the pool resembled where Annabelle had danced in the video, but then again, hundreds if not thousands of pools in Palm Springs resembled each other.

"Would it surprise you to know they're here to seek faith?"

Marriner turned, saw Rev. Joy, dressed now in casual slacks and white shirt and a Panama hat against the sun.

"It's the only thing they're missing," Marriner replied.

"We must look beyond appearances. To the sinner's immortal soul. Detective . . ."

"Pinckney. First name Perry…Just don't call me PP." The Reverend Joy didn't laugh. He motioned at the estate and grounds.

"My headquarters. Some question whether the ministry needs a place so extensive. So ostentatious, if you will. I told them it's not ostentatious enough. This place is not mine or the ministry's. It's the Lord's."

"Does he golf in the morning or evening?" The Reverend ignored the crack.

"The stones in the fence come from all around the world. Including the Holy Land."

"Blocks the view though."

Joy indicated the interior of the building. "It's cooler inside."

Marriner asked, "Big place. You ever hold parties here?"

"We call them celebrations."

As they moved toward the patio sliding doors, they passed the 3-piece hulk who had been watching them from the beginning.

"Marvin oversees a security force on duty 24 hours a day." They approached the patio entrance to the house.

"So you see--Perry"--he slid open the glass patio door, held it for Marriner to enter—"even the devil would hesitate to trespass."

"If I were him, I'd stay by the pool."

"No, you are wrong. This home was designed to be a place just short of Paradise. Let me show you around. Assuming, as I do believe, you can ask questions and admire at the same time."

The ground floor took time. One capacious bedroom led to another, and another and another. "Temporary lodging for those faithful who need succor in a time of crisis and doubt. That is one reason you came to me, yes? As you said. You are not here just to investigate. Or am I wrong."

"Like you preach, Reverend. The way and the truth. Nice bedrooms."

They had every comfort and were spic and span to the max, with a very large Bible placed on the huge, hand-embroidered pillows.

Marriner quipped, "No one here reads frippery magazines." The study was huge, lavish, bedecked with photos and mementoes of Rev. Joy and the ministry.

"Here we counsel and educate and sometimes, heal." The kitchen and dining room lay off in an L-shaped side branch of the house, with a fountain in the middle of a patio. A replica "of the holy cross" doubled as object of worship and water source, pouring out in a continuous stream.

"We've tapped into a spring. Some of our enemies call this bad taste-"--meaning the cross--"but Our Lord gives the water of life."

They went up to the second floor. There was a gym, cinema screening room, and Joy's bedroom, which was about as big in space as Marriner's Banning house.

"Well, what do you think, Officer Pinckney?"

"Impressive. Amazing to think it was all paid for by a bunch of people with horny pricks."

"I don't understand what you mean."

"The House of Ecstasy. And who knows how many others in cities all around this country. Hell, the department doesn't care if you own a few sex joints. Just saying, you know."

"Thousands of dollars pour into our ministry every day. We have to invest it somewhere. Regrettably, I can't keep track of where it all goes."

"You should."

"I checked with your department. It seems you were taken off active investigative duty. So I am asking myself, why are you here and why am I talking to you?"

"For one very good reason. You know damn well who Annabelle Angel is and you want to know how much I know."

"She joined our ministry. I can tell you that."

"Yeah. I'm betting she was one of those damaged souls you keep alive at halfway houses so they can come out here and root you on when you stand up there on stage. Hell, I half expected them to do the wave."

"You have no jurisdiction and no clues--correction, no clue--so you are wasting my time. And yours. Annabelle was a very beautiful girl, but no more than that. To put it in crude terms, she was just a piece of tail."

Marriner had another flash of deepseated anger and never being someone anyway who respected certain respectable mores, he grabbed the good reverend, spun him around and proceeded to slap him silly. One after another, whap whap. Joy's head jerked from one side to the other, whap whap.

Marriner stopped short of knocking him unconscious. He shoved Joy against the wall.

"Talk or I'll kill you," Marriner hissed. "And you know damn well the Lord won't take you in."

Joy had to muster strength to speak.

"Film."

Marriner looked puzzled, but a short time later he saw what Joy wanted him to see.

#

They had moved into the cinema room. Joy said, after he'd recovered some from his shellacking: "We show instructional videos and scenes from our celebrations." He had riffled through a shelf of categorized DVDs and found the one he wanted to show. Light filled the room, splashing from a full-sized cinema screen.

Marriner stayed standing, watching. On the screen he saw, after various shots of the estate grounds, people arriving at a party, then more guests, some of whom amused themselves by mugging for the camera.

Joy took a stance near the screen.

"She came to me in an hour of distress." Annabelle came into view for a moment, moving through a group of guests. Marriner peered closer.

"I told her faith could lighten her handicap. Her burdens. I invited her to join our community, our celebrations."

The dancing images in the dark created an atmosphere of menace.

"When was this?" Marriner asked.

"Over a year ago."

Joy hit fast forward to a shot of guests dancing. The camera moved in closer, and there was Annabelle, dancing her solitary dance to her solitary dream.

"She tried to believe, but love had clouded her judgement. Selfish, imperfect human love." Rev. Joy's eyes could well have been misting over as he watched Annabelle. "She was so beautiful."

Annabelle concluded to the applause of the guests. Rev. Joy was among them.

Marriner's eyes were riveted on Annabelle, on screen. "In the end she rejected us," Joy said.

On the screen they saw a man from the back, walking over to Annabelle. She embraced him…the photographer moved in…As Annabelle and the man were about to turn Joy said, "But that's not why I had Marvin kill her."

The screen was ripped open by the force of a projectile. Marriner doubled over, fell to his knees. He looked down--a dart had been shot into his stomach.

Marriner jerked it out…eyed it in a kind of stupor…it dropped to the floor. Marvin came out from behind the shattered screen, now in tatters.

The DVD continued to run, sending images onto and through the screen. But the picture was so distorted to his eyes, Marriner could no longer tell what he was seeing.

Joy said, "In a New Testament sense, I suppose I was responsible."

Marriner groped for his gun…his fingers were not responding. He got the gun, laboriously pulled it out, dropped it onto the floor.

Marvin picked it up. Marriner was woozy, wobbling. Rev. Joy leaned down to him. "You'll retain consciousness but have little if any control of your faculties. Rather like Annabelle, I imagine."

Joy said to Marvin, "Here are your tickets to ride. I was saving them for a rainy day but it never rains here in Palm Springs. Take Mr. Marriner and dispose of him. And this time, don't let the body come back to haunt us."

23. TRAM

If a living, breathing and functioning man who had not passed to the far side and come back devoid of volition and any faculties that did not resemble involuntary reflexes--a zombie--that is what Marriner had become.

Marvin had no trouble leading him down and out of the house and into the passenger seat of his own car. He willingly and easily surrendered his keys, and Marvin drove them to the gate.

The guard smiled at the sight of the two, and especially Marriner's vacant, unfocused eyes. "Wish I could come with you," he said to Marvin.

"Do your fucking job," Marvin said bluntly. He drove away from the compound. He had placed Marriner's phone on the dash, and it now buzzed with an incoming call from: "Gwen." Marvin let it ring to message, and as he'd cut the sound, he didn't hear her plea for Marriner to call her.

The Palm Springs Aerial Tramway was a bustling horde of tourists departing or arriving on the trams and mingling among the snack bars and souvenir shops. Marvin hurried Marriner toward the tram and entered just before it began its journey.

The conductor looked askance at Marriner's state but said nothing, closed the door.

The tram began its ascent from the desert floor to its destination near Mt. San Jacinto peak, nearly 10,000 feet. Marriner slumped down and back on the row of seats. His head lolled back groggily.

One of the passengers eyed him with amazement. An acrophobe, he hunched in terror as the tram rose higher and higher.

"How can he sleep?" he asked.

Marvin made a spinning motion with his finger around his temple: crazy.

Marriner's view was of a mass of blurred shapes and swirling figures, amid which he could just make out the two figures of the conductor and Marvin--the two persons most important to him at that dangerous point in time. He knew he had to do something--he just did not have the faculties to do it.

Exactly midway on the ascent the downward tram passed. The crisscrossing passengers smiled, yelled and waved to each other.

On the last stretch of its journey the tram ascended precipitously, almost straight up.

Marriner blinked his eyes, trying to clear his head. With the altitude he felt he was losing consciousness. Marvin worried that he would. He leaned down and said softly to Marriner, "Don't go counting no fucking sheep."

Marriner held it together and moments later the tram arrived at its mountain terminus.

The tram doors opened onto a spacious station and dining room, filled with tram passengers in line for the return trip or dining and milling about among the shops. Marvin led Marriner off through the crowd. He took the hiking trail that led toward other sites in the mountain wilderness. Take one and it would lead them to another peak. Take another and it would lead eventually down the mountainside to the small resort village of Idyllwild where Marriner and Gwen had passed yesterday afternoon.

Marvin took the peak trail. They passed an elderly couple on their way back to the tram station, and next a young hiker with backpack. Then they were alone.

Marriner slowed and uttered something slurred and unintelligible. Marvin shoved him forward. A few paces later he led Marriner off trail.

They picked their way through the thick brush and pine tree forest.

Marvin stumbled often as he awkwardly thrashed his way, frequently cursing. He kept brushing his shirt and trousers, as if every speck of dust or leaf would infect him.

He had changed from his slick suit to garb more suited to the outdoors, but clearly he was not meant for the great outdoors.

They arrived at a precipice. Down below they could see the desert floor, thousands of feet of sheer fall. Zombie or not, Marriner knew that now it was do or die.

He shook his head, tried to regain force.

Marvin pushed him hard from behind, but although Marriner lurched forward he returned to his stockstill stance. Marvin shoved him again; Marriner remained at a standstill.

Marvin smiled. "Okay. We'll do it this way." He drew out his gun. "Won't be anything left anyway when I roll you down. Just a bunch of mush."

Marriner mumbled a word that sounded like "snack," but could have been "snake." Enough for Marvin to ask, "What?" Marriner made all the effort he was capable of to articulate the word: "Rattlesnake!"

Marriner's trips to the desert and his numerous evenings in Banning watching wildlife had given him, as he said to Gwen, some experience with rattlesnakes. He had not become deft enough to actually catch and pin them, like Juan, but during a long afternoon when they'd first met, and after an appropriate number of beers, Juan had shown him how to imitate the snake's rattle.

"It's like you got rocks in your throat and wind in your teeth. And it's easier after a few beers. Loosens up the gullet."

On the porch at night he'd practiced the trick sound to amuse himself--if not others. He'd posed a question to Juan: "What the hell kind of use does this trick have?"

He'd stumped Juan there. But now it seemed to him even in his half-sentient state that he might use his talent, and being half-sentient as from too many beers, the gullet would do good work.

And he was right. The volume and sonority and accuracy of the rattle astounded him.

And Marvin, who literally almost jumped out of his shoes trying to avoid a snake that wasn't there.

Marriner punched him in the same way as Pinckney, but Marvin still managed to fire off a shot on his way to the ground.

Marriner pinioned his gun hand and kicked Marvin full in the face--which made him loosen his grip. Marriner was able to reach down and take the gun, but the movement pumped up the drug still in his system and sent him reeling backward, dizzy. He stumbled toward the mountain precipice, trying to recover balance before falling. He wobbled on the edge for a long moment.

When he regained equilibrium, he looked up and saw that Marvin had gone.

#

At the tram station Marvin hurried toward the departing tram, jostling people out of the way. At the elevator he encountered a line of people waiting to board.

A ticket operator barred his way. "Tram's leaving. Wait your turn for the next one." Marvin punched him out of the way. Seeing what had happened, the tram conductor closed the door. Marvin rushed over, banged on it. The conductor shook his head no and mouthed the words, "Too late."

Marvin turned, saw Marriner hurrying through the crowd toward him.

The tram signaled the beginning of its descent.

Still groggy, nevertheless Marriner charged forward.

Marvin jumped down onto the roof of the descending tram. Marriner arrived when the car had begun descending and it was touch and go if he could make the leap.

Marriner went. He leapt down onto the tram car and onto Marvin. The impact sent them sprawling, both groping at opposite ends of the tram car for the connecting poles. The gun fell out of Marriner's grasp and went spinning onto the car roof.

As the tram car plunged out into the open air and began the steep descent to the valley below, Marriner and Marvin regained balance and watched helplessly as the gun slowly slid off the car and into the abyss.

Marvin pulled a knife. He moved toward Marriner, using the support bars for balance.

Marvin stepped gingerly, holding the knife before him. Inside the car the passengers heard the footsteps above. Marvin took a couple of swipes with the knife at Marriner, who managed to duck though still groggy. On the third try Marriner dodged, grabbed Marvin's knife hand and banged it hard and repeatedly against the tram bar. Marvin grimaced in pain. They struggled for a moment, then Marriner finally knocked the knife loose.

It went clattering to the end of the tram. The tram car approached one of several steel towers on the line route as the two men struggled, locked in each other's grasp, both trying to retain balance. As the car reached the tower it jerked upward and down abruptly.

Marriner lost his balance from the jolt. Seeing an opening, Marvin karate chopped him twice on the back of the neck.

Marriner fell down to the side of the car and over the edge, clinging by his fingertips to the side of the car. His body hung perilously over the vast drop below.

Inside the car the passengers screamed in horror as Marriner dangled there outside the window, a slip away from death. As he scrabbled with his fingertips, trying to climb back atop the tram car, Marvin--holding onto the tram cable bar--began to stomp on Marriner's hands, which began to bleed from the battering.

Marriner kicked in the tram window, the glass fragments flying into the tram car and eliciting screams from inside. Once he had shattered the glass Marriner was able to get a quick foothold. He grabbed Marvin's foot, sent him tumbling backward. Marriner began to pull himself back up the tram car by means of Marvin's legs. Marvin could do nothing but hang for his life to the tram bar. He kicked feebly at Marriner with his other leg, but Marriner pulled himself steadily upward.

Midway up Marriner was caught squarely in the head by one of Marvin's kicks. Still doped, he gripped Marvin's leg, hung on for dear life. His vision was a whirling mass of shapes, the dizzy vastness of air and space below him.

Marriner's grip relaxed...then suddenly as if from a second wind, he became lucid again. In a frantic burst of energy he pulled himself back onto the tram car.

The fight began in earnest. The two men exchanged punches, fell back, balanced precariously on top of the car. Inside the tram the occupants remain horrified at the peril the men above faced. They could hear the thumping footsteps and falls above on the roof.

The conductor held up his arms helplessly.

Above, Marriner swung, caught Marvin flush on the jaw--he slumped to his knees.

But before Marriner could apply the finishing touches another wave of dizziness hit him.

He turned, hung onto the tram bar for support. The yawning gulf of empty air loomed below.

Marvin saw his chance. He punched Marriner on the back of the neck, karate style. Marriner slumped. . .

Marvin turned and scrambled to the other end of the car. Holding onto the tram bar with one hand, he reached to the edge of the tram car for the fallen knife.

Marriner's view was of a blur of shapes gradually coming into focus. Below the tram car and down the line route where he was facing he could see a large dark shape. Marvin got the knife, turned and started toward him.

Marriner's sight came into sharp focus. He saw that the dark shape was the other tram car, ascending. The stunned passengers inside the car were looking on in horror at the two men, some filming the extraordinary sight.

As Marvin swiped with the knife Marriner suddenly whirled and kicked him squarely in the face.

Marvin fell over the side of the tram. He grabbed vainly at the roof edge, fell over the side, managed to grab the sill of the window Marriner kicked in.

The glass shards ripped his hands . . in a moment they were streaming with blood. Marvin screamed in agony. Marriner yelled to the people inside: "Grab him!"

Several men moved forward to haul Marvin inside but he could hold on no longer. The oncoming tram was now even with them and he saw a chance. He leapt for the roof of the other tram.

His hands gripped the roof's rim. He tried to scramble up toward the roof bar, but his hands were too bloodied.

Slowly, in a motion that horrified both sets of tram passengers, Marvin slipped down the side of the tram. As he plunged to the desert below his scream gradually diminished. On the descending tram Marriner slumped exhausted against the cable car bar.

As the tram approached its dock, a large crowd, drawn by the sight of the fight, had gathered and was buzzing at Marriner's arrival.

The tram docked.

Marriner leaped down into the crowd and into the grasp of two local police officers.

Marriner waved his badge. "Officer Perry Pinckney. LAPD!" he shouted. The officers noted the badge. "That man was a hired killer, a hit man," he explained. "Pick up the pieces. We've got to have his DNA. Hurry! I'm going after the son-of-a bitch's boss."

He moved away quickly, leaving them to their task--which, when they gave it a moment's thought, brought a certain queasy expression to their faces.

24. JUST DESERTS

Marriner knew that the Rev. Joy trusted in the Lord for salvation, but not physical protection, and once he learned of Marvin's inconvenient demise he would hire extra beefeaters with earplugs and big guns.

But he would not have extra lead time to wire the whole house and grounds, and during his first visit Marriner had scoped out the property even as he laid on the flattery like marmalade. Joy knew he wasn't sincere, but his self-importance and pride in the loaves and fishes and earthly fruits he'd gained from spreading the gospel had overcome judgement and care.

Marriner doubted that Joy would expect a seeker of salvation in the modern world to go to the trouble of trekking over a desert hillside in dirt and sand and cactus, plus rattlers, to press the Reverend's flesh and find forgiveness. Salvation could wait for easier access to a more comfy venue.

Gwen wasn't happy driving Marriner to his self-blazed trailhead.

"Me, I am so scare," she said.

"It'll be a long night but we'll have breakfast together tomorrow, promise."

"You promise?"

He did. En route he received a call from Turkey, who was as excited as Marriner had ever heard him.

"I got him! I got the SOB. Had to work through I don't even wanna tell you how many DNA DBs--"

"What's a DB?"

"God, now we know what happened to some of those Neanderthal genes. My rate just went up by a cool thou for having to explain basic tech language to a Neanderthal."

"Tell the cave man what you found."

"Well, his family bred like rabbits and came from all over. I had to work back from God knows how many brothers and sisters and cousins but I locked in, man. I got the SOB."

"Does his first name begin with an M, as in Marvin?"

Turkey went dead silent on the phone and Marriner and Gwen drove a good mile it seemed before he could find speech.

"If you know that, you know he's living in Palm Springs. Right around the corner."

"So to speak. Right now a few buzzards are nibbling on him."

#

Marriner had seen only a few dales but plenty of hills in Afghanistan and he had no problems trekking across the desert mountainside and arriving at the rear of Joy's house. Desert rats like Juan who roamed at night had long been eliminated from the city, as if the Pied Piper had come and done his work and taken up residence in Palm Desert, on permanent call.

Marriner had also done some free soloing in his time, and the minute cracks in the stone wall posed no difficulty. He crossed and came down at the poolside where Annabelle Angel had danced toward her tragic destiny.

He was prepared to shoot his way in, taking out any guard he had to, but doubtless they were all at the front entrance, biding time till dawn--or Marriner--arrived.

No one had bothered to lock the patio sliding doors, and Marriner slid his way in and made his way to the bedroom suites. He moved softly, quietly. It was very late, or early depending on perspective.

He glanced at the first bedroom. It contained a king bed where two very attractive followers slept very well. Perhaps they'd exerted themselves earlier. The other guest bedrooms were empty.

Marriner moved upstairs. The master's bedroom was decorated in garish colors that reminded Marriner of Graceland.

He saw no cross, but many framed photos of Joy receiving plaques and commemorative honors from the rich and famous.

Joy's bed outkinged kingsize, and amazingly enough, had only one occupant this night. Marriner corrected his prior assumption that Joy had relaxed earlier in the evening. Perhaps he'd sensed that nobody knew the trouble he might see, and felt in no mood for cavorting.

Joy had taken care to place a handgun on the bedside table. Marriner picked it up, saw it was loaded, and pressed the gun barrel firmly to the Rev. Joy's forehead.

When he didn't stir, Marriner tapped him lightly, then more strongly on the side of his head.

This woke the sleeping dog. Marriner said softly, "Avenging angels always come at night. Shut up, get up and put on your clothes. I need a ride."

Joy did as he was told, always watching Marriner warily. "You got any jeans?" Marriner asked. Joy nodded. "We're going for a little hike. Like the guidebooks say, dress accordingly."

Marriner kept an eye on him, moving over to a side table where a Bible rested under a glass case. "Which museum did you steal it from?"

Joy said, "It's worth a million, easy. Take it. It's yours if..." Marriner didn't answer. He opened the glass case and thumbed through the pages.

Joy had donned sandals. "Perfect," Marriner said, "except maybe when you brush up against cactus."

Marriner turned the pages to a passage in the New Testament.

"40 days and 40 nights. Some fast."

"He was the Lord God and Savior."

"You're neither. You kill young girls and go right on living and preaching like you're without sin."

"Look, it was an arrangement. For influence. They were going to shut me down."

"On the ride you're going to tell me all about it. And not with pronouns. I want proper names."

"Put all the heat on me you want. I'm not telling. I'll be finished if I do."

"The Lord God who made heaven and earth is going to provide the heat. Now you're all dressed and presentable, you're going to show me your pharmacy."

Marriner had brought along a roll of duct tape and it came in handy to seal Joy's lips as they made their way silently through the house, toward the garage, past rooms in the side wing that housed servants and sleeping security and whatever hangers-on who'd cadged lodging for the night in the Master's home.

After Marriner installed Joy behind the wheel of one of his 4x4s, he explained the ground rules--first ripping off the tape in the most efficient way possible--brutal.

"Goddamn!"

"Taking the Lord's name in vain. You should be ashamed. But then, if you had any shame, you wouldn't have buried a girl who hadn't gotten around to dying."

"Marvin did that. I just said, get rid of her, clean and quick. He is afflicted by sadism."

"Was. The wages of sin and all that."

Marriner hunkered down in the well of the back seat. "Now listen as carefully as you ever have in your life, if you want to have a life. The guards are going to be surprised out of what serves as their minds seeing the boss go out for a tour this late, but they're not trained to second guess. If anybody hesitates, you look and act impatient--like you're in a silent movie. If they don't get the picture from your expressions, we're going to have one hell of a shootout. And you do know hell."

Joy managed a nod. "I figure it'll take thirty seconds for them to open the gate. A second more and I'll know you're fucking with me."

"You're a sinner and a scumbag and the devil won't take you in-- but you're not a murderer. You won't shoot me."

"It's called divine retribution. And me, the Lord's servant. He will push the trigger. No guilt and all. Or hesitation."

He pushed the gun barrel hard into the seat back until it almost hit Joy's body. "Drive."

Joy started the car and raised the garage door, eased the car out of the garage. It had been backed in, so it took only a short few seconds to arrive at the front gate. "You're on the clock," Marriner said quietly to Joy. He heard the driver's window rolling down and thought Joy might be gesturing.

The seconds ticked down--Marriner heard Joy shifting in his seat and even though he'd been told not to speak, he panicked:

"Move!" he shouted to the gate guard. At the 30-second mark the Rev. Joy hit the gas and Marriner felt the speed bump at the entrance gate, then the smooth pavement of a chic neighborhood Palm Springs street. Marriner raised up and looked back at Joy's compound. The guards were nowhere to be seen.

"Hit a right," Marriner said to Joy, and they continued down a side street until Marriner told him to stop. He gestured with his gun for Joy to move over to the passenger seat, and in an instant he'd taken place behind the wheel. He resealed Joy's mouth with duct tape, then pulled out the syringe he'd forced Joy to prepare.

"The same shit you gave me," Marriner said, and injected the drug.

The Rev. Jubal Joy passed several hours in the netherland zone of blur, surreal images and garbled sounds.

When he finally woke up to sufficient clarity, he saw clear blue desert sky and gradually realized he was in a sand and dirt hole too deep to climb out of.

Suddenly Marriner peered down from the rim of his newly dug gravesite. The sun blazed.

"Hey there, Chucklehead," Marriner said. "Been a long day. Lots of scenery and you just slumbered through all of it."

"Give me a drink of water and get me out of here. I'll tell you everything you want to know."

"Oh, I've got it pretty well figured out. Anyway you talked a lot already. Must be some truth serum in that zombie juice. Here, drink up."

He tossed a canteen down. It was about a third full and Joy guzzled all of it. "That's not good survival tactics but hey, it's your life. What's left of it."

"You're going to kill me."

"Hell no. Like you said, I'm not a murderer."

"Where are my shoes?"

"Damn. Must have fallen off the burro. He packed you in."

"Listen Mister. I can make it happen that you never have to work again. Big money. Lots of it. The Lord's been good to me and he can be good to you, too. Let's make a deal."

"Porno money. I wonder what the Lord would say about that."

"The needs of the flesh. When they're satisfied, hearts and minds open up to other needs."

"You know what I think? You're a wasting asset and the Lord knows when it's time to cut his losses. I'm not Marvin. I'm not going to turn you into compost.

"Night's coming on and it'll get damn cold but you should be able to claw your way out of this hole in a few hours. Dawn at the latest. Then all you have to do is follow our tracks out. We took the long way in and if you take the right shortcut and your feet don't burn off in the hot sand, you may find a dirt road that'll lead you to a 7-11. Civilization. Not much of a civilization if it's got worthless scum like you, but maybe the Lord wanted to make an example of the wages of sin. Careful though. These canyons can fool you."

"Why are you doing this? For God's sake..."

"Not for God's sake. Annabelle's."

"Look, she was a nut job. Who was going to miss her?"

"Somebody did. Or you wouldn't be here. Better start digging. Maybe I'll see you again. Maybe not." He moved out of Joy's line of sight.

"Hey!" Joy screamed, "if you don't want money, tell me what you want. Tell me and it's yours!" He went on but as time passed and Marriner didn't respond, he turned to the task of freeing himself from his grave. The sand and dirt were firm but if he scrabbled hard, the earth came tumbling down, piling at this feet.

If he could dislodge enough, he would be able to climb out, like a mole or when the walls of Jericho came falling down. Then his ordeal would truly begin. He would have to walk fast, on bare feet, and find his way. But the Lord would guide him.

Wouldn't he?

#

Marriner led Bucky back to Juan de la Costa and repeated, "Any trouble comes to you because of this loan-out, you lay it all to me."

And Juan said again, "I don't know nothin' about nothin'. Bucky makes his own decisions, you know. Hell, I didn't even notice he was gone. I'm just a daffy old desert rat, like the rangers say. How about a beer. You look fried."

"Yeah. Hot one today."

"Like every day out here."

They shared beers and discussed world affairs. It wasn't till Marriner was leaving that Juan posed a question.

"That poor girl I found. She resting in peace now?"

"As much peace as we can give her."

Juan nodded. He knew something about something now.

Marriner parked the Rev. Joy's car at the entrance to Long Canyon, then hiked to a Desert Hot Springs cafe. Gwen joined him there and they shared the nice aforepromised breakfast.

She had a lot of questions but he fended them off by saying simply, "We have other priorities."

"Like what?"

"First, a good shower. Not cold. Then us." He and Gwen spent another day and night back home in Banning enjoying each other's company. He learned more of the French language.

25. GORTON

The Diner in downtown LA was a fixture since the 1930s and its basic menu for breakfast, lunch and dinner had hardly changed over the years. It was a historic greasy spoon distinguished by the quality of its basic food and the waiters, most of whom had done time and needed a job on the way back to wherever they were going, or might be going, frequently back to the slammer but the Diner had a rep of second, third and even 14 chances.

Sometimes the toast arrived burned but few customers had the nerve to complain. Gorton hadn't been thrilled when Marriner invited him to lunch and insisted on the Diner, and he looked uncomfortable when he arrived and took a seat at the table where Marriner had been installed for a hour, drinking coffee and waiting for his good friend.

"I put that guy away," Gorton said about the waiter who'd exchanged tables with his colleague so he wouldn't have to serve them.

"Apparently he didn't stay away."

"Justice system's fucked, you know that. I give him a month before he goes right back where he belongs."

"Where do you belong, Ed?" Gorton looked puzzled. "And while you're pondering that existential question, give me one good reason why I don't put a bullet right between your goddamn eyes."

Gorton's puzzlement gave way to shock.

"The holy reverend Jubal Joy's missing, but you know that. Just like you knew exactly what happened to Annabelle Angel. 'Trail went cold, John.' Bullshit. Easiest one I've ever followed. No one bothered to hide their tracks. You couldn't have missed it. Unless you wanted to. And you did."

Gorton stared at him for a long moment.

"I went crazy over her, John. About as crazy as she was. But that excited me. You know me. Straight arrow, upstanding citizen and father, good husband. What do you do when a woman upsets your whole world? It was like she cast a spell over me and I couldn't resist or shake it. And I didn't want to. Until she got demanding. Too demanding, scary demanding. I made a deal with Joy to get her off my back. I never said, kill her.

"But he knew if he did, he'd have me by the balls. I've been doing him favors. Sold out in a big way."

"He knew I'd be coming. Thanks to you."

"I just told him to be careful."

"You are one naive motherfucker. Or just stupid. Or plain evil."

"Look John, when you fall for a woman like I did...I just couldn't control it. Still can't. I see her night and day. Dreams, nightmares. Dancing like she did that night at Joy's party. He was working us, LAPD, we knew that. But hell, we work offduty for Hollywood, don't we? After hours pocket change. Let me tell you, he showed us a good time. Drink and wham and bam and outta there, but I made a mistake. I met her, and I stayed over. Dancing under the moon like that...I ought to say I regret it, but deep down I don't. I'm ready to burn in hell."

"And you will. But if I don't fire that bullet, you've got time."

"They identified Joy's goon. That had to be you. And the reverend?"

"All I know is what I read in the papers. If they don't find him, there goes our witness. You'll be off the hook."

"The hook's in deep."

"Lucinda and the kids need you. The Chief and I both know that. He promised to fix you up with the best security agency in town. Night duty maybe, but paid enough to make a living. Pension plan and all that." Gorton was at a loss.

"Pinckney's going to replace you. Who cares if folks all around this crazy world hatch conspiracy theories that it wasn't him on the tram and in fact, he was spending his off day sniffing seaweed on Venice Beach. Better if the Department gets credit for finding a killer. Yeah, Chief's corrupt too, but he can't let one of his men out-corrupt him. Bad for the force but mostly, his pockets. When I speak, he tends to listen, you know. Unlike some people, I don't lie."

Marriner rose to his feet. Unlike Gorton, he'd had no problem chowing down the excellent burger prepared by an ex-felon turned excellent cook.

"You fucked up, Ed. Got in deep and then fucked up world class. Don't do it again, 'cause I'll be watching with that bullet. Pick up the check."

As he turned to go: "Hey, let's go hiking in the desert sometime."

Gorton didn't watch him leave. He had other things on his mind--like how he was going to get through the rest of his life.

26. MOTHER SUPERIOR

Annabelle Angel's grave lay in a far corner at Forest Lawn, far away from celebrity names. The Mother Superior stood with Marriner in front of the grave. "She wanted to succeed, to be somebody. But she was always somebody."

The Mother Superior paid weekly visits, and she was surprised when she arrived and saw Marriner standing there.

He confessed: "I wanted to come and see her."

The Mother Superior nodded. She had dressed in the more traditional hood of the Order. "I come here when I can," she said.

They stayed for awhile, not saying much, then turned and walked away together.

"Do you always come on Thursdays?" he asked.

"Usually."

"Then we might meet again. "

It was a cloudy, lowering day, so atypical for the Southland that the papers gave as much space to the meteorological phenomenon as to the principal local news of Rev. Jubal Joy's demise.

His body had been found not so very far from Long Canyon, victim of heat and thirst. As speculation had it among followers and television news commentators, his noble desire to emulate his Master and find cleansing in the desert had overcome caution and a proper assessment of how long 40 days and 40 nights could be in reality.

"Penance, I guess you could call it," Marriner said to the Mother Superior when he explained the case. He'd meant to do it at the convent, but they had met by accident and truly it seemed more fitting here.

The Mother Superior said, "The devil in disguise of a man of God. Horrible. But not the first time or last."

He had not given details as to how the Rev. Joy had gone into the desert. That would be a matter for his own penance, in the event he ever felt guilty.

But he did not spare Gorton.

"The sins of the flesh," she said.

"And he sinned big time."

"There is one thing I can believe," she said. "That he loved her. I sometimes think, the Lord got impatient to have her with all the saints and all the justified, where at last she could find where she belonged."

She looked up at the sky, which was growing darker. It was a long way from the rainy season and if rain did come, it would be a disturbance in the historical order of things rarely seen in LA.

She said, "It was a tragic mistake, his. We will have to leave justice to his conscience. The case is finished."

They walked in silence for a few moments before Marriner said, "Your retainer covered my work. I won't accept any more."

The Mother Superior gave him a look that resembled admiration. "I thought you might say that. One can read a person's soul sometimes, you know. So I sent a check by mail and asked your assistant to deposit it immediately."

"So that's why I couldn't make out her message, what with all the excitement in her voice."

"When people depend on you, you shouldn't refuse manna from heaven. Christ's followers didn't."

The Mother Superior held out her hand to shake.

"Go with God, Mr. Marriner. And don't refuse the ride if offered. Whether you believe or not, He may believe in you."

27. ONCE MORE UNTO THE BREACH

The door in the Santa Monica apartment remained unfixed, and Gwen had met several of Tony's disgruntled girl friends, some of whom refused to accept the prefix "ex."

At first they had been jealous of each other, for the most part, but in the end under Gwen's benign influence, which after all was that of a French woman accustomed to the vagaries of men--"Despite everything, we do not regard them as enemies. They are just *faible,* that's all. They can be seely"--they banded together and became close.

In the grand tradition of American jurisprudence, they decided to take class action and hire Marriner to find Tony. He'd hoped to leave off missing person/dogs work, but Tiffany, the girl from Bel-Air, seemed to own half of that ultra posh neighborhood and funds were not wanting. Marriner graciously accepted the case.

He paid his back rent in Banning, and paid a handyman out of his own pocket to repair the Santa Monica apartment door. It did not take long, and it did not cost much.

"He could have done it for a song," the handyman said. Marriner knew how voluble Joe was, and rather thought his lax attitude to home security afforded him a chance to BS and commiserate with Tony's exes--or "pending exes," they said to him when he took the case. Joe's welcoming attitude changed when the lock did, and Marriner realized new digs were needed.

He and Gwen ran through the possibilities over a few weekends on the Banning terrace while they ran through the rest of Marriner's wine contraband.

"Should I stay or should I go," mused the back-in-business-in-LA private detective. The Chief had been amenable to negotiation, only requesting in no uncertain terms that Marriner remain "forever and for eternity" out of his line of sight.

Officer Pinckney had indeed been reinstated, with a new badge. Marriner had sent him a very brief note with the admonition to take it easy on less fortunate citizens because "I'll be watching."

Spoke Lacey had a load of legal troubles brought on when Elfego and Bob took Marriner's advice to sing like birds. There was talk of the slammer for a very long period.

Turkey went back to Farmer's Market and said he was very happy to do so, given as how in working for Marriner, he had not only felt redundant, but was. Marriner countered that if need be, he had a future in the insect eradication business.

Marriner knew he could always find work in the city named after heavenly angels that had themselves bailed out on it many decades ago. But at what cost of lifestyle and soul? "I've gotten used to the desert," he said to Gwen over a bottle whose name he couldn't pronounce, Romanée Conti.

Any discussion of him and them and their future necessarily had to include Bobby the boa. He would have to be fed, and as he grew older, he would outstrip certain living accommodations. It was too dry in Banning. Or so he imagined.

Gwen said, "You can maybe make this decision in France."

"How's that?"

"It's summer and I need to see my family. Don't you want to go?"

After a nanosecond of reflection, "Yes." Marriner realized that if she wanted him to meet her family enough to overcome her embarrassment when he tried to speak French, she was getting serious. But then again, so was he.

"In France I will not be so scare for you. It is so dangerous sometimes, your business."

"Sometimes. I won't have much to fear from Tony, though. His girl friends, yes, if I don't manage to find him."

"I have confidence in you."

They sat in silence for a few moments and finished the wine. Marriner noticed she had tears in her eyes and felt like he might be falling in love.

"Look, don't be scare--scared. Everything's going to be ok..."

"I am so emotion and proud. Little Bobby caught his first rat. He is growing up."

Marriner did look and saw Bobby in mid-swallow. He seemed significantly bigger than a few days ago. Well, Marriner thought, perhaps naively, if she can have so much love in her heart for a snake's baby steps--slithers--she might have room for me.

6. FIRST LOVE. PART 3.

Rachel went on her honeymoon the same month Matt's film hit the theaters, so she missed it and the hostile reviews. When she returned the film had long gone from theaters, a boxoffice flop. She feared that Matt would fall into the LA oblivion caused by failure, and would need time and all he could do to maintain his career.

A part of her, the realistic and pragmatic part, told her she had made the right choice with Max.

A letter arrived from Matt. He had learned about her marriage and wished her much happiness, but he could not hide his anguish and regret.

Rachel did not reply.

"I don't drive," Rachel said to Karen, "never had a license. So I don't need to look into the rear view mirror." Karen noticed that she hadn't used Matt's name. Rachel had so much to do after marrying Max, what with their four children who arrived in succession and by design as she lived closer to forty, that she never had time for rear views, and indeed, after her first child Richard arrived, made a conscious decision to live always for the present and future.

Many years later Karen mentioned that she'd seen Matt's name on the credits of a film screening at one theater near Times Square. It came and went in one week, and Rachel allowed herself to wonder if Matt could recover from another ignominious flop. Certainly she hoped he would, and wished him the best.

The years passed, and Rachel could say with reason that she had everything she'd always wanted, loving children and husband and the comfort of her faith and community. Max was as devout as she. His business thrived. They were able to buy a huge apartment in Manhattan and had become part of the city's successful upper middle class.

Rachel had moved the music box to her parents' farm very soon after marrying Max as it didn't seem right to have to explain to their numerous guests where it came from and how, in front of her husband. Among his many qualities was trust in her and lack of jealousy, but she saw no reason to listen to Debussy when so many other composers abounded, and each year a new season brought more wonderful operas to the Met. As major gift donors, they had all the privileges possible.

One day one of the farm cats leaped onto the mantelpiece and knocked the music box down, damaging the mechanism irreparably. It fetched a few dollars at a yard sale. Rachel had kept Matt's love letters and locked them in a metal box in the attic of the farm, where all kinds of trunks and suitcases and other bric-a-brac was stored, and when her mother passed away, a year after her father, and she sold the farm, she had been too busy to thoroughly vet the possessions she truly needed to possess and they vanished in the general chaos of movers and painters and plasterers readying the property for sale.

She regretted the loss, even if she had not reread the letters in 40 years.

#

Rachel saw Karen more rarely as work and commitments and family matters occupied her time, but when Bill passed away and Karen had to learn to live without her husband and risked falling into moroseness and worse, depression, Rachel found time on her incredibly busy schedule to have one of their oldtime coffee sessions. It had to be in mid-Manhattan, between Rachel's engagements--plus a new decorator was re-designing their apartment, and he needed "room for reflec-tion," Rachel laughed. "I didn't know one needed a room to reflect. So I asked him to design one for me and he took it seriously. I had to explain I was kidding. It takes me nanosec-onds to reflect."

"So I know," Karen agreed. "Nothing gains on you because you never look back."

"Why should I? Max and my family are the joy of my life. I don't know if I deserved them, but I'm so thankful." It oc-curred to her without reflection that this might not be the moment to vaunt her happiness to Karen, and she added, "like you were so happy with Bill. How are you doing? Listen, I'm always there for you, you know that."

"I've been doing pretty well. When you have time to prepare, you know..."

"Tell me about your trip to the reunion. You said you weren't going."

"Well, think about it. 50-year reunion. You look around and see all these old people you don't recognize and then you see their badge and you have to stop yourself from saying 'My God, is it you, Sally? You're so obese and you used to be a beanpole.' Plus you can't say hey, I'm the same old Karen, because they'll be thinking yeah, old is right. "

"So why did you go?"

Karen hesitated a moment. "I just said to myself, these people were part of my life. Part of me. And I was part of theirs." She hesitated again before continuing: "Jim was there with his second wife."

"The first crush? How did he look?"

"Well preserved, I have to say."

"Any sparks fly?"

"Are you flattering me? No. But for a while I could have used a Valium. Still some feelings, can you believe it? Luckily he made me laugh like he always did and feel comfortable. Plus his wife was nice, really bright and pleasant even after she figured out I was an old flame. We sat together at dinner and had a great time. She told me, 'I'm his second go-round and let me tell you, I wouldn't have wanted any part of him while he was sowing his wild oats. Thank goodness you came out of it okay.' I told her, 'You are so right.' "

Karen went on, "It was great to see him again. He was my first love. Bill came along and we got married and as the years went by I forgot about him. Almost. Like you and Matt, I guess."

"So that's why you always put in a good word for him," Rachel smiled, meaning Matt of course. "I don't think I would have gone. I enjoy my comfort zone, you know. It's been very very good to me. My wild oats got sown a long time ago. In the desert. Not a great place for wheat."

"Well, the desert can surprise sometimes. It did you."

#

When she looked out the airplane window now at the Utah desert, Rachel remembered that conversation with Karen. In a few minutes she knew they would pass over the Grand Canyon and the El Tovar, and she could don again the armor that time and destiny had forged.

A deep clear day like today, at just this hour of the afternoon--she knew she was lucky to have a chance like this, and she strained to look down and delineate the canyons where she'd been.

It occurred to her that when Matt died--if he had not already--no one else would ever know what happened to them down there. It occurred to her that quite possibly no one had ever found love in that remote canyon as they had.

The love and passion of those days and nights came rushing back, the dancing pine tree elves, the wonder and excitement of her first love, and soft tears came to her eyes. She tried to wipe them away so she could see more clearly.

The plane passed over Navajo Mountain and the westward sun put the terrain in brilliant relief. She could see the Colorado River clearly and the canyons that emptied into it. Even at this altitude she felt sure she made out Bridge Canyon.

Nonnezoshe lay down there, majestic and serene. She recalled how it had been, the Bridge and the sinuous trail that followed the stream on her way back to camp that day long ago, the light of the afternoon sun on the soaring canyon walls. Most of all, how he had sat there on the warm sandstone, waiting for her.

ABOUT THE AUTHOR

Martin Copeland is a screenwriter, playwright and author of the novels MANHUNT IN FRANCE, THE BOYS FROM DOGTOWN and A STAR FALLS IN CANNES.

www.ingramcontent.com/pod-product-compliance
Lightning Source LLC
Chambersburg PA
CBHW070105280626
47159CB00016B/1325